Critical acclaim for

# SHALLOW GRAVES

"A fast-paced story with an interesting hook, and a thoughtful look at what it means to be human versus what it means to be a monster. The end result is a superbly crafted debut bound to entrance."—ALA *BOOKLIST* (starred review)

"Constantly entertaining, intriguing, and suspenseful." —*KIRKUS REVIEWS*

"Kali Wallace has created a world that's both natural and unsettling and reminds us that true terror is not a monster but what lurks in the dark corners of human nature."—MADELEINE ROUX, *New York Times* bestselling author of the Asylum series

"*Shallow Graves* is a stunner. Gripping, gory, and insightful." —KENDARE BLAKE, *New York Times* bestselling author of *Three Dark Crowns*

"A fast-paced ride through a dark, imaginative world." —MINDY MCGINNIS, author of *The Female of the Species* and *A Madness So Discreet*

"A phenomenally written, spine-chilling story, *Shallow Graves* is sure to keep you up all night."—KIMBERLY DERTING, author of the Body Finder series

"Writing in Breezy's pragmatic and engaging voice, Wallace weaves an unsettling tale that explores Breezy's strange existence, while also thoughtfully examining a life cut short. Her struggle to reconcile what she has become with the human she used to be forms the heart of this bittersweet story."—*PUBLISHERS WEEKLY*

## Also by Kali Wallace

*The Memory Trees*

# SHALLOW GRAVES

## KALI WALLACE

KATHERINE TEGEN BOOKS
An Imprint of HarperCollins Publishers

Katherine Tegen Books is an imprint of HarperCollins Publishers.

Shallow Graves
Copyright © 2016 by Kali Wallace
Library of Congress Cataloging-in-Publication Data
Wallace, Kali.
    Shallow graves / Kali Wallace. — First edition.
        pages      cm
        Summary: After waking in a shallow grave, Breezy, a high school senior, crosses the
country seeking answers about her death and resurrection, discovering along the way a host
of supernatural creatures, as well as a human cult determined to "free" them at any cost.
        ISBN 978-0-06-236621-4
        [1. Dead—Fiction.    2. Supernatural—Fiction.    3. Cults—Fiction.    4. Murder—
Fiction.    5. Racially mixed people—Fiction.    6. Horror stories.]    I. Title.
PZ7.1.W353Sh   2016                                                                    2015005855
[Fic]—dc23                                                                                   CIP
                                                                                              AC

Typography by Ellice M. Lee
17  18  19  20  21   PC/LSCH   10 9 8 7 6 5 4 3 2 1
❖
First paperback edition, 2017

FOR MY PARENTS

# ✦ ONE ✦

THE FIRST TIME I killed a man it was an accident.

He didn't have any identification on him. He was white, probably in his midfifties. Average build, average height. Smoker. No tattoos or distinguishing scars. His fingerprints matched those found at a thirty-year-old crime scene in North Dakota: a family murder, both parents, son and two daughters, all killed one night at the dinner table. Nobody was ever arrested.

A real estate agent with the unfortunate name of Poppy Treasure found him three days after I killed him. She opened the back door of an empty house to air it out before her clients arrived, and there he was, facedown on the lawn, dead. The police released a description and pleaded for information, but nobody came forward. Nobody admitted to seeing him. They didn't even know how he had gotten to Evanston, much less how or why he had ended up dead in the yard of a foreclosed house in the Backlot. There wasn't a mark on him. The medical examiner blamed the death on a heart attack, but the "unusual circumstances" of where he was found made them suspicious.

They meant my grave. There was a hole in the backyard of that empty house, about five feet long and eighteen inches deep, and in that hole they found hair, blood, fibers. Everything I left behind was too degraded for identification purposes. That's what you become when you die but don't manage to do it properly: *too degraded*.

This is how I killed him:

I woke in the dark, choked on a mouthful of mud, and I panicked. I clawed my way through the soil and sod until I found air, and there was a pair of hands, his hands, scooping the dirt away from my face. He was murmuring as he dug, "Oh, you're perfect, you're beautiful, you're *perfect*." There was dirt in my ears, packed around my head, but I could hear him. His voice was breathless, excited but quiet. "Calm down, sweetheart, calm down."

He cupped his hands around my head and tugged at my hair. I couldn't see. I couldn't breathe. I didn't want him touching me. I grabbed his wrists, and I *pulled*. I didn't make a decision. My mind was blank with fear. Everything was wrong, twisted and nauseating. There was something foul in him I wanted to destroy, a dark quivering thread stretched taut between us, and I broke it.

He died. He died, and two things happened.

My heart, limp and lifeless, began to beat again.

And all of the man's memories about the murders he had committed thirty years ago flooded into me.

I remembered children slumped over their dinners of pork roast and potatoes. The littlest girl had fallen out of her chair. Blood soaked the tablecloth, the carpet, streaked the wallpaper in bright splashes. I felt the kick of the shotgun and my bloody hands slick on the knife. The winter wind was cold and howling through an open door. I smelled rosemary and beer and piss. The children had wet themselves. The woman took her last breath. It gurgled in her throat, and she was gone.

I remembered it all as though I had been there.

I still remember. It's faded now, but the memories I steal never disappear entirely. That family, whoever they were, they died almost fifteen years before I was born, in a state I had never visited, but I am the only person left in the world who knows what happened to them.

Their killer was there when I woke up. He was dead before I saw his face. I know what he did, but I don't know his name.

It was an accident, the first time I killed. It was an instinct I didn't know I had. I never made a choice.

The second time was on purpose.

# ⫴ TWO ⫴

IT WAS LATE AFTERNOON and a storm was coming. The wind was picking up, and there were towering thunderheads stacked high in the west. Down the interstate lightning flashed through a black curtain of rain. I was sitting outside a truck stop west of Omaha, Nebraska, perched on a low brick wall that enclosed a bed of wilting flowers. I had my backpack hooked around one arm, my skateboard at my feet, my eyes hidden behind a pair of pink heart-shaped sunglasses. I watched strangers stop, park, head into the convenience store or the restrooms, return to their cars. They frowned at the storm and drove away.

I couldn't decide who to approach. Families were out of the

question. Nobody invited a stranger into the car with their kids, not even a stranger who looked as harmless as I did. Same with most elderly couples. Young couples or groups of college students were a better bet, the right mix of careless and sympathetic. Some of them would give me a few bucks or offer to let me use their phones or buy me a meal. I took the money but turned down the phones and the food. I didn't have anybody to call, and I don't need to eat anymore.

I wasn't the only suspicious teenager hanging around. Across the parking lot, a short guy with black hair and black clothes and a lot of piercings was approaching drivers at the pumps and outside the restaurant. He talked to them for a few minutes, handed over a blue paper from a stack, walked away with a thank you and a smile. In between conversations he tucked fliers beneath the windshield wipers of parked cars.

I watched him work, not all that curious, until I realized he was watching me too.

I looked away. I didn't want to attract any attention, but it was too late. The guy wandered over, taking his time. He looked like he couldn't decide if he should speak or not. His face was round and pink cheeked and spotted with acne. He had a soft gray shadow around him, the kind of shadow I could feel but not see, but I didn't think it was a killer's shadow. It was too feeble for that.

"Hey," said the kid. His voice was deeper than I expected, but his smile made him look all of twelve years old. "You seem like you're in some kind of trouble."

"Not really," I said. I didn't offer anything else. If he was a thirty-year-old creep hanging around a truck stop pretending to be a fresh-faced teenager, I didn't want to encourage him.

"Sure, okay," he said with a shrug. "But if you are, here." He peeled one of his blue papers off the stack and held it out to me. "I'm not saying you need it, because you're not saying you need it, but if you're heading west and you need a place to stay, it's an option. They're good people."

I took the page from him. NEED HELP? it asked in all caps printed across the top. Below, in smaller letters, it encouraged me to visit the Church of the Prairie. There was an address, a little square map with a star marking the spot in western Nebraska, and the promise of a bed, a shower, a hot meal. At the bottom, a Bible verse: "For I was hungry and you gave me food, I was thirsty and you gave me drink, I was a stranger and you welcomed me." Matthew 25:35.

I folded up the paper and shoved it into my backpack.

"Just tell them Danny sent you," the kid said. He said it like he had said it a hundred times, reading from a script that didn't particularly interest him anymore. "Not Daniel. Daniel's somebody else. Not that it matters—he's a good guy too—but I'm Danny."

"Thanks, Danny, not Daniel," I said. I didn't even try to make it sincere. "But I'm fine."

"They're not, like, Jesus freaks or anything," Danny said. He shook his black hair out of his face. "I mean, they are, but they don't care if you aren't. They won't ask any questions. They'll just help you figure out what to do next."

"That's nice of them," I said. I wanted him to go away. He wasn't offering a ride and he wasn't a killer; he didn't have anything that interested me. "I'm still fine."

"Sure, okay, but sometimes you don't know you need help until it's too late, you know?"

Danny waited. Maybe he wanted me to give in and admit that I had no money, no ride, no one to call. Maybe he could tell just by looking at me that it had been ten days since I'd managed more personal hygiene than a cold water splash in a gas station bathroom.

I let him wait. I stared at him until he shrugged and he said, "Suit yourself."

He walked away. He looked back a few times, like there was something he wanted to say. I felt a pang of worry, but I ignored it. I looked suspicious enough for perfectly ordinary reasons: a dirty teenage girl in stolen clothes and stupid sunglasses, lurking around a truck stop, alone. He didn't recognize me. It had been over a year, and what had made the local news in Evanston was of no interest in Nebraska. He was just a kid who got paid a few bucks to hand out church fliers in his free time. I lost track of him and went back to searching for my next ride.

I didn't have a plan. I hadn't had one since I left Chicago. My first ride had taken me south to Indianapolis before I decided I wanted to go west instead. I hitched a ride with a friendly stoner heading to Iowa City to pick up his little sister from her first year at college. He smoked joint after joint and listened to Phish bootlegs for the entire five-hour drive, and when we got to Iowa City he gave me a twenty-dollar bill and told me to enjoy life. After we parted ways, I hung around a big interstate gas station, looking as helpless as possible, until I met a gray-haired trucker named Dottie. She grunted with disinterest when I told her my made-up life story: I was a college student whose roommate and ride home for the summer had copped out at the last minute. Dottie only said, "You don't look like trouble," and she said, "You're too young to be out here alone," and, "I can take you as far as Omaha, then my route turns around."

The cab of her truck smelled of cigarette smoke, stale coffee, fast food. She didn't say much during the hours I rode with her, and when she did talk, she talked about her son, who was twenty-nine years old and missing. In December he had taken a business trip to Pittsburgh and never came home. The cops didn't bother looking. Dottie had taken time off a couple of months back to go and search for him, but she didn't know anything about his business, didn't know his friends or girlfriends or enemies. She spent two days driving aimlessly around Pittsburgh in the slushy gray winter. Her son was gone and she didn't know why.

Drug dealer, I decided. Being uncharitable toward a stranger made it easier for me to avoid thinking about my own mother and what she didn't know.

"You can't trust anybody anymore," said Dottie. "Not even your own kid."

Her voice was rough, her eyes sad. Her hopelessness felt like an empty space beside me, a hole eating away the fading echoes of a life. I was relieved when she dropped me at the truck stop and drove away.

As the thunderstorm gathered in the west, I rested my feet on my skateboard and rolled it back and forth, back and forth. Across the parking lot Danny was in conversation with a white-haired old lady. He was smiling and she was charmed; I looked away when he glanced toward me. A few more hours and the gas station employees would notice I was still sitting outside. I had a story ready, but I didn't want to linger. I wanted to keep moving.

A few minutes later, my ride showed up.

I felt him before I saw him. The sensation was sudden and unmistakable.

*Killer.*

It was a busy truck stop, dozens of cars passing through, and it took me a moment to pinpoint him. Second row of pumps, number five. His car was a blue Corolla. Minnesota plates. He had an eye on the approaching storm as he filled the tank. He didn't clean the windshield. When he was finished, he ripped the receipt from the pump and got back into the car.

If he had driven away, I would have put him out of my mind. I would have watched his blue Corolla leave and felt him recede, a fading murmur under my skin, until he was gone.

But he didn't. He parked beside the store and went inside. He came out a few minutes later with a soda and a bag of pretzels. He looked so very ordinary, but he felt like a tangled mess of shadows. Weeds and vines and oily black worms beyond the edge of my vision. Dark squirming shapes at the corners of my eyes. The taste of ash at the back of my throat. All of those things and none of them. It made me think about bonfires, graveyards, dark damp holes in the ground, about waking up with dirt packed in my mouth and bruises in the shapes of fingers around my throat, and the excruciating, exultant pain of a beating heart after a year of stillness. It was the best feeling I knew, and the worst.

He wasn't the first person I had found who felt like that. He wasn't the strongest, or the sickest, or the most tantalizing. But he was right there.

I looked up and caught his eye.

He stopped, and he smiled.

"Hi," he said. "Are you waiting for somebody?"

I sighed, loud and exaggerated. "No," I said. I tried my best to look annoyed with just a hint of worry. "I mean, maybe? I don't know. My roommate was supposed to give me a ride home for the summer, but she changed her mind at the last minute and decided to go visit her boyfriend in New York instead. Her boyfriend she met on the internet. She doesn't even *know* him."

That's what had happened to Maria Garcia's cousin last Christmas break. Two Christmases ago, now. I had missed one. I remembered Maria reading text messages and saying, "That's what she gets for rooming with such a slut." Maria had a million cousins and she loved to gossip about them. It was easy to borrow their lives for my temporary lies.

The man asked, "There's no one you can call?"

"My parents are in Europe," I said. "They told me to buy a bus ticket but I figured, well, it's just as easy to get a ride, you know? Save me a couple hundred bucks."

"Where's home?"

"Denver," I said. I had no idea which direction he had been heading before he pulled off for gas. I didn't know the first thing about Denver. "Well, near Denver. Close."

The man's smile grew wider, but he checked himself and put on an expression of false concern. "I'm headed that way."

"Yeah?"

"I know this is weird, but it's a long drive and I wouldn't mind the company to help me stay awake."

I pretended to think about it. "I don't know."

"Right, I know," he said, too quickly. "I understand. Do you want money for a bus ticket or something? I don't have much cash on me, but I hate to see you stuck here."

I stood up slowly, hooked the backpack over my shoulder. "Where did you say you were going?"

He was headed to Utah to visit his mom, and he didn't mind taking I-70 through Denver instead of I-80 through Wyoming on the way. He liked the scenery, he said. Prettier mountains.

"I know how much it sucks to be stranded." He laughed, and it was almost believable. It would have been if I couldn't feel what he was. "I'm not a serial killer, I'm promise."

"That's exactly what a serial killer would say," I said.

"Good point. But it's really not safe for you to hang around here. You look like you could use the help."

I made him wait while I thought about it. I caught sight of Danny walking around the pumps. He was talking to somebody, but he looked over, like he felt me watching. He wasn't smiling his cherubic little kid smile anymore. The storm was blowing closer, the wind growing stronger. The afternoon was dark enough for the cars on the highway to switch on their lights. Those coming from the west were splattered with rain.

He wasn't lying about one thing: He wasn't a serial killer. Not yet. He had killed before, but only once. I didn't know his story or his real name yet, but I knew he was a murderer.

I couldn't read his thoughts. It's not like that, not until they die. I don't know if they're bad people or good people, if they enjoy their lives or hate them, if they look forward to every new day or dread it. I don't know if they've been arrested, convicted, imprisoned. I don't know if it was on purpose or an accident. I can only sometimes feel if they regret it; guilt and regret are such slippery, untrustworthy things. I don't know if they have parents or spouses or children, if they're going home to their wives or if they've left everybody behind. I don't know if they ever had anybody at all. I don't even know if they're human or not.

But I always know if they've killed someone.

It's not much of a party trick.

"Okay," I said. I kicked up my skateboard, caught it in one hand. "Thanks. I'm sick of being stuck here."

The man led the way back to his blue Corolla. I put my skateboard in the backseat and let him open the passenger door for me.

"What's your name?" he asked.

"Melanie." I felt stupid as soon as I said it. My real name is Breezy, and I had meant to name one of Maria's endless supply of cousins, like I had when Dottie the truck driver asked. But Melanie's name was out before I could stop myself. Saying it aloud felt like a spark of electricity, quick but painful for the moment it lasted.

"Nice to meet you, Melanie," he said. "I'm Tate. Let's hope that storm up ahead isn't as bad as it looks."

# ⋙ THREE ⋙

THE STORM WAS just as bad as it looked. The rain broke over
us with shattering noise. Thunder crashed and I jumped, laughed
uneasily. The man who called himself Tate switched on the wipers
and the headlights. He sat forward in the driver's seat, both hands
on the wheel, and followed too close behind a minivan slicing wet
channels across the asphalt. The traffic marched in lines of white
from the west, red straight ahead, blurred and indistinct in the
downpour. It was too loud to talk. We crept along for forty-five
minutes, maybe an hour, barely making any progress before the
rain slackened.

The man eased back into his seat and turned the wipers down

a notch. "At least it's not a tornado."

"You had to go and say that, didn't you?" The air conditioner was blowing cool air across my skin, raising goose bumps on my arms. I leaned forward to peer through the windshield. "The sky doesn't look green. I hope you didn't jinx us."

"I have better luck than that," he said.

I had always been afraid of thunderstorms before, ever since I was little. My dad had tried to explain to me what they were and how they worked: air pressure and temperature changes, electrical discharges and cloud formations. He thought laying it all out in scientific terms would help. But knowing how lightning happened didn't make it any less frightening, not when I was ten.

That was before. There wasn't much point in being frightened anymore. I stared out the window at the rain-battered fields and wondered what it would be like to be caught in a tornado. Lifted up and tossed around, scoured and stripped and dropped miles away, a bloody piece of debris in a pile of rubble. I could add it to the list.

The traffic grew heavier when we passed through Lincoln, dissipated on the other side. It was evening on a Tuesday or Wednesday; I had lost track of the date. The man asked if I minded a short stop to grab some food. He chose a roadside diner with a neon sign and a dirt parking lot. I didn't want anything but he insisted, so I asked for a milk shake. It was chocolate but tasted like ash. He ordered the special, pork chop and mashed potatoes and soggy green beans, and he smothered the entire plate in ketchup.

He talked about himself while he ate. None of it was true. He told me he was an economics professor from Michigan. I made the appropriate impressed noises to keep him talking, but I couldn't look at him. The smell of his dinner reminded me of a faraway house splattered with blood and small bodies collapsed over their plates. Outside a rainbow curved over the landscape. The clouds broke briefly to let shafts of evening sun shine through.

I blinked, the clouds closed, and the sunlight faded again. I excused myself to the bathroom to throw up the milk shake. My body doesn't digest food anymore.

When we were on the road again, the man who called himself Tate laughed self-consciously and said, "We've got a lot more hours of this great scenery ahead of us, and it only gets more boring from here. Tell me about yourself, Melanie. What are you studying in school?"

I invented a story for him. I wove together pieces of Maria Garcia's cousin, Sandra Ulster's stepsister who lived in her parents' basement and played the banjo, Marcus Reyes's brother who had won a swimming scholarship and might be training for the Olympics, bits and pieces of secondhand acquaintances and friends of friends. I told him I was a freshman at the University of Chicago, studying biology or maybe chemistry, and I was going to work as a lifeguard for the summer. I was an only child and my parents were lawyers.

"Not, like, criminal lawyers," I said. "Car accident lawyers. You know. Like the kind you see on TV."

I offered a silent apology to my parents for forcing them into such an embarrassing profession.

I didn't tell him one true thing about myself. It was easier that way. I was a patchwork person, stolen scraps stitched together with the frailest threads. If he cared at all, he would have seen the lies for what they were.

But he didn't care that I was lying to him. Every few moments he tapped nervously on the steering wheel and glanced my way. I didn't need to read his thoughts to know what he was thinking. He was planning. Wondering how long he had to drive before he could find an isolated place to pull over. Thinking about what he would say, how he would deflect my worries, what excuse he would give. How it would feel.

I leaned into the door and hitched one leg up, hugged my knee to my chest. I hadn't bothered with the seat belt. If we crashed, that could be another item on my list.

I knew I ought to be scared. But all I felt was a faint flutter beneath my ribs that was a little like excitement, a little like hunger. He thought I was helpless, but I knew something he didn't know: he couldn't hurt me.

I had never before had that kind of power over someone.

I tucked the feeling down in my gut in a tight little ball, small and black like a frightened roly-poly bug, and kept it in the same place where I kept my real name, my real story.

When we were back in the car and on the road, I leaned my head back against the seat and faked a yawn.

"Tired?" said Tate.

"A little."

"You can go ahead and sleep," he said. "I was just kidding about making you keep me company."

I yawned again. "Thanks."

The night grew darker as we drove west. I pretended to drift off, but I don't sleep anymore. Rain came and went in quick taps on the windshield. The air smelled like ozone and exhaust and manure. The man murmured to himself from time to time. I couldn't make out the words.

A couple of hours outside Lincoln, he turned the signal on, slowed the car, and eased to an exit. I kept my eyes closed. I felt us stop for a moment, then we turned right. The road was rough and loud beneath the tires. He drove for another twenty, thirty minutes before stopping.

He turned off the engine. His seat belt clicked and rasped as it retracted.

"Nobody will know," he said, a whisper under his breath. "It's okay. It's okay. Nobody will know."

There was a soft thump as he hit the steering wheel with both palms. I waited for the fear. He had made his choice. I should be scared now. But all I felt was tired. Tired, and disappointed that I had been right. He could have kept driving through the night and into the morning. He didn't have to stop.

"Nobody will know," he said again.

I opened my eyes. He was looking right at me.

"Don't move," he said. His voice shook. He gripped the steering wheel. His lower lip was trembling, his shoulders tense, the line of his neck taut as a steel cable. "Don't move. You—you stupid, you freaky bitch, what are you doing?"

I didn't say anything. I wasn't moving. I wasn't doing anything except waiting.

"How stupid are you?" He hit the steering wheel again. "What the hell did you expect, getting into a car with a stranger? Didn't your mother tell you that's asking for trouble?"

I clenched my hands together in my lap. I could barely remember how it had happened before, when I'd woken in the grave with the stranger kneeling over me.

"You should have known better," he said.

"I know," I said.

He launched himself across the car and slammed my head into the window. The angle was bad, he was shaking and grasping, but I felt his fingers dig into my neck, pressing against my windpipe. He wasn't strong enough to hold me. He didn't know what he was doing. But I didn't try to push him away. All I did was close one hand over each wrist, and I *pulled*. The shadowed vines wrapped around us, an impenetrable tangle.

His eyes went wide with surprise and anger—anger that I would fight back, anger that it wasn't going to be easy. His face turned red and beads of sweat formed on his brow. His pupils were dilated, his mouth open slightly, pink tongue pressed between crooked front teeth. He was trying to say something. His lips moved, fishlike, but the only sound he could make was a weak kittenish mewl.

Something dark and oily inside him snapped.

I felt his heart beat once, twice, stuttering—and no more.

I was standing in a kitchen. I was raising a baseball bat. I was swinging it down. A small body crumpled before me.

The man's hands dropped from my neck. I shoved him away and he slumped against the steering wheel. His eyes were open, his mouth gaping. He was dead.

I pushed the door open and tripped out. My heart was racing, my breath coming in quick, painful gasps. I dropped to my knees, gagged and spat on the ground. I felt like I was buzzing on caffeine, on adrenaline, trembling so bad it was all I could to do crawl away from the car. I curled onto my side and lay there for a long time in the glow from the headlights, and I remembered.

A little kid. A boy. He had killed a little boy who liked baseball and video games and had come home early to get a snack of peanut butter and crackers. The brat wasn't supposed to be there, not while his mom was at work. There was an open jar of peanut butter on the counter, a glass of milk beside it. The kid was always sticking his fingers in the jar. His blood spread across the yellow linoleum floor. He wasn't supposed to be there. His baseball bat was supposed to be in his room, or in the garage, not right there in the living room. He was always sticking his nose where it didn't belong. He would still be alive if he had put his bat away. If he knew how to keep his mouth shut. If he for once in his life had used a knife to spread the peanut butter instead of sticking his fingers in the jar.

A long time passed before I was able to sit up.

A mosquito whined in my ear; I waved it away. We were parked on a rutted dirt driveway by a narrow road. Lights of isolated farmhouses shone in the distance. The car clicked as the engine cooled. The night was quiet, the prairie grass damp with rain. My hands shook as I rubbed them through the wet blades, wiped them over my mouth. I spat again.

When I was certain I could move without my heart bursting in my chest, I walked back to the car and took my backpack and skateboard out of the backseat. I found the man's wallet in his pocket. I didn't steal anything; I only wanted to know his real name. I tucked my sleeve over my hand and wiped my fingerprints from the inside of the car. Anything else they found, if they looked, would be too degraded to identify me.

Natural causes. That's what they would decide. His heart had stopped. Suspicious, out there on that empty road, so far from home, but there was no sign of foul play. I looked at him closely. He didn't look any different. He wasn't gray or shriveled or pale. The clinging black tangle that had hung around him was gone. What I felt in its place was an electric hum beneath my skin, the steady thump of my heart, a deep dull ache in the bruises around my neck.

I slammed the car door; the light went out.

I wanted him to look on the outside as he did on the inside. I wanted to feel guilty or sick or scared about what I had done. I wanted to regret it.

I didn't. He had been a murderer. Now he was a dead murderer.

I walked to the road and dropped my skateboard to the asphalt. I was only 50 percent sure I was heading toward the highway. I didn't care. I pushed myself faster and faster, much faster than I would normally go on a rough road in the dark, racing and reckless. The night air was cold and damp on my face, in my hair, on my tongue. It felt wonderful, the cleanest exhilaration you can imagine. I never wanted to stop.

# ✤ FOUR ✤

HIS REAL NAME was Duncan Palmer. He was forty-seven years old. He had been a bank teller in Minneapolis, but he had recently been fired from his job for losing his temper and making threatening comments to customers. He told his friends he was going to take a vacation to get his head together before he found another job.

He had been arrested two years ago as a suspect in the death of his ex-girlfriend's son. No charges were filed and he was released.

The boy had caught him with the sixteen-year-old babysitter while his mother was at work. The girl had run away, humiliated, and Duncan Palmer had panicked. He hit the kid repeatedly over the head with a baseball bat. The bat had been a birthday present from Palmer a few months earlier; he had spent too much money on a good one, never mind that the boy was the worst player on his Little League team and the mother wasn't impressed.

The boy had died on the kitchen floor. Duncan Palmer wrapped the body in plastic and drove out of the city to dump it. A woman walking her dog found the boy the next day.

The cops suspected the man from the start, but the babysitter lied and Palmer lied. The mother lied and swore he would never hurt her son. Maybe she even believed it. The case went unsolved. They blamed it on a home invasion gone bad.

Not all of that was in the news, but there was enough in the memories for me to put the story together.

By the time I met him, Duncan Palmer was thinking about doing it again. The possibility was there in the back of his mind, wrapped up on those vines and thorns that tasted of ash, deep and thrumming like a distant drumbeat. He had gotten away with it before. It had been the most exciting day of his life.

He was the second man I killed.

Some days I feel bad about it. Most days I don't.

The kid was short, chubby, with dirt brown hair and brown eyes. He only wanted a snack. I can still smell the peanut butter.

# ᴑ|ᴑ FIVE ᴑ|ᴑ

DUNCAN PALMER HAD driven us several miles along a county road north of I-80, through gently rolling fields surrounded by wire fences. It was a dark night, most of the sky covered with clouds. The pavement was uneven and rough, difficult to skate on, but I barely noticed. I kicked and kicked and my legs never grew tired. I was energized, my nerves sparking, my blood flowing, my heart beating so strong I could feel it in my ears and my fingertips.

I wound my way along the grid of country roads for miles. Trees loomed beside the road, dropped away as I passed them, and insects buzzed in the darkness. A few cars passed, headlights bright and white. Some slowed when they saw me, but none stopped. The rich night air rushed over me, soft on my skin, cool through my hair. My mind was empty.

I crashed once, not entirely on purpose. I knew I was going too fast when I crested the hill, but I didn't slow down. I hit a pothole in the asphalt near the bottom, on the outside edge of a sharp turn. My skateboard went left and I went right. The momentum carried me straight into the trunk of a tree.

I lay on the ground for a few minutes, dazed and hurting.

I moved my head, neck, arms, hands. I probed at the abrasions on my face. If there were hairline fractures in my ribs or cracks in my skull, they would heal themselves. If there was blood collecting in my brain, it would drain away. The scratches on my chin and cheek bled sluggishly for a minute or two, then stopped. I would have fading yellow bruises and new scars by morning.

The worst of the pain passed. I sat up, took my notebook out of my backpack. It was too dark for me to read what was already written on the page, but I didn't need to. I knew the list by heart. I had started writing it shortly after I woke up. A record of experimental trial and error: all the ways I could not die.

I added one more line:

8. *Skated face-first into tree.*

As failed deaths went, that one was pretty embarrassing, but in the spirit of scientific inquiry I couldn't leave it out. I sat cross-legged beside the road until the sting in my skin faded, then I found my skateboard and I kept going.

The clouds gathered and parted through the night. It rained a few times and my hair and clothes grew damp, but it always passed. I stopped once at an empty intersection, not because I needed a breath and not because I cared that I was lost. I only wanted to taste the cool damp air and listen to the quiet. There was enough of a clear patch overhead for me to recognize the broad *W* of Cassiopeia, but I couldn't see much else. As I watched, the clouds drifted over her.

It figured that now that I was here, in the dark in the middle of nowhere, no cities to speak of for hundreds of miles, it was too cloudy to see anything.

But I didn't have to leave.

The thought drifted into my mind, curious and bright, like a fish behind the curved glass of an aquarium.

I didn't have to keep moving. If I wanted, I could lie down in one of these fields. It wouldn't matter if it rained because I couldn't get sick. I didn't have to worry about the cold. I didn't have to eat. I didn't have to sleep, or find a safe place, or do anything at all. I could lie beneath a shade tree and use my backpack as a pillow and wait through the day, watch the clouds clear, watch the sunset, watch the stars come out again. I could do that for as many nights as I cared to count. I could never see anybody again.

No murderers. No memories.

Eventually the hollow cold that wasn't hunger would fill me again, but I could wait it out. Maybe my heart would slow, my blood would grow sluggish in my veins, my lungs would spasm and shudder when I tried to breathe, and maybe I wouldn't mind so much, out here with nothing around but grass and stars, with no people dragging their guilt and grief and anger behind them like oily dark banners.

I had left home after I woke up because it was impossible for me to stay. There was a Breezy-shaped hole in the life I had once occupied. The girl I had been was gone. I didn't know what I was anymore.

I went west because it was as good a direction as any, and because I thought I might like to reach the Pacific Ocean before I made another decision. But I didn't have a plan. For the first time in my life I didn't have any idea what I could or should do next. I didn't have anywhere to be. Nobody was waiting for me. Nobody was expecting to see me ever again.

Grass rustled nearby and I started, spun so quickly I nearly lost my balance. It was only the wind pushing leaves against each other. I let out a loud breath, shook my head, and turned again.

There was something in the intersection.

It was pale and translucent and drifting a foot above the asphalt. It had the basic shape of a human body: limbs, torso, smudge of a head. The legs ended in shredded rags, the arms in spidery threads.

I thought: Mom and Dad would be so disappointed.

They had always told us there was no such thing as ghosts. No ghosts or spirits, no heaven or hell, no afterlife. When my youngest sister, Sunny, asked what happened to us when we died, our middle sister, Meadow, had scoffed and said, "You rot and worms eat your brain, stupid." Mom and Dad had hushed her, told her not to frighten Sunny, and they had explained that all that remained were the memories our loved ones carried with them and the impact of the things we had accomplished. Nothing in their view of the world allowed for the possibility of ghosts in empty intersections, shadows clinging to murderers, or the half-dead thing I had become.

"Hi," I said.

The ghost had no face. It drifted in the breeze, like a tattered flag on a pole, but it gave no sign that it had heard me. It didn't come closer. It didn't move away. It didn't do anything. I walked around it in a slow circle; it didn't turn.

I reached out to touch it. It felt like nothing at all, not even a cool puff of air. It had dark smears where its eyes ought to be.

I stopped bothering the ghost and headed west along the road again. When I looked back, it was still there, a pale drift above the road, tiny in the dark prairie night.

# ᛁᛁᛁ SIX ᛁᛁᛁ

THE NIGHT I DIED was warm and clear. I remember joking with Melanie when we slammed the doors of her mom's car, the mini-van with the stick-figure family displayed on the back window. Two parents, two kids, two dogs. I remember laughing as we dodged sprinklers on somebody's lawn and slipped on the grass. Everything was laughter and light and fun. There was nothing before us but our last summer of high school stretching long and open.

Later she would recoil, and my face would sting where she slapped me, and I would leave the party alone.

Later still I would grow cold and stiff in a backyard grave, but I don't remember that.

On the day I came back to life, hundreds of birds within a two-mile radius dropped dead with no warning and a freak storm covered the city with frost.

I don't remember much of the year in between.

I don't remember the police, the searches, the interviews. I don't remember the headlines: EVANSTON TEEN MISSING. I don't remember the articles: "Breezy Lin, 17, was reported missing by parents David Lin and Erin Donahue after she failed to return home from a party on Saturday night." I don't remember the interviews, the speculation, the online comments, the inevitable school assembly. I don't remember my parents giving press conferences, my sisters beside them. Sunny cried and Meadow scowled while Mom and Dad held my picture and pleaded, but I don't remember it. I don't remember that picture appearing every night on the local news: last year's school photo, taken when my hair was longer and I was wearing an electric blue shirt I had since given to Meadow. I don't remember the posters stapled up around town. I don't remember the police dogs barking and tugging through the neighborhood.

They had no chance of finding me. I don't smell like myself anymore. I'm too degraded.

I don't remember any of it. I read about it afterward.

You don't sleep when you're dead, but you can dream. During that year I lay buried in my grave, I dreamed about darkness and space and silence. During that year, I was alone.

I always wanted to be an astronaut when I grew up. Not in the casual, halfhearted way all kids want to be astronauts when they go through their drawing-pictures-of-Saturn phase, but truly, earnestly. I was going to be a member of the first manned mission to Mars.

I decided when I was seven, and when I was eleven I worked it all out: the classes I would take in high school and what I would study in college, how long it would take me to get my PhD in astrophysics or planetary geology or engineering, the research projects I would do, the grants and internships I would get, all of it with the space program in mind. I seriously considered joining the air force but decided a career in scientific research was a better option. I had a long-term plan and a carefully annotated schedule in my desk drawer. I convinced my teachers to let me create independent math courses so I would already know calculus by the time I enrolled at MIT. I signed up for swimming lessons so I could ace NASA's swimming requirement. I wrote practice answers to imaginary interview questions. I asked my parents if I could go on a parabolic flight for vacation rather than our usual summer at the cottage on Lake Michigan. I had files and calendars and an entire shelf full of astronaut biographies. I had a map of Mars on my bedroom wall, another of the moon, and a space shuttle poster signed by Sally Ride and Mae Jemison. I had a T-shirt with a drawing of the cosmonaut dog Laika and would tell anybody who asked all about how she had died a horrible death alone and in pain above the earth.

Melanie said it was creepy that I knew that and I probably shouldn't talk about it if I wanted to keep my friends. I thought twice about wearing my Laika T-shirt after that, but I didn't stop. I just wore it when Melanie wasn't around.

A future in space was the only thing I had ever wanted.

My parents encouraged me. They were proud of my dreams and my determination. They told me I could do it, and I believed them.

I imagined hundreds of times what it would be like to float above the earth, a clear marble of green and blue and white below me, the stars at my back, specks of light in the cold and the silence, and the vast, incomprehensible beauty of the universe. Every astronaut, every cosmonaut, all the women and men who have gone into space, they all say the same thing: they went up expecting to be awed by the moon and the sun and the stars, but what astonished them most was the earth. Michael Collins, the astronaut who orbited the moon in the Apollo 11 Command Module while Neil Armstrong and Buzz Aldrin left footprints on the surface, once said that what he thought when he looked down at the earth was, "My god, that little thing is so fragile out there."

Being dead isn't like that.

Unfamiliar white stars pinpricked the darkness all around me, tiny and bright and impossibly distant. There was no earth, no moon, no sun. No strange planets wrapped in rings. No colorful nebulas or vast clouds of gas. Only stars.

No matter which way I turned, drifting and spinning helplessly in slow circles, nothing new ever came into view. My heart wasn't beating. I didn't breathe. I didn't think about anything.

The year passed, but I didn't feel it. All I felt was cold.

I didn't know I was waking up until it had already happened.

The birds started dying after midnight. The first people to notice were the early morning birders out before dawn, armed with their notebooks and binoculars, wrapped in scarves and puffy down coats against the surprise cold. They saw their blue jays and orioles and herons all struck dead on their migration north. The bird-watchers called animal control, and animal control called an environmental consultant, and the consultant called a wildlife biologist, and before the morning was over dozens of little feathered bodies were packed away in plastic bags and coolers and carried off to be tested. All over the city people were checking their backyards and gutters and warning their kids not to touch the corpses. In homes and pet stores, parakeets and finches and parrots were dropping dead in their cages.

The frost melted away before noon, and the birds kept dying. On the news a scientist insisted the freak cold snap had nothing to do with it, never mind that it was the middle of June and Illinois was ready for summer.

The last birds died just before midnight, and I came back.

One moment I was in the darkness, surrounded by stars, and the next I was coughing and choking. I couldn't move. There was something crushing me from all sides. When I tried to open my eyes, I felt a sharp, stinging pain. I couldn't see. The stars were gone, and there was no light. I tried to breathe, my lungs heaving and burning, but my mouth and throat were packed with dirt.

I kicked and clawed, and slowly, slowly, the soil above me loosened. I wasn't buried very deep. Eighteen inches, no more, but I was so weak I couldn't break through to the surface. I was thrashing and squirming, trying to push the soil away, and that's when I felt the man's hands on my face and heard his excited whispers.

Somebody besides the birders and the scientists had noticed the dying birds. Somebody who recognized the signs and knew that no natural weather phenomenon was responsible.

I grabbed his wrists. A thick, nauseating darkness washed over me, more suffocating than the soil, oily and slick and sickening.

I thought: *killer.*

I thought: *murderer.*

I only had to touch him and I knew what he was. I was holding his wrists, but it wasn't his flesh and bone I was feeling. It was the sick slippery guilt inside the meat shell.

I pulled without thinking, without hesitating, and he snapped. He was there one moment and gone the next. A lightning bolt of memories and blood and exhilaration exploded through me.

My heart shuddered, squeezed, began to beat again.

I hauled myself out of the grave. I fell onto my hands and knees, heaving and vomiting. I began to shiver. I was crying, tears streaking down my face, painful sobs shaking my body. I dug my fingers into my mouth to clear the dirt away, gagged and vomited again until my stomach ached and my throat burned.

I wiped a hand over my mouth and looked at the man lying on the ground. I checked his pulse because I thought I should, not because I didn't already know. His face was turned into the grass. He had a spot of thinning hair on the back of his head.

He had killed five people one winter night thirty years ago.

My ears rang with gunshots and screams. A woman's pleading voice. Only after several gasping minutes did the images soften, the smells fade, and I understood it was a memory.

I didn't feel weak anymore, but the nausea lingered. My blood was humming in my veins and my lips tingled. I spat on the grass; there was dirt in my teeth. My heart was thundering in my chest. I could feel the air filling my lungs, the muscles of my abdomen clenching, the nerves in my skin waking and pricking with pain. I could feel all of it. The awareness was overwhelming. In the darkness, surrounded by distant stars, there had been no time, but now I was counting the seconds with every breath and every heartbeat.

I breathed until my head stopped spinning. Every gulp of cold air was the best thing I had ever tasted. I lifted my head, waited to make sure I wasn't going to topple over, and stood.

I was in the backyard of a two-story house. There was no light through the back door or any of the windows. Somewhere nearby dogs were barking, angry and insistent. I realized I had been hearing them for some time.

I crossed the lawn, fumbled at the gate, pushed it open.

I kicked something soft and looked down: a little bird, still and brown and dead. I stared at it, waiting for a pang of revulsion, but I felt nothing. I brushed over its feathers with my bare toes. It was such a tiny thing, barely the size of my fist.

My eyes were gritty with dirt, scraping with every blink, but I recognized the neighborhood. I was only a couple of blocks from home.

# ⫸ SEVEN ⫷

IT BEGAN TO RAIN as dawn crept over western Nebraska. Within minutes I was soaked through, head to toe, but it was another few miles before I skated into a small town and found shelter in the local McDonald's.

My shoes skidded on the tile floor when I stepped inside. Shivering with cold, I went into the bathroom to change into the clothes I had taken from a Laundromat before leaving Chicago. The jeans were so long I had to roll them up, and the Wonder Woman T-shirt was meant for a little girl with a flat chest. I couldn't do anything about the shoes; I didn't have another pair. I finger-combed my hair into a ponytail, wrung out my scarf, and wrapped it again around my neck. It was clammy and uncomfortable, but it was better than letting people stare at the bruises.

My grandmother used to say, "You look like death warmed over," when my mother was tired or sick or worn down. I always thought it was a funny thing to say; I imagined coffins lined up on a baking sheet, sprinkled with sugar and frosting and ready to go into the oven. Grandma Elaine had died when I was eight. We went to San Francisco for her funeral, an open casket service, and I remember looking down at her thin white hair and pale face, stiff and unnatural beneath the heavy makeup, and knowing better than to ask my mother if it was time for Grandma to be warmed up now. It was cold in San Francisco that spring, rainy and gray everywhere we went, and I was worried Grandma would feel that way forever.

I didn't look like death warmed over. My face wasn't going gray. My skin wasn't shriveling up. My nails weren't yellowing and long. There were no hollow holes of rot opening in my face. I looked like a drowned rat in ill-fitting vagrant-chic clothes, but otherwise I looked like myself. There was a faint flush to my cheeks and my eyes were bright. I looked alive.

The cashier behind the counter raised her eyebrows when I walked up to order. "Get caught out?" she said.

"A little bit," I said.

"What can I get for you?"

"A small coffee, please." I dug into my backpack for the twenty the friendly stoner had given to me when we parted ways in Iowa City.

"And?" She was a middle-aged woman with graying hair and

deep lines around her eyes. Her fingers twitched over the register.

"That's it," I said.

I can't eat anymore. Everything tastes like dust.

I walked to a seat by the window. My shoes squelched. I felt the familiar tug as I passed a group of old men and women chatting over coffee and Styrofoam plates of pancakes: *killer, killer.* Their shadows were old and frail, spider-web wispy. The men were veterans. One of them was wearing a POW/MIA hat, another a US Navy jacket.

One of the old women, too: *killer.*

That would have surprised me before, when I was first feeling out the limits of my new sense, but an old lady in a pink cardigan is just as likely to be a murderer as anybody else.

The woman caught me staring. I turned away.

The rain showed no sign of letting up. Trucks passing on the interstate sent waves of water over the guardrails. I sat at my table by the window and shivered. I tried not to think too much about what I was doing and where I was going. I would worry about that when the rain stopped.

I took the notebook out of my backpack and unhooked the pen from the spiral. I turned to the third page and wrote: *Duncan Palmer. Little boy with a baseball bat.*

I breathed in the scent of the coffee to chase away the phantom smell of peanut butter.

The only other words on the page were: *Man by grave. Family of five with shotgun and knife.*

One didn't mean anything, but two was a body count. I was

tempted to number them, neat digits at the front of each line, but I didn't want *1* and *2* to imply there would be a *3* and *4*.

Instead I turned to a clean page and drew a long vertical line down the middle, another line across the top. At the top of one column I wrote *REAL*, and atop the other I wrote *NOT REAL*.

On the first line of the first column I wrote: *Whatever I am.*

Below that: *Ghosts.*

The Not Real column remained empty for now.

I drank my dust-flavored coffee as slowly as I could, but soon the cup was empty. It was still raining, I was cold and filthy and uncomfortable, and I smelled like a bum who had been sleeping in a Dumpster. There was grime underneath my fingernails, and my hair was tangled in knots. The nighttime exhilaration of racing along country roads in the darkness was gone. I wasn't sure how long I could hang around McDonald's before the employees asked me to leave.

I found Danny's blue flier, unfolded the paper, and smoothed it down on the tabletop. Church of the Prairie. I had no idea where I was in relation to that cross on the map. Nebraska had a lot of prairie and a lot of churches. I didn't need help. I definitely didn't need a hot meal. But a shower and clean clothes would be nice.

I grabbed the flier and walked over to the table of old men and women.

"Excuse me," I said. I held out the blue paper and tried to look as pathetic as possible. "I didn't mean to bother you, but I was wondering . . . Do you know where this is? Is it near here?"

One of the women smiled. It was a kindly grandmother's smile, crinkling up her face and warming her eyes. I wondered who she had killed. Her guilt was delicate and sharp, like brittle rose thorns in an old, old garden.

"It's not too close, sweetie, but it's not too far either," she said.

"Can you tell me how to get there?"

She took the flier from me. "Oh, we can't let you go out in that storm again. You're so little you'll get swept away."

They all laughed, and I laughed too. They invited me to have a seat. I looked harmless.

# ⊪ EIGHT ⊪

I DECIDED SHORTLY after waking up that I needed to take a rational approach to figuring out what happened to me. The first page of my notebook contains the record of that brief burst of scientific enthusiasm.

On the top line in block letters I wrote: *RESEARCH*.

And beneath it:

> *Preliminary research indicates that subject is not a living human person anymore. A review of the available literature is unclear on whether this state is permanent.*

By "review of the available literature" I meant I had googled "how do I not be undead anymore" and come up empty.

*Subject is still able to breathe, but respiration is not necessary. A similar situation persists with the circulatory system. The subject's heart will beat if instructed to do so, and sometimes when subject is not paying attention. There are no negative consequences to stopping the blood flow. Experimental evidence suggests this state can persist for at least six hours and forty-two minutes. Longer time periods have not yet been investigated as the subject grows bored with testing. In spite of the intermittent blood flow, there are bruises on the subject's skin that have not faded and show no signs of healing or yellowing. The bruises are arranged in a ring around the subject's neck. The pattern of bruising suggests the injury occurred*

My scientific report on my own apparent mortality stops midsentence. I told myself as I was writing that I found my own affected detachment silly and mildly embarrassing, the same way it became embarrassing to play make-believe with friends long after you knew it wasn't real but long before you were ready to admit it wasn't fun anymore.

I keep my notes in an ordinary seventy-page wide-ruled spiral notebook. On the cover is the NASA seal and a picture of the space shuttle *Discovery*. I've had it since the summer after sixth grade, when I wrote an essay about what space exploration means for the future of humanity and won a trip to a two-week space camp in Houston. They gave us the notebooks on the first day, but I never used mine except to write my name inside the front cover: *BREEZY LIN, ASTRONAUT,* in outrageously bold block letters. I didn't want to ruin the rest of the clean empty pages with my looping childish handwriting. They gave us NASA pens too, which didn't even last the full two weeks, and pins and stickers and patches to iron onto our backpacks.

When I got home from space camp I put the notebook in my desk and forgot about it. After I woke up in my backyard grave and went home, it was still there, sitting at the bottom of the drawer beneath a pile of birthday cards and postcards, notes Melanie and I had traded during ninth grade geometry, bad poetry and embarrassing lovesick letters sent to me by a persistent crush. The notebook and a pen were the only things I took from my room when I left. Nobody would miss it.

On the first page there are a couple of blank lines below the paragraph, then:

> *I've been missing for one year. I woke up buried in somebody's backyard.*
> *I don't remember dying.*
> *I don't remember.*

# ⑪⑪ N I N E ⑪⑪

THE LIST IS on the next page.

### 1. Sleeping pills

An entire bottle, choked down in several handfuls. In retrospect, it was a pretty stupid thing to try. If you can't sleep when you're dead, you definitely can't sleep deeply enough to never wake up.

That's also how I discovered that all of the things I had learned in anatomy class about the digestive tract being controlled by the autonomic nervous system didn't apply to me anymore. I can make myself breathe, can make my heart beat, but I haven't quite figured out how to make myself digest what I swallow. It sloshes around in my stomach until I make myself throw it up. My gag reflex works just fine.

### 2. Drowning

Lake Michigan is right there. I entertained brief and undignified thoughts about a future as a deep-sea treasure hunter while I was beneath the surface, but otherwise suffered no ill effects.

### 3. Rat poison

Our neighbor Mrs. Feely left her garage open one night. Same result as the sleeping pills, only with more self-induced vomiting.

### 4. Gunshot

Heart, not head. The biggest risk was the number of houses I sneaked into before I found a loaded weapon in somebody's bedside drawer. I was trying to be undiscriminating in my search, but it turned out the middle-aged white guy with the pickup truck and the racist antigovernment bumper stickers did not responsibly lock his weapons in a safe. I was so shocked.

### 5. Electrocution

It only occurred to me afterward that if I hadn't picked the right spot, completely by chance, I would have given some train operator or security guard a heart attack. I ruled out public locations after that.

### 6. Hanging

Boring. Also: hard to get down once I was dangling there.

### 7. Stabbing

Bathtub, kitchen knife. I knew by then nothing was going to work.

I couldn't die. No matter what I did, the wounds healed. They hurt, every single one, pain like I had never felt before. They bled, they burned, they left scars. But they healed. The list was pointless, but it was all I had. I didn't have any answers. I didn't even have the right questions. All I had was data, and all the data told me was that sometime between the moment I had died and the moment I woke up, I had become something unnatural, something not alive but not dead either, and I wasn't going to figure it out sticking knives in my stomach and watching my blood trickle down the drain.

## ❮|❯ TEN ❮|❯

THE OLD WOMAN'S name was Helen and she insisted I let her buy me another cup of coffee. I smiled shyly and sat with my backpack in my lap, my skateboard leaning against the side of the plastic booth. I told them the story about the irresponsible roommate and the change of plans. I only needed a place to get cleaned up, I said, and a ride to the nearest Greyhound station.

They made the appropriate noises of sympathy and agreed that while they didn't know anybody who attended that church—they were Methodists, you see, and went to First Methodist on Grove Drive when they went to church at all—Pastor Willow at the Church of the Prairie sure seemed like the right person to ask for help.

"We'll get you set right up, Katie," said Helen. "Don't you worry."

Katie was the name of Melanie's older cousin, the one who had run off years ago to be a jazz musician in New Orleans and stayed after Hurricane Katrina to rebuild houses for charity groups. The real Katie was tall with dyed red hair and had a voice like an alcoholic gospel singer.

"I don't want to be any trouble," I said. That was the only protest I offered. I had willingly gotten into the car with a murderer the day before, just to see what would happen. I wasn't worried about accepting help from strangers.

Helen patted my hand and volunteered to make the call when I admitted I didn't have a phone. Her skin was liver spotted but her touch was warm, and I let myself be reassured. For two weeks I had been on my own with my secrets. It was a relief to have somebody else take over, if only for a little while.

Even if she was a killer.

Helen couldn't hurt me. Her frail old shadows barely felt like guilt at all.

Her car was a boatlike brown Buick that coughed and trembled. We drove north out of town, away from the highway, until there was nothing but muddy fields striped with young crops as far as I could see. Helen never pushed the car above forty-five. We made awkward small talk during the long, slow drive. She was happy enough to chatter about her children and grandchildren who were coming to visit in a few weeks, even though they always complained there was nothing to do in Nebraska in the summer. Riding bikes and climbing trees in the sunshine and fresh air wasn't good enough for kids anymore, not like it had been when she was young.

She didn't mention a husband. I wondered if he was who she had killed.

The better part of an hour passed before Helen slowed the car and said, "Here we are."

The sign beside the road announced the Church of the Prairie in bold white letters, and below that: "Jesus is help in times of hardship. Sun Service AM," but there was no time specified. There was a cross atop the sign, the name and number of a Bible verse painted on the wooden frame.

Helen put on her blinker and turned off the road, over a culvert running with rainwater, and into a gravel parking lot. The church was a boxy wooden building, topped with an old-fashioned spire, white paint peeling and faded. Beside the church the heads of white crosses and gray headstones peeked above the grass. An old man stood at the edge of the cemetery, shoulders hunched in a blue jacket, head bowed beneath a brown fisherman's hat.

Next to the cemetery was a small playground wrapped in a chain-link fence. The structures were metal, rusted, paint falling away in patches, and the swing set was crooked, as though half its double A-frame was sitting on quicksand. Two kids kicked on the swings in the rain. A woman in a red raincoat watched them from beneath a black umbrella. She turned as we passed, but she didn't wave. Her face was shadowed by the hood of her jacket.

At the end of the muddy driveway was the farmhouse and barn, both surrounded by a quivering cluster of cottonwood trees. The house was desperately yellow, weathered, as badly in need of fresh paint as the church. The windows on its upper stories looked toward the road like twin rows of eyes. Small purple flowers poked out of the wood-chip mulch in front of the porch.

"Oh," I said. I swallowed and rubbed my palms over my knees. "It looks nice."

It was anything but nice. It was bleak and cold and unwelcoming. It was the ugliest shade of yellow I had ever seen.

There was nothing nearby. No other houses, no farm buildings. I couldn't even remember when Helen and I had last passed another car on the road. My heart was thudding and I felt a nervous twist in my gut. I wanted to tell Helen to turn the car around and take me away.

She parked in front of the house, but she didn't turn off the engine. "This is the place. They're expecting you."

I hesitated before putting my hand on the door handle. "It's kind of in the middle of nowhere, isn't it?"

"Right in the heart of God's country." Helen's smile was brief and watery. "Go on. No need to be shy."

I forced myself to return to smile and thanked her for the ride. I ducked into the rain and jogged to the front porch of the house.

As I climbed the porch steps, the door opened.

"There you are!"

The girl in the doorway wore a long flower-print dress with an old-fashioned lace collar, and her red hair was split into twin braids over her shoulders. She could have been cosplaying *Little House on the Prairie*, but I had a feeling this wasn't dress-up. She was in her twenties, fresh faced and pretty in a forgettable way, except for her astonishing green eyes. The color was so startling I wondered if it might be contacts.

"Hi," I said. Behind me Helen was already leaving. I fought the urge to run after her.

"You must be Katie," the girl said. She waved at Helen, received a brief horn tap in response. "Pastor Willow said you were on your way. Lunch is just about ready."

Then she smiled, and I nearly missed the last step.

I recognized her. I had seen that smile before.

My mind flicked through *school* and *camp* and *summer*, but nothing fit. I knew I had seen her before, that smile and that pretty red hair, the freckles across her nose and those green eyes, but I couldn't remember when or where.

"Yeah, I'm Katie," I said. For the first time since I had left Evanston, I felt guilty about lying to a stranger.

"I'm Violet," she said. She stepped aside to let me in. "I hope you like potato and cheese soup. I know it's more of a winter food, but it's so gloomy today I thought it was right. Come on in."

The front hall of the house was just as virulently yellow as the outside. The walls were papered with an alarmingly cheerful sunflower pattern, and an array of photographs in white frames marched in neat lines down the hallway and up the stairs. There were dozens of photos, more than I could count.

"Those are all the people Mr. Willow has helped," Violet said. "We keep the pictures around to remind ourselves how important our work is."

"Wow. There are a lot of them," I said.

Some of the photographs were old, with faded colors and fashions right out of the seventies or eighties, but most were more recent. They were all posed portraits of men and women looking toward the camera, but rarely directly at it, distracted, their minds elsewhere in spite of the photographer's best efforts. Some were smiling vacantly; most weren't.

"Mr. Willow has been helping people for a long time," Violet said. "That's him and his father."

She pointed to a photograph of a broad, unsmiling bear of man in a winter coat, standing beside a much skinnier teenage boy in corduroy and a patterned button-down, with a tragic bowl haircut and a vague frown.

"His father founded our congregation," she explained. "It's a very sad story, but Mr. Willow always says that adversity is an opportunity for us to learn our true strength."

The men in the photo weren't touching. They didn't look much like father and son. In the corner somebody had written the date: 1973.

"What happened?" I asked.

Violet's smile softened. She wasn't a killer. She had no shadows clinging to her. Her smile was so light, her expression so kind, I wondered if they would even dare. "It's better that he tells you. Do you want to get cleaned up before lunch?"

"I guess I should. Do I really look that bad?"

"You can do laundry too," she said with a laugh. "I have some clean clothes you can borrow. I'm glad you're here. It's been so quiet this week. Usually there are a lot more of us. Oh, here's Esme. Say hi, Esme."

In the front room there was a woman sitting in a wheelchair with a blanket folded over her knees. Her face was slack and she was thin in a wasted, unhealthy way, and she had a faint scar stretching from the corner of her eye down to her chin. Her shoulders hunched under a threadbare bathrobe and her hands were clenched on the arms of the chair. There was a towel tucked into the collar of her shirt; somebody had covered her up to help her eat but had forgotten to take it away when they were done.

The woman turned her head when Violet said her name. She stared at me, her wide brown eyes unblinking, until I looked away.

"She's a little shy," Violet said, and she smiled again, that same friendly smile, and I remembered where I had seen her before.

Not in person. We had never met.

But I had seen her face and her smile, and I had heard her voice.

That's what I remembered most clearly: the sound of her voice when she screamed.

## ◦⫴◦ ELEVEN ◦⫴◦

EVERY YEAR SINCE first grade, Diane Fordham invited a group
of us over for her birthday party at the end of the summer, and every
year I went to her big white house with a gift in hand. The inside of
the house was just as white as the outside: white sofas, white carpet,
white walls, white artwork in white frames. The only thing in the
living room that wasn't white was the cross on the wall, about six
inches long, plain polished wood hanging above the white fireplace.

I hated walking through that living room to the stairs. I worried
I would leave tracks on the carpet and Diane's mother and father—a
tall stern couple who worked for an investment firm—would look
down their thin noses and scold me for bringing dirt into their

home. It felt like a test, crossing that white living room, and I never exhaled until I reached the stairs and the relative safety of Diane's second floor family room. All through the night we would make excursions to the kitchen for snacks and soda, to the front door when we ordered pizza, but we were always quick, always careful, and every single time Diane said, "Don't spill anything." Every time. She had been hearing it her entire life; she blurted it out without thinking.

It was fun when we were little, that yearly sleepover with so little supervision, but Diane and I grew apart as we grew older, and her birthday party became a tiresome obligation. The rest of us changed, started caring more about sports and boys and music and college and the future, but Diane was still Diane, with her bedroom of girly ruffles and lace in that albino mausoleum of a house.

The August before our sophomore year of high school, the invitation came like it always had: a pink card in a square pink envelope, my name and address written in Diane's curling cursive. My mother had left it on my bed with a copy of *Scientific American* and another letter in a regular white envelope. I recognized the handwriting on that one too. I set it aside without opening it. I already had a collection of Ricky Benning's awkward notes and terrible poetry in my desk drawer. Melanie thought it was hilarious, and at first I had agreed, secretly pleased to be the object of somebody's attention, even a loser like Ricky Benning, but now it was only embarrassing.

I opened Diane's invitation and called Melanie.

"I can't believe she invited you," Melanie said, laughing. "I thought for sure you'd be off the list this year. You have a reputation now."

I was lying on my bed in my basement bedroom. The day was hot and sticky, but the basement was always cool, even through the long summer afternoons. The glow-in-the-dark sticker stars on my ceiling were faint yellow smudges against the off-white paint. Melanie's words stung, but I wasn't about to let her know. I remembered my aunt Colleen giving me a warning a few years before, as we were fixing Thanksgiving dinner. Colleen had said, "You have to be careful, Breezy. I know it doesn't seem like a big deal now, but nobody ever cares about having a reputation until they've got a bad one."

Melanie loved that I had a bad reputation now, but she hated it too. She hated that there were things I had done before her, without her help, without her input. Her jealousy was petty, needlelike, deployed at unpredictable moments. I didn't have any defenses against it. Not against Melanie. Not against my best friend. All I had was the naive hope that after three months of summer nobody would care any more about the rumors that had raced around before the end of the school year. Mostly true, but not completely: I did have sex with Michael Chaffert, my first time and he knew it, but I didn't know he had a girlfriend at the time, and I definitely didn't beg him to introduce me to all his friends for a whole summer of repeat performances. I don't think anybody even believed that last part; everybody knew Michael couldn't tell the truth about girls or sex if his life depended on it. But what they believed and what they laughed about were two different things.

After a few weeks I had realized that denying Michael's version of events wasn't making any difference, so I chose another tactic. I told anybody who mentioned it that fucking Michael had been the dullest three minutes of my life and I couldn't even be sure it had happened at all, that's how little I felt, emphasis on the *little*. Maybe it wasn't in line with Aunt Colleen's well-meaning advice, but I had decided, as soon as ninth grade ended, that it was better to be scornful than shamed.

It didn't matter anyway, not after Cherie Kostova turned up drunk on the first day of school and wrecked her car on the third, and not after a junior named Samantha French announced that he was now Samuel French and the teachers and counselors scrambled to put together sensitivity groups and stumbled over pronouns, not after Lindy Oliver went off her meds and threw a chair across the room during Mr. Park's class discussion about *Ethan Frome*. There was always somebody doing something more shocking, more out-rageous, more interesting. I was completely irrelevant by the time our sophomore year began.

But I didn't know that yet, during the last week of summer, and I was tired of not knowing how much to care.

I put my feet up on my windowsill and dropped Diane's invitation on the bed beside me.

"Well, she did," I said. "Are you going?"

Melanie laughed again. "No way. Don't you think we're a little old for pizza and stupid horror movies now?"

I did, but I went to Diane's birthday party anyway, mostly because I was angry at Melanie for deciding who among our acquaintances would still want me around and who wouldn't. I wrapped up a present in gold and white paper, rang the doorbell, smiled when Diane's mother answered.

Mrs. Fordham's expression was distant and cool. "Diane and the others are upstairs. I'm so glad you could make it."

She didn't greet me by my name; I wasn't sure she even knew it. After the party the year before, as I had been rolling up my sleeping bag and shoving my clothes into my backpack, I had heard Mrs. Fordham saying to her daughter, "Why don't you ask that nice Oriental girl to help you study? They're very good at school, you know. It's part of their culture." I didn't hear Diane's answer, but she never did ask me to help her study.

I hurried through the white living room, conscious of my shoes on the carpet, of Mrs. Fordham's eyes on my back. I gave her a quick smile before running up the steps. Diane was there, of course, and her two best friends Courtney and Julie, but so were Maria and Tatiana. I was relieved to have at least two real friends for the night.

Diane unfolded herself from her corner of the sofa and stood to take the present from me.

"Thank you," she said stiffly. "I didn't want to invite you, you know."

I was surprised by her directness. I knew Diane didn't like me very much and inviting me to her birthday party was more habit than anything else, but we usually pretended. We were pretty good at pretending.

"But my mom would wonder where you were if I didn't," Diane went on. "She doesn't know what a slut you are. I wasn't going to tell her."

"Jeez, Diane," Maria said. "You don't have to be a bitch about it."

But she laughed, because Maria laughed at everything, and I had to laugh too. Melanie would love to know she had been right. I had managed to get dirt all over Diane's pretty white house even without spilling a thing.

Diane ignored me for the rest of the night. We watched a movie about college kids getting murdered by a professor possessed by the spirit of a serial killer, and when it was done Diane ordered pizza and dragged Courtney downstairs to fetch soda and chips. When they came back, Diane had a DVD case in her hands. It was plain on the outside, printed words and no pictures; she tucked it between the arm and cushion of the chair before we could see it. Tatiana asked her if she had any alcohol, just to see how she would react, and Diane informed us that nobody in her family would *ever* drink.

The pizza arrived, we scattered paper plates and napkins all over the room, and Maria launched into a story about her cousin in Mexico who had decided to hitchhike through Central and South America, all the way down to the tip of the continent, and the trouble he was getting into, the people he was meeting, the mornings he woke up confused and disoriented after partying with strangers. It sounded equal parts fun and terrifying, and when Maria was finished, Julie said she would like to do something like that, something brave and adventurous, maybe after graduation. The rest of us agreed in the way of girls who had three long years before *after graduation* meant anything, a safe distance from which all wild ideas were possible.

But not Diane. Diane only said, "That's awful. He's going to get himself killed." Then she carried the DVD over to the player, put it in before any of us could get a look at it. "We're watching this next."

"What is it?" Courtney asked.

"My youth pastor gave it to me," Diane said. Courtney groaned and rolled her eyes; Diane glared at her. "It's not like *that*. It's not a church thing. It's better than a horror movie, because it's real."

"It better not be a church thing," Courtney said.

Julie asked, "Is this the hot youth pastor you told us about?"

Diane blushed. "He's married," she said, and we all laughed, almost like we were friends again.

She turned off the lights again, took the remote, and pressed play. The first minute or so was completely black, no title or credits or anything, then the film began. It was low quality, like it came from a cheap old camcorder, or a found-footage movie made to look like it did. There was a plain bedroom with a twin bed, nightstands on either side, a single lamp, and dull beige walls. The camera was at the foot of the bed.

There was a girl sitting on the bed. She was maybe seven or eight years old. She was wearing blue flannel pajamas and playing with a stuffed rabbit, making it hop across the bed to one side and back again, narrating its progress in her little girl voice. She called him Mr. Rabbit. Her red hair was messy, her smile sweet. If she knew she was being filmed, she didn't show it.

"What is this?" Maria asked.

"Shhh," Diane hissed. She was staring at the screen, rapt.

Footsteps sounded and a man passed in front of the camera,

and another approached the bed from the side. The one on the left held a Bible and wore a priest's collar. The one on the right said, "Hey, sweetie, you remember Father Matt?"

The little girl smiled at the priest. She looked happy right up until her father took the rabbit out of her hands, then she began shaking her head and squirming. The men grabbed her arms and legs to hold her still, but she didn't make a sound.

"Oh, you've got to be kidding me," Maria said. "Come on, Diane. This is dumb."

Diane ignored her and turned the volume louder.

"I have like thirty Catholic aunts and uncles and cousins, and all of them know stuff like this is bullshit," Maria said. "We should be watching *The Exorcist* instead. At least that's not boring."

"If this is real, it's child abuse," Julie said. She looked sick to her stomach.

"They're helping her," Diane said.

A second later one of the men on the screen said, "We're helping you."

"It's not real," Maria said. She didn't sound like she doubted it, but she was still watching.

The two men held the girl long enough to tie her down. They used cloth straps on her wrists and ankles. A woman's voice was speaking off camera, saying over and over again, "Don't hurt her, don't hurt her, don't hurt her," stuck between a plea and a prayer. I wanted the camera to rotate. I wanted to see what kind of mother would let men do that to her daughter.

Even if it was fake. Diane's youth pastor had to be seriously messed up to give that to a fourteen-year-old girl and tell her it was real.

Courtney said, "Definitely fake. It's some kind of stupid viral marketing thing."

And Julie said, "Nobody even thinks movies like this are good anymore."

The man on the left picked up the Bible. He didn't open it, just held one hand over the cover, and he began to speak. He had a weak voice, too quiet for the camera, and most of what he was saying was monotonous and dull. After he had been listing names of saints for a while, Maria and I began talking about something else, and when Diane shushed us, we settled for folding her discarded gift wrap into paper planes and chucking them at each other. On the recording, the girl struggled a little against the bindings, more annoyed than pained. A few times she looked beseechingly toward her father and the woman offscreen, but still she did not speak. Her lips were pressed together so tight they were a thin white line.

The priest hesitated in a few places, watching the girl warily. He made it through addressing the unclean spirit, ancient serpent, impious one, et cetera, finally landed a firm *amen* and fell quiet. His face was red, as though the recitation had exhausted him. He touched his hand briefly to his chest and winced.

The other man said, "Try again."

So he did, from the beginning. But the girl had had enough. She began to whine and whimper, tugging at her bonds with restless impatience. The priest stuttered, and he reached out to touch her head. The girl jerked away and shrieked.

It wasn't an expelling-demons-from-her-soul shriek, more like a tantrum-in-the-grocery-store shriek, but the adults reacted like she had started screaming bloody murder. The girl's father flung himself at her, clapped his hand over her mouth with an audible slap, and in the background the mother was saying, "Oh, no, no, honey, you know you have to be quiet!"

The girl twisted away from her father's hand and shrieked again. "I don't want to!"

The words were so much louder than they had any right to be. Each one landed like a stab in the ear, piercing and sharp. Julie grabbed the remote control from Diane and turned the volume down. Diane didn't look away from the screen. The girl shrieked again. The girl's father clasped his hands to his ears.

The priest stared at the girl in shock. "You're not—"

The girl screamed again, and that time her shout stretched out into a wail, rising louder and louder until it drowned out whatever the priest was saying. His face grew redder, his eyes wider. He touched his hand to his ear, stared at a spot of blood on his finger. He pressed his hand to his chest again.

"What's wrong with him?" Tatiana said. We were all watching the video now, our conversations and wrapping paper planes forgotten.

The girl screamed one more time, and the priest collapsed.

The woman shouted, "Father! Are you okay?" She and the man jostled around the bed and knelt beside the priest. The man said, "Go call 911," and the woman sprang to her feet. She knocked the camera askew as she went by, so that it was pointed at an empty corner of the room, but we could hear the little girl saying, "Is Father Matt okay, Daddy? Is he okay?"

The screen went dark, and white words appeared: *Father Matthew was dead before the paramedics arrived. Officials refused to investigate.*

The video ended. There was no *Coming Soon*, no title, no studio name, no credits.

"That's it?" Courtney said. "I can't believe you made us watch that, Di. This is so dumb. It's not even scary."

"Did your pastor get that off YouTube?" Julie asked. "That was so stupid. Let's watch a real movie now."

Diane clicked the DVD carefully into its case. "You shouldn't joke about it. A man died."

"Not for real," Maria said.

"Put on whatever you want," Diane said. "I don't care."

She vanished downstairs for a long time. We were most of the way through *Carrie*, the original version with crazy Sissy Spacek, all the way to the start of the prom, before Diane came back to her own birthday party. None of us mentioned the video she had made us watch. We were afraid to find out just how seriously she took it.

Tatiana found the video online a few days later. It had about a million hits. It was widely acknowledged to be a hoax, but there were still dozens of comments asking if anybody knew if the priest had really died, or if the little girl had ever gotten rid of her demons.

I didn't get an invitation to Diane's birthday party the next year, and the last time it would have been possible I was dead and buried. I wondered if Diane even cared that I was gone, or if years of routine childhood friendship meant nothing in comparison to the triumph she must have felt given the general agreement that I had gotten what I deserved.

# ✦ TWELVE ✦

VIOLET SHOWED ME to a bathroom on the second floor. I took my time in the shower, lingering until the water was lukewarm. It had been far too long since I last felt clean. When I was done I toweled my hair dry and dressed in Violet's clothes. The flower-print dress was too big, but the scratchy collar was high enough to hide the bruises around my neck.

I sat down on the closed toilet seat and took my notebook from the backpack. I held the pen over the page for a minute or two, but I couldn't decide if I needed to add demonic possession to the Real list yet. I didn't know what I had seen on the video at Diane's house. I was less willing to dismiss the possibility that it was real now, but

I tucked my pen and notebook away without writing anything. I needed more information.

When I emerged from the bathroom, Violet was nowhere to be seen. I poked my head into the only open room on the hallway. A middle-aged woman sat by the window, knitting a pink baby blanket.

"Hi," I said.

The woman didn't react. Her wooden needles flashed with astonishing speed. She wasn't watching her hands as she worked; she was staring out the window with wide, unblinking eyes.

"That's really pretty," I said. "I like the color."

The woman gave no sign she knew or cared that a stranger was standing outside her room. I watched her for a minute or two, waiting for her to notice me, but she never did.

The stairs creaked as Violet returned. She smiled and said, "You look better."

"I feel better. Thanks."

I glanced at the knitting woman, looked to Violet for an introduction, but Violet only said, "It will be a little while before lunch is ready. Would you like me to show you around first?"

"Sure. That would be great."

I didn't care about the tour and I didn't care about lunch, but I was curious about Violet. I wanted to know how the screaming little girl in Diane's video had ended up at a church in Nebraska.

I remembered that I was supposed to be stranded, so I added, "I do want to go online and check the bus schedule, if I can. I don't even know where the nearest station is."

"Oh, don't worry about that," Violet said. "We'll get you where you need to be."

Esme was no longer alone when we went back downstairs. Two men had come in while I was in the shower. One was young and dark-haired and unsmiling. Violet introduced him as Esme's brother, Lyle. He had pulled a chair close to Esme's side. He plucked the towel from her collar and smoothed the blanket, tucked it around her legs, his motions hesitant and awkward; he wasn't used to taking care of her. He glanced up when Violet and I stopped in the doorway. Esme made a sound in her throat. Lyle answered with a soft *shh-shh* murmur.

"And this is Pastor Edward Willow," Violet said.

Pastor Willow wasn't what I expected. Part of me had expected him to be the exorcist in Diane's video, and part of me was looking for somebody gawky and young, like the boy in the photo. But he was middle-aged and clean-cut, his blond hair lightly mussed, his smile warm and welcoming. He wasn't as broad as his father in the picture, but he wasn't skinny anymore either. There was a mist of rain on his hair and a shadow clinging to him that only I could feel. He was a killer.

I smiled and shook Mr. Willow's hand. I didn't let myself grimace when I felt the darkness coiled and quivering inside him. His shadow was small, so feeble it seemed to vanish the moment I noticed it.

"Welcome to our home, Katie," said Mr. Willow. He clasped my hand with both of his and looked me in the eye. "I'm so glad you found your way to us."

"I really appreciate the help," I said. "I feel stupid for getting stuck like this."

I gave him an abbreviated version of my made-up story: flaky roommate, missed ride, traveling parents. I had repeated versions of the story so many times it was taking on a life of its own. This time I told them my roommate had run off with a girlfriend, not a boyfriend, just to see how they would react. I was a little disappointed when Mr. Willow didn't even bat an eye.

"We'll get you where you're going," Mr. Willow said, exactly as Violet had said only five minutes before. "How did you find us?"

"Danny," I said, "not Daniel. I met him in Omaha. He told me if I needed a place to crash, I could come here."

A quick glance passed between Violet and Lyle, but Mr. Willow wasn't looking at them. He grinned and said, "You were lucky to run into him. Danny's always felt very strongly about paying forward the kindness shown to him by sharing it with others. Is lunch ready yet, Violet?"

"Not yet. Maybe half an hour, if that's okay? I thought I'd show Katie around first."

"That's just fine," said Mr. Willow. He touched Violet's shoulder and gave it a gentle squeeze. "You know how we appreciate everything you do for us."

Violet ducked her head and stepped back, her cheeks pink. I glanced away. I wasn't the only one averting my eyes; Lyle was staring fixedly at the floor. He only looked up when Esme made a small, animal sound in her throat. She lifted her head and turned slowly, so very slowly, to look at me.

Lyle took her hand and held it. To me he said, "You're upsetting her."

"Oh," I said. "I'm sorry."

"She doesn't like strangers," Lyle said.

"Esme is closer to angels than most of us ever will be," said Mr. Willow.

It sounded like a non sequitur, but his voice glowed with so much fondness, so much pride, it was like a father praising his daughter for an unexpected accomplishment. If it weren't for his shadow cowering and quivering, tucked away like a rodent in a burrow, I would have sunk into the warmth of it.

Mr. Willow's tone was familiar, almost conspiratorial, when he turned to me and said, "It is her gift and her curse, because it means she's closer to demons as well."

I blinked.

"We're so glad you've found your way to us, Katie," he went on. "Even if only for a little while. Go on with Violet and have a look around. The sun is coming out."

He knew.

I didn't know how. I had no idea what he saw when he looked at me.

I had to look away first.

He *knew*.

It was impossible. Nobody knew what I was. I had hitchhiked halfway across the country without anybody noticing. I was being paranoid. Paranoid and stupid and irrational.

I might have convinced myself of it too, if I hadn't seen what

Mr. Willow couldn't see.

Behind him, behind his open expression and relaxed posture, his kind smile and kind eyes, Lyle was clutching Esme's hand so hard their joint grip was trembling, and his face was pinched with rage. Esme's lips worked but no sound came out. A shiny line of drool gathered at the corner of her mouth. Her upper lip pulled back in a snarl, revealing white teeth in red gums.

Violet touched my arm. "Come on, Katie."

At once Lyle's expression cleared, the anger replaced by a mild mask. He wiped his sister's mouth and patted her knee.

"I'll show you the church," Violet said. "How does that sound?"

I tried to smile. "That sounds great."

# ∗||∗ THIRTEEN ∗||∗

THE RAIN HAD stopped and the sun was shining through the clouds in bright rays. The prairie smelled fresh, clean, not a hint of a manure or fertilizer. Violet skipped between the driveway puddles, stopped after a few feet, looked at me, and laughed. "I'm sorry. I'm just tired of being stuck inside. It's hard to get used to being all the way out here, where it's so quiet."

"Have you been here long?" My voice was steady, but my throat was tight. I didn't let myself look back to see if Mr. Willow was watching.

"Not long. We used to have a church in Colorado," Violet said. "In Boulder. That's where the congregation started. But it was . . .

It's a little remote here, but it's better. I like it."

On the playground the kids had moved from the swings to the merry-go-round, and the woman's umbrella was folded up and tucked under her arm. Beyond the playground, the old man in the brown hat was still standing by the church graveyard. He hadn't moved at all.

The woman turned toward us as though she was going to say something, but her gaze flicked over me and she spun away.

"That's Gail," Violet said. If the woman heard, she gave no sign. "She's still getting used to it."

"Getting used to what?"

"To who she is now," Violet said. "It can be hard to give up something that's hurting you, even if you know how much harm it's causing. Mr. Willow is letting her stay here for a while, until she's feeling better. The children help, I think. She likes watching them."

Drugs, I thought. She was talking about drugs. The coded language, the damaged people with blank stares, all the unsmiling photographs in the hallway. This was a halfway house for addicts. That's what Danny had seen when he looked at me, unwashed and bedraggled and alone in my ill-fitting clothes, stranded at a truck stop between nowhere and nowhere. He had looked at me and thought, hey, there's a girl who needs to break a really bad habit. That's what Mr. Willow and Violet thought I was.

The merry-go-round creaked as the kids pushed it around. They were a boy and a girl, about the same age, maybe twins. They weren't talking or laughing or making any noise at all. There was only the faint squeak of the merry-go-round.

"Where are their parents?" I asked.

"Their mother isn't ready to give up everything she's holding on to," Violet said. "She's a danger to them, for now. They're better off with us."

When I glanced back, I saw Gail's face in profile: sharp, almost birdlike, the briefest flash of teeth when she hissed at the children, hidden again when she fell silent.

"How long have you been with the congregation?" I asked.

"Long enough that it feels like I never belonged anywhere else," Violet said. "Here we are."

She climbed the steps of the church and reached for the wide wooden doors. I was right behind her, but I stopped as soon as the doors were open.

There was no movement in the air, no change in pressure, but I felt something flowing out of that church like breath from a gaping mouth, so sudden and so strong I backed down one step and caught the railing for balance.

"Katie? Are you okay?"

"Fine," I said between gritted teeth.

Still holding the railing, I started up the stairs again. Goose bumps rose on my skin and I grew nauseated with the effort.

"It's okay," Violet said. There was a mournful edge of disappointment in her voice. "You only have to come as far as you can."

If I had been paying attention, I would have realized what a strange thing that was to say.

But all I could think was: I shouldn't be here.

I was as certain of that as I was of all the other new truths in my world. I had been dead and now I wasn't. My heart could stop and it wouldn't hurt me. I didn't need food or drink or sleep anymore. Murderers dragged shadows of guilt behind them for the rest of their lives.

I could kill with a touch.

I shouldn't be here.

"It's okay," Violet said again.

I was breathing heavily when I reached the top of the steps. Six broad church steps and I felt like I had sprinted up a hill.

"Can you come inside?"

My throat was raw. "I'd rather stay out here."

"I think you should come inside. This is our way of being sure."

Violet reached for my hand.

We stood side by side, backs to the road and the endless prairie, looking at those open church doors. There was a smear of reddish-brown paint across the threshold, stretching from one side to the other.

When Violet stepped over the threshold, I did too, suppressing the quiver of nausea that rolled through me. There were boxes and chairs stacked inside; the vestibule was being used for storage. Sunlight slanted through high stained-glass windows, illuminating a room cluttered with old furniture and crooked pews. Nobody had held services in that church in a long time.

"I know it's frightening," Violet said. "You have a darkness in you."

A darkness. I almost laughed, but I couldn't make a sound. The darkness wasn't inside me. No priest standing over my childhood bed could call out demons while my parents watched in fear and hope. There was no voice whispering in my mind, no being controlling my body.

"It's like a cancer," Violet said. "It's inside you, this terrible thing. Maybe it feels like it's part of you, but it isn't. It isn't, Katie. That's the lie it's telling you. You won't be free until you cut it out. Whatever you are, we can help you."

"I don't need help." My voice was hoarse. "I'm not—"

I had seen beneath my own skin. I had opened wounds in my own guts. I knew what was there. Inside of me was flesh and blood and bile and bone, same as it had always been. The darkness was all around, in the endless sky, in the crumbling soil of an empty grave, in the grasping shadows that clung to people who had done terrible things.

"I'm not *possessed*." I spat out the word, but if I expected it to hit Violet like a blow, I was disappointed. "I don't have a demon inside of me."

"I know you don't," she said. "That's only an easy way to think of it, for people who are too scared to understand. But you don't have to be scared. Just because you've always been this way doesn't mean you have to stay like this. Let us help you, Katie."

I thought: but I haven't always been this way.

And I thought: that isn't me.

But what I said was: "How? What can you do?"

Violet was quiet for a long time. Clouds drifted over the sun. The inside of the church dimmed, darkened, brightened again.

"We all used to be like you," she said.

I felt a spark of wild hope. "You?"

"Yes."

"Exactly like me?" The painful shrieks, the bloody ears. I couldn't do that. Whatever Violet was—or had been—it wasn't the same.

"Oh, no. Not exactly. There are so many different kinds of darkness."

"But you—" I swallowed. There was a sharp, sour taste at the back of my throat. "But you're not anymore? You're not . . . what you were?"

"Mr. Willow helped me," Violet said. "I'm not anything but ordinary now."

I had a dozen more questions, a hundred, clamoring and clashing in my mind. What Violet was telling me, if it was true, was fantastic. It was incredible. There were other things like me in the world. I hadn't dared imagine it might be possible, but that's what she was saying. Ever since I had woken up I had assumed that dying was like walking through a one-way door. I had come out the other side as something else, something inhuman and different, and most of all alone.

It hadn't occurred to me there might be others.

I hadn't thought I might go back.

Violet was still holding my hand, so tight I felt my bones grind. Her palm was damp. There were tears in her eyes.

If it was true.

"That's what he's done for all of you?" I said.

"That's what we do. We can help you too."

"What about Esme?" Silent Esme, growling Esme with the towel tucked into her shirt. Had they done that to her? Was that their idea of help? "Did Mr. Willow help her too?"

Violet didn't answer.

"And that woman upstairs? Those kids out there? What did you do to them? What kind of help? You have to tell me *something*. Violet. Please."

"Mr. Willow helps them," Violet said.

"How? What does he do?"

"He doesn't do it himself. He's not alone. None of us are alone. He takes them—us—to a friend. A very special friend. Not here," she added, when I glanced around the church. "She stays somewhere else, where she can be safe. Whatever we are when we go to her, we come back better."

"Mr. Willow? He used to—"

"Oh, no, no, not him. He's human. He only wants to help."

"What about Esme? What did she used to be?"

"She was—" Her voice caught, choked with an emotion I couldn't identify. "Dangerous."

I thought of all the photographs in the house, the vacant expressions, the empty eyes. Decades of photographs. Dozens of people, if they were even people anymore inside those blank shells. Charming Mr. Willow was human. Helpless drooling Esme was dangerous. I was cancer and darkness. None of us were special or alone. That's what Violet was telling me.

I remembered, suddenly, with a painful shiver, the day my father took me to an empty parking lot to teach me to drive, to change a tire and check the oil, and how he had laughed when I drove over the curb trying to parallel park, and laughed again when I hit my own nose with the jack handle. He had reached over to muss up my hair—I had squirmed and protested, "Dad, don't!"—and he had said, "It's all right, Breezy, at least we know you'll always have your brains." He couldn't have known how right he was. I might be dead, I might be walking around with a heart that didn't have to pump and a touch that could kill, but I was still *me*, and I didn't like the picture Violet was drawing.

I couldn't know how many of Mr. Willow's people were like Violet, functional and sensible, and how many were like Esme or the silent children on the playground. I wanted to believe it was possible. I wanted to believe Violet was proof of that. But what would it matter, to have flowing blood and sucking breath again, if it turned my mind to mush? What would it matter, to discover I wasn't alone, if all I could do with that knowledge was watch silent children drift listlessly on rusty swings? I didn't trust those odds.

"The only help I need," I said, speaking slowly, "is a ride to the bus station."

I expected her to argue, but Violet only squeezed my hand. "If you're sure."

"I am."

She lifted her free hand to my face, and I flinched. She touched my jaw and leaned close to whisper, "You have to run."

I looked at her in surprise. "But—"

"You have to run. You can't go back to the house."

"My stuff," I began.

"Forget it. You can't go back. He won't let you leave." She released my hand to take my elbow, turned me around to face the church doors again. "You have to go now."

But when we emerged from the church, Mr. Willow was waiting.

"I was wondering where you went," he said. He smiled up at us, so warm, so convincing. His combed hair had been teased out of place by the wind. "It's time to come in and talk about your plans, Katie."

"We'll be right in," Violet said.

Willow's hands were tucked into his pockets. He looked up at the sky, squinting in the patchy sunlight. "It's turning into a beautiful day, isn't it? There'll be plenty of time to talk after lunch."

Violet let go of my elbow. "In a minute, Edward. We're looking at the church."

Mr. Willow looked at me, and at once I saw what I hadn't seen before, the subtle shift in expression that before had made me think he knew more than he was saying.

He was afraid of me.

Nobody had ever been afraid of me before.

"Come in now," he said, and his smile was gone.

If I gave him a chance, he would take that away.

Violet said, "Katie."

I jumped down the church steps in two bounds. I stumbled at the bottom, recovered, and I ran.

# ·⫶· FOURTEEN ·⫶·

THE GRAVEL CRUNCHED under my feet and muddy rainwater splashed my legs. Mr. Willow shouted, but I didn't look back. I ran to the end of the driveway. I didn't know which way to go. I picked right, hit the asphalt, and kept running.

I couldn't stay on the road. They would catch me in a minute with a car. I veered left, slid into a ditch and scrambled up the other side. I ducked through the barbed wire and risked a look back.

Willow wasn't chasing me, but Lyle was.

He was running down the road in long bounding strides, each one stretching longer than the last, and he was *fast*. I gaped for too many seconds at the impossible blur of his legs, then shook myself and broke into a run across the field. The ground was muddy and spotted with puddles. I splashed and skidded and crushed young plants beneath my shoes.

I wasn't fast enough. Lyle was at the fence. He cleared it in a single jump, and he caught up with me in seconds. He hit my back with such force I felt—*heard*—something crack. Fiery pain burst through my ribs, and I went down hard. Lyle's hand was on the back of my head, driving my face into the ground.

I tried to shout, gulped a mouthful of mud and water instead. It was in my nose, in my throat. Lyle was on my back, his fingers digging into my neck and my side—not fingers, no, but claws, sharp enough to tear my clothes and break my skin. He hadn't had claws in the house. I would have noticed claws.

I thrashed and kicked, but I couldn't push him off. His breath was hot on my neck.

Whatever you are, Violet had said.

They didn't know what I was.

They didn't know I didn't need to breathe.

Against every screaming instinct, I stopped fighting and let myself go limp. I had been here before, mud in my mouth, grit in my eyes. I wasn't even underground this time.

All I needed was a chance. I had done it before. I could do it again.

Lyle didn't let go, but the weight on my back eased. He flipped me over easily, as though I weighed no more than a doll. The man-handling twisted something in my rib cage and I gasped, spit the mud from my mouth, and coughed.

I swung at Lyle with my free arm, struck him on the side of his face. He cursed and tried to grab my hand, but I was ready for him. I caught his wrist and I *pulled*.

Nothing happened.

There was nothing there. Nothing for me to grasp, nothing for me to stretch and break.

Lyle jerked his wrist away. I grabbed it again. *Nothing.* There were no vines of darkness trailing Lyle or gathered about his head like thunderclouds. He wasn't a killer. I couldn't do anything to him.

I tried to squirm away, tried to kick at his legs, but he was bigger than me and every bit as strong as he was fast. I bent one of my knees up into his groin. Lyle grunted and loosened his grip just enough for me to break away. I scrambled backward through the mud, heels digging into the ground, the broken rib a hot fist of agony in my side.

"Wait!" I gasped. "Stop! What are you—"

Lyle leaped at me. He landed with all of his weight on my right knee; I didn't hear a crack that time, but pain exploded through my leg. I yelped as Lyle wrestled me to the ground again.

"Shut up!" he roared.

He struck me across the face with so much force my head snapped to the side. His claws raked through my cheek, and something in my jaw cracked. His face was only inches from mine, his breath hot on my skin, and his hand slipped from my face to my neck. His long fingers and claws closed around my throat, right over the bruises already there, the ones that never healed, and through the throbbing pain I smelled green grass and spilled beer and I saw my own face in the slick curve of a car windshield and a reflection behind me and I couldn't breathe I couldn't breathe I couldn't breathe—

The pressure on my neck vanished. My ears were ringing, but it wasn't until I saw Lyle's wide eyes did I realize I had been screaming.

There was a flash of something on his face—pity, almost—but he quickly stamped it down.

"You can't get away." His voice was ragged and oddly high. He couldn't be much older than me. "I can't let you get away. I'm sorry."

I wasn't much persuaded by his apology. I kept fighting, beating and scratching at his arms and face, but it was no use. No matter how much damage I did to him, he had broken my rib and my leg and probably my jaw, and I wasn't healing fast enough. He lifted me easily, swung me over his shoulder. The motion sent a fresh wave of pain through every part of my body. I felt the cracked rib shifting as his shoulder dug into my abdomen, and his arm hooked around my legs made my knee hurt so much my vision blurred.

Lyle carried me to the fence and jumped the ditch—that hurt too, but groaning in protest only made it worse. He walked me up the road, up the driveway, past the church and the playground. Violet was nowhere to be seen, but the woman and children were still there, watching me like spectators at a funeral procession.

Lyle stopped, shoes scuffing in the dirt, and Mr. Willow said, "I'm proud of you, Lyle."

I couldn't see him, slung as I was over Lyle's shoulder. Trying to lift my head for a better view only made my jaw feel like somebody was ripping it away with their hands.

"I know you must have been tempted to let her go," said Mr. Willow. He sounded so understanding, so gentle. He wasn't angry. He wasn't blaming anybody.

Lyle said nothing.

"You have a good heart," Mr. Willow went on, "and I know you don't wish to do anybody harm. You only want to help."

"I only want to help Esme," Lyle said, sullen, like a child tired of having to explain himself.

"I know. But you understand Mother does not see these things as we do. It would be dangerous for you to ask a boon of her without bringing a gift." He said *Mother* like a title, an honorific, solemn rather than familiar. Footsteps on gravel, and Mr. Willow came around Lyle's side to look at me. He grabbed my hair to lift my head. "She will like this one. Take it inside."

In the front room of the yellow house Violet was holding Esme and rocking her, murmuring reassurances. Esme's eyes were squeezed shut, but they snapped open as Lyle passed the doorway.

"You have to hide," Esme said, her voice so clear and so strong it made Lyle jump. "Lyle, Lyle, you have to hide. You have to hide. They're coming. You have to hide."

"Violet will see to your sister," Mr. Willow said as Lyle paused in the hallway.

"You have to hide. You have to hide." Esme pushed Violet's hands away and shook her head. "You have to hide. I'll stop them. Lyle. Lyle. You have to hide."

"Into the kitchen, please, and wait for me." There was a trace of impatience in Mr. Willow's voice. "The floor is easier to clean in there."

Lyle kicked one of the chairs away from the kitchen table and sat me in it. I tried to stand and lurch away, but my leg gave out from under me with an agonizing pop. Lyle lifted me again, and this time he used both hands to hold me in place, one on my shoulder, the other curling around my neck.

"Move and I'll rip your throat out," he said. Then, softer, close to my ear: "I'm sorry. Don't move. I'm sorry."

I didn't try to answer. My jaw was swollen and hot, my entire face burning with pain. I heard a soft drip, drip, drip. I was bleeding on their white tile floor. I hoped it stained the grout so deeply no bleach could ever get it out.

In the other room, Esme was still talking: "You have to hide. Lyle. You have to hide."

Mr. Willow returned to the kitchen. He was on the phone. "Of course, of course. We all have our doubts, but we must remain strong. I know you can remain strong. Give my love to Barbara, and my apologies for dragging you away from her again." A pause, a warm chuckle. "You're lucky to have her. We'll be there by six, if the road construction isn't too bad. Is the other one secure? Good, good. It will be good to see you, Brian. I know Lyle is looking forward to learning from you. He is eager to do his part. Take care."

He set the phone down and turned to me.

"I don't like to do this," he said, "but you leave me no choice. It would have been easier if you had chosen this willingly."

He came a few steps closer. I kicked him with my good leg,

splattered mud all over his khakis. He frowned and stepped back again; he wore the expression of somebody disappointed by a badly behaved puppy. The peculiar little beetle of shadow he carried deep in his chest began to unfurl, but I couldn't reach him. I had grabbed the wrong man. I could have avoided all of this pain if only I had touched Mr. Willow's hand and killed him.

"I spoke to Danny earlier, while you were with Violet," said Mr. Willow casually, as though sharing news about a mutual friend. "He said he's never seen anything like you before. He has found so many different creatures for us, but you're new. He was quite repulsed."

Danny, who had been staring at me like I was a puzzle to be solved, seeing something in me nobody else saw. The understanding was like needles under my skin. He had never wanted to help. I spat a wad of mud and blood onto the floor. Lyle's claws pressed into my shoulder.

"But we know what you are. You are a foul lying thing that masquerades as human."

Mr. Willow opened a cupboard and took out a few metal containers, the kind tea comes in, but old, dented, the labels long ago worn away. In another cupboard he found a glass, filled it with water, and set it on the counter.

"Sometimes you do it very well, well enough to fool even yourself, but your true nature will always be revealed in the end."

He spooned a scoop from each tin into the water; metal clinked on glass as he stirred. A moldy, earthy scent filled the kitchen. He opened another cabinet and brought out a jar with a metal lid. It wasn't until he unscrewed the lid and carefully tipped the jar did I see what it contained: beetles, each about the size of his thumbnail, scurrying and crawling over each other. Mr. Willow nudged a couple into the glass.

"The world is full of things like you," he said. "Most people refuse to see, but a few of us know better."

With the backside of the spoon, he crushed the beetles. Each collapsed with a quick wet snap.

"It's not an easy thing to know about the world. Knowing also means carrying the burden of protecting the world from its worst creatures. Open its mouth, Lyle."

I clamped my jaw shut—the pain made spots dance in my eyes—but Lyle was already digging his fingers into my gums and pressing down on my tongue. I thrashed at him with my free arm, scraping at his face, at his hands, but he hunched behind me and wrapped an arm around my chest to hold me in place.

"It used to be that when terrible things came into a community, we knew how to destroy them. The abominations, the evil creatures. Things like you." Mr. Willow tapped the spoon on the side of the glass and set it aside. He didn't look as calm as he sounded. He was still afraid of me. "Now, if there are monsters that wear human faces living in our cities, or hunting through our schools, or inviting darkness into our homes with whispers in the night, we have no defenses."

Lyle's claws dug into my chin and my tongue as he pried my mouth open. I tasted blood, felt it pooling under my tongue. I tried to throw my head from side to side, tried to spit, bite, flail, but Lyle was too strong.

In one smooth motion, Mr. Willow tipped the glass into my throat. Lyle forced my mouth closed before I could spit it out.

My teeth ground together. The concoction had the texture of muddy leaves and dirt, but it tasted of rotten meat left in the sun, rancid and green, with a tangy bitterness. Sharp edges scraped my throat and tongue. I gagged, but Lyle pressed his big hand over my mouth, and I couldn't spit it out.

Mr. Willow stepped back. I felt his shadow unfolding long and thin, a filthy smudge spreading through the white kitchen.

"No defenses except for us," he said, "and Mother, who is our salvation and our strength. There is too much evil in the world for us to fight it all, but with her help we do what we can. We will help you. You can't go on like this, this terrible monstrous thing. She will be so happy to see you."

I wanted to tell him I didn't want to meet his mother. I might be a monstrous creature now. I might be unnatural. I might even be evil, but I didn't want his help.

But I couldn't say a thing. My tongue grew numb, and the numbness spread, dampening my anger, cooling the throbbing pain of my damaged bones, a heavy blanket of relief creeping through my entire body as a cold dense fog. My heart slowed, then stopped. The room darkened.

The stars began to emerge.

# ⫴ FIFTEEN ⫴

THE UNIVERSE IS mostly empty space.

The ground beneath our feet and the moon in the sky, the sun in the day and the stars at night, the feeling of being surrounded, embraced by matter and light and weight and heat—that's all misleading. That's the comforting lie we tell ourselves to avoid thinking about the truth, because the truth is darkness and emptiness and deep, deep cold.

A woman named Karen Garrow told me that. Karen was my mother's closest friend. She was a physicist, and Mom was in neuroscience, but they worked together to study how people perceive space and time, how our minds comprehend things so much bigger and weirder than our everyday experience. Karen was tall and dark haired, with copper skin and gray eyes. My sister Sunny told her once she looked like Nefertiti, and Karen had laughed and said she had her father to thank for that, whoever he was.

Karen was always being invited to appear on television shows about physics and astronomy. She was the one they interviewed when they wanted to prove that science was for minorities and young women as much as old white men. Every time she was on the Science Channel, I recorded the episodes and kept them on the DVR. I watched them all more than once and told myself it was because she was Mom's friend and I found the topics interesting.

The summer after my freshman year of high school, Karen came with us to the lake cottage for a few weeks. She and Mom were writing a paper. They worked every day on the covered porch, articles and laptops spread before them, lemonade sweating in glasses, lunch forgotten on plates.

And every day I tucked myself into a wicker deck chair with a book from my summer reading list. I pretended to read while I watched Karen work. She wore glasses when she was writing, heavy black frames in the best sexy librarian style. They slipped down her nose every couple of minutes; she pushed them up without thinking.

One afternoon, after lunch, my sister Meadow shouted for Mom inside the house, and Mom went to help her find her bathing suit, her sunscreen, her hat, whatever she was looking for. Meadow never kept track of anything. The screen door snapped shut, and Karen tilted her chair back on two legs, stretched her arms above her head.

"Your mother is a slave driver, Breezy," she said. "Do you think she'd let me take the afternoon off to the go to the beach?"

"She might," I said.

I had been watching them and I knew Mom was the one who was restless, Karen the one so lost in her notes she was surprised every time she looked up to see the sunlight had crept a little farther along the painted floor.

"She'll just have to deal with it," Karen said. She pulled her long dark hair out of its ponytail, ran her fingers over her scalp, twisted her hair up again. There were faint lines along the back of her neck. Wrinkles, I thought, but when Karen rolled her head from side to side, I knew they were scars.

"What are you working on?" I asked.

She opened her eyes. "Nothing."

Now that I had spotted the scars, I couldn't take my eyes off them. "Really?"

"Really. Literally nothing." Karen leaned forward and rested her elbows on the scattered papers, tapped a pen with one hand. "Have you ever heard of the supervoids?"

I wanted to say yes and impress her with my knowledge, but I had no idea what she was talking about. "I don't think so. Super what?"

"Voids," Karen said. She straightened her shoulders and lifted her chin, shifting effortlessly into the chatty professor persona she wore when she went on television to talk about black holes and parallel universes. "Voids in space. Regions where there are no stars, no galaxies, hardly any matter at all. There's simply nothing."

I felt like she wanted me to be more impressed than I was. "How big?"

"The Boötes void is two hundred and fifty million light-years across, and it's nearly completely empty. Can you imagine that?" Karen was facing me now, gesturing with her hands. I couldn't see the scars on her neck anymore.

"It's crazy," I said.

"No, no, not so fast." Karen's ponytail swung back and forth as she shook her head. "Think about it before you answer. If our corner of the universe was as empty as that, we wouldn't have even known there were stars besides the sun until we had the telescopes we built in the 1960s. That's how far away the nearest stars would be. But would we have ever built telescopes at all if we didn't know there was anything out there worth looking for? Can you imagine?" Her eyes were wide and bright. "Try. Try to imagine what that would be like."

I bit down on my initial response and did as she asked. I thought before I answered. There on the sunporch of our lake house, the summer day warm and blinding, I felt the hard wicker chair through the cushion beneath me, under my arm where I leaned. I smelled the dusty pages of my father's copy of *Frankenstein* and felt the soft old paper against my fingers. Through the screened windows I saw sunlight on water and sand, the wind turning through the tall grass. I heard Sunny giggling in that excited way she had when she forgot she was trying to be more grown-up, and in the house Mom and Meadow were arguing, but not angrily. Their voices rose and fell as the floorboards creaked. A door slammed, and Meadow ran by the porch, a wide hat on her head and a bag over her shoulder. She slowed to a walk when she reached the sandy trail to the beach.

Karen was watching me through her black-rimmed glasses.

I closed my eyes and tried to put myself in outer space. Tried to push away our blue and green Earth surrounded by its artificial constellation of metal and mirrors, push away Mars ruddy and cold, Jupiter with its angry spot, Saturn black and white and wrapped in rings like it was in the *Cassini* photographs, beautiful blue Neptune with its captured moon Triton, our entire solar system in concentric ellipses around one lonely star. And farther out, the Horsehead Nebula in all its bright false color, the pale blur of the Andromeda Galaxy, the clean curl of a black hole devouring its sister star. I pushed it all away, deleted the stars one by one, wiped clear the smear of the Milky Way and emptied the sky.

I opened my eyes.

"No," I said. "I can't imagine that."

"Exactly," said Karen, grinning in triumph. I saw what she must be like as a professor, tall and captivating before rows of awed students in a windowless lecture hall. "Our brains aren't designed to handle that much emptiness. But it's real. It's the nature of our universe, whether or not we can comprehend it. The universe doesn't care if our tiny human brains understand anything. What do you know about quantum mechanics?"

"Schrödinger's cat. The one in the box. It's both dead and alive."

Karen laughed. "A grossly inaccurate oversimplification of the concept, but I guess that's okay for a layperson. How about multiple universes? Entanglement? Quantum tunneling?"

Mom opened the screen door. "Really, Karen, I don't think you need to give my daughter an advanced physics lecture today. She's not your postdoc. She's on vacation."

"I'm only trying to instill a sense of wonder in your depressingly sensible kid," Karen said.

The words stung. I didn't want to be a kid, a layperson, a sensible child with no sense of wonder. I wanted to be more impressive than Karen's students. I wanted to dazzle her with my insightful questions and surprising knowledge.

But she was already going back to work. I unfolded my legs from the old wicker chair and dog-eared my page in *Frankenstein*.

"I don't mind," I said. "But I'm gonna go have a sense of wonder at the beach now."

Mom kissed my forehead. "Don't forget your sunscreen."

I changed into my swimsuit and headed down to the water. Meadow was lying on her stomach on a plaid blanket, head pillowed on her arms. She didn't stir when I sat down beside her, but a few minutes later she said, "If you can get over your girl crush on Karen long enough to notice, that guy with the kite is totally checking you out."

"He is not," I said. Then: "I don't have a crush."

Meadow didn't even look at me. "Yeah, right."

I don't, I thought.

I like boys, I thought.

It's not like that.

I worked down the list of possible responses in my mind. All of them sounded unconvincingly defensive.

"So what if I do?" I said.

Meadow's voice was sleepy and slow. "So what if you what?"

"Like girls too. As well as boys. Both."

Meadow groaned and threw her arm over her face. "Oh my god, I don't care. Go tell the kite boy if you want to share. Maybe he's into it. Guys think bi girls are hot."

I glared, but her eyes were closed, so I grabbed a handful of sand and threw it at her. I scrambled to my feet and skipped away before she could get me back.

On this planet, at least, in this universe, there was only one star in the sky and not a cloud in sight. I caught the kite boy's eye, and I smiled.

A couple of months later Mom and Dad were talking about Karen Garrow during dinner.

"She's taking a sabbatical in Italy as soon as she gets out of the hospital," Mom said. "She wants to work on her next book."

"Hospital?" I said, startled. "Why is she in the hospital? Is she sick?"

They exchanged a glance, one of their quick, silent conversations. Dad cleared his throat. Meadow and Sunny were paying attention too. Our parents didn't lie to us, not if they could help it, but that didn't mean they always told the truth.

"Karen's ex-husband is not a very nice man," Dad said.

And Mom said, "For all that she's a genius about everything else, she can be really stupid about men." It was an uncharacteristically nasty judgment from my mother, but she got that way sometimes when she was upset.

I thought about those fine scars on Karen's neck, faded and hidden beneath the rich curtain of hair, but Dad changed the subject before I could ask what had happened.

# ⚜ SIXTEEN ⚜

## THE STARS BLINKED OUT.

I woke up, and everything hurt.

I was lying on my side on a hard floor. I could still taste Mr. Willow's concoction at the back of my throat, sour bile mixed with the metallic taint of blood. I had no idea how long I had been gone.

My limbs burned as the feeling came back. I could make my heart beat again, but erratically. One by one I identified my injuries. My jaw, my knee, the rib Lyle had snapped, they all ached, but the pain was muted. I could open my mouth, move my toes, inhale, and exhale. There was a hot, tight burn in the slashes on my side, but the cuts on my neck and face seemed to have healed. My head felt like somebody had hit me with a hammer.

I opened my eyes. The room was dim but not completely dark; faint light flickered behind me. It took some effort, but I managed to sit up and look around. I was in a closed room. A trio of fat candles sat in the center of the floor. There was no furniture except a flat, stained mattress slumped against the wall. There were two windows, both boarded up on the inside. I couldn't tell if it was day or night.

The walls, the floor, the ceiling, the crown molding and closed door, the plywood over the windows, it was all painted red. When I looked straight at it, the paint was a dull, dirty reddish brown, sloppy and uneven. The wallpaper underneath showed through in spots, a pattern of flowers and birds and delicate trees. But when I glanced to the side, the walls almost seemed to glisten in the unsteady candlelight, slick and shimmering as though streaks of paint were still wet, and in those sidelong glances it was all red, a deep and suffocating red wrapped all around me.

*Thump.*

I wasn't alone.

There was a woman sitting in the far corner of the room. She lifted her bare feet—they were bound together—and brought them down again. *Thump.* There was a wide strip of duct tape over her mouth, and her hands were behind her back. *Thump.* She tossed her head impatiently, a motion that reminded me of a skittish horse.

"Okay," I said. "Just a second."

I wasn't sure I could stand, so I crawled. Caked mud and blood flaked from my clothes and skin. I was filthy, completely disgusting from head to toe, and the effort of creeping across that eerie red room made my head spin. When I got too close to the candles I felt a shivery chill, so I kept my distance. I paused to let the nausea subside, then crawled the last few feet to the woman.

"This is going to hurt," I said.

She rolled her eyes. I ripped the duct tape from her mouth and she exhaled loudly.

"My hands," she said. She slid away from the wall and twisted around. I tore the tape from around her wrists. She balled it up, tossed it away, and began peeling the tape from her ankles. "You're awake."

"I guess so," I said.

"You were out for a long time."

"How long?"

"And when I say out, I mean you weren't breathing."

"Heavy sleeper," I said. "How long?"

"How should I know? It's been at least a day since they dumped you here."

I rubbed at the grime on my face. It hurt to talk, hurt to sit up, hurt to move. My tongue was still sore from the punctures of Lyle's claws.

"You look like shit," the woman said.

"Thanks. I feel awesome."

Through the torn dress, I could feel the four hot, swollen slashes on my side, scabbed over but not yet stitched back together. Maybe they were too deep to heal by themselves, or maybe Lyle had venom in his claws. I tried to remember the colorful diagrams I had learned in tenth grade anatomy class. Was my liver on that side? My appendix? I couldn't remember. We had only ever looked at pictures of human bodies. The only real corpses we cut up were euthanized cats. Mr. Beautiful. That's what Melanie and I had named ours, because he was the ugliest cat we had ever seen. Melanie did most of the dissecting. She wanted to be a doctor someday and cutting up Mr. Beautiful was the most fun she ever had in school.

I stopped bothering my wounds and rubbed my hands over my face, winced through the pins and needles. The room was small and square. No closet. The door was closed. The candles smelled like vanilla, cloyingly sweet, but it wasn't enough to hide the stink. Bleach, and beneath that, unwashed bodies and sweat, piss and shit, the faint metal stench of blood.

Everything was red. So dull and dirty and red.

The woman was staring at me.

"Where are we?" I asked. "Are we still in the farmhouse?"

"What farmhouse?"

"At the church. In Nebraska. Mr. Willow's church. Isn't that where we are?"

"Oh, is that how they got you?" The woman laughed. It wasn't a friendly sound. "That's perfect. Did they tell you they wanted to save your immortal soul and take away everything that makes you evil?"

"Something like that."

"And you walked right into it."

Walk right into it was exactly what I had done. I hadn't seen the danger until it was too late.

"I have no idea where we are," the woman admitted. "We're in a house, but I don't know where. It might be Nebraska. We could be on the freakin' moon, for all I know. I was in Colorado when they grabbed me. This guy bought me a drink." She made a face and touched her jaw with one slender hand; there was a fading bruise on her left side. "Tasted like shit. Never trust a frat boy in a Steelers jersey who wants to buy you a drink. I can't figure out what you are."

"What?"

"You. What are you? I'm usually good at this, but I can't figure you out at all. You're breathing now."

She unfolded her legs and stood, walked closer and sat down again on the other side of the candles. She was strikingly beautiful, so beautiful I felt guilty for my initial impression of horsiness. She had auburn hair cut in a severe pageboy, pale skin, and wide golden eyes, and her limbs were long and ballet elegant. I guessed she was in her thirties, but I wouldn't have bet on it. She wasn't a killer. There were no shadows of guilt clinging to her.

"Come on, share," she said. "I'll show you mine if you show me yours. What are you?"

"Schrödinger's cat. Nice to meet you."

She snorted, unimpressed. "It's not like it will matter by the time they're done with us. What's your name? Will you tell me that, or do I have to keep thinking of you as Smelly Girl?"

"Breezy," I said. I could have lied again, but it didn't seem to matter anymore.

"Seriously?"

"Seriously."

"Were your parents hippies or something?"

My parents had named me Breezy because they were young and sleep deprived and overly fond of marijuana when they found themselves in possession of a newborn neither of them had planned for. They were graduate students, Dad in biochemistry at MIT and Mom in neuroscience at Harvard, and they wrote their theses in a one-bedroom Somerville apartment while a fat, red baby squalled in the crib. As an infant I looked like a lumpy red potato with a smear of black slime mold for hair. It's not like they were planning on getting any sleep anyway, Mom liked to say, so after they got their PhDs, they decided they might as well get married and make more screaming, red-faced, half-Chinese, half-Irish babies. Two more, also girls, Meadow and Sunny, because Mom and Dad never got over the embarrassing-names phase of parenthood. We all grew up to be short and black-haired and looked mostly Chinese except for our freckles, which came from Mom's side of the family.

The woman's question put a tight, cold knot in my stomach. I didn't want to think about Mom and Dad and my sisters.

"Yes," I said. I halfheartedly considered a new version of the patchwork girl: my sixth-grade locker neighbor Free Farmer had wannabe hippie parents, never mind that they had been born in the late seventies themselves, and she had rebelled by going full Goth as soon as she was old enough to pick out her own clothes. But that all felt like too much effort for the sake of a lie, so I only said, "It could have been worse. It could have been Zen or Soulfire or something. I can't even imagine what kind of names they would have stuck on my siblings if I had any."

The woman laughed. "Hey, I'm not judging. You can call me Rain."

"Great. Together we can be the weather report."

My leg didn't ache quite as much anymore, so I stood up, paused to get my balance, and walked to the door.

"It's locked," Rain said. "And it's—"

I didn't think it would be as simple as opening the door and walking out, but I wasn't expecting what happened.

I reached for the knob and there was a cool, solid pressure on my skin. Before I could react, the cold turned to heat, searing heat like putting my hand on an electric stove coil, and I was overcome with a dizziness so intense my vision darkened. I stumbled away from the door, gagging and gasping.

"That," said Rain. "It's locked. Just for us."

There was no burn on my hand, but I could still feel it.

Rain leaned back on her elbows and watched me make my way around the room. The same thing happened when I tried to touch any of the walls and when I got too near the candles. I couldn't even get close enough to pry around the plywood over the windows.

When I gave up, Rain said, "They wouldn't be very good at catching monsters if they didn't know how to monster-proof a room."

*Monsters.* There it was. A word I had been deliberately not thinking for two weeks.

"It's . . ." I didn't want to say it out loud. "How?"

She raised an eyebrow. "Magic. How else?"

And there was the other one: *magic.*

"Like in *Harry Potter*?" I said stupidly.

Rain laughed. "Yes, exactly like that. Gosh, if only we had our unicorn hair wands, we could get Professor McGonagall to help."

I tried to glare at her, but my heart wasn't in it. "I'm kind of new at this. I don't know how it works."

"See the walls? That's how it works."

I picked at the edge of a ruddy brown floorboard. I had no trouble touching the floor. "What is it?"

"Well, it's not paint, and it's not ketchup."

I shuddered and wiped my hand on my dress. I didn't want to believe her, but magical force fields made of blood weren't much of a stretch after everything else that had happened.

"But who does this?" I asked. "How do they know how to do it? How does it even work?"

"You really are new at this, aren't you?"

"Yes. Very."

"That's . . . kind of interesting, actually. Most of us are born into it."

"Born into *what*? What are you talking about?"

"Sit down," Rain said. "You're making me dizzy. Why don't you start by telling me what you know, and I'll tell you how you've got everything wrong."

I sat across from her and tried to find a position that didn't make every part of my body ache. I barely knew where to begin. Since I had woken up—come back—I had been assuming I was the only one. I had tried to figure out what I was by looking on the internet, naturally, but the internet insisted giant four-foot-tall frogs stalked unwary travelers in the wilds of Ohio. I couldn't believe any of it. Then there was Violet, telling me there were other things like me in the world, not just a few, not rare, but everywhere. Common enough that people went looking for them at truck stops. Common enough that Mr. Willow had built an entire church around hunting them down.

Us. Hunting *us* down. I wasn't on the outside of this, looking in at the monsters and marveling at their bad luck. I was in the cage.

Monsters and magic. It was a little late for me to be having a *This can't possibly be happening* freak-out, but I felt one coming on anyway. I needed to stay calm. Take the logical approach. I had spent my entire life before I died knowing exactly what I wanted to do and exactly how I was going to do it, and now all I could think was that I really wished I had my notebook so I could add to my Real/Not Real list. That might make me feel better. I was a little bit disgusted with myself.

But I did have questions.

"Some people aren't human," I said. "Right?"

Rain snorted. "Gosh, really? Maybe some of them are in this very room."

"And some people can do magic."

"Sometimes they're even the same people."

"Only sometimes?"

"Sure. Not always," she said. She was delighted by my ignorance and not bothering to hide it. "Mostly it's humans who do magic."

"Like . . . wizards?"

That earned a deep, throaty laugh. "They don't call themselves wizards."

"What do they call themselves?"

"Magicians, mostly. Sometimes the old ladies or Wiccan chicks call themselves witches. There was this dude in Palm Springs who called himself the Grand Majestic Sorcerer of the Imperial Valley, but he was a douche and I think somebody ate him. The rest are just magicians. And, no," she said, before I could ask, "I don't mean the top hat and rabbit on a stage in Vegas kind of magician."

Too late. I was already imagining the top-hat-and-rabbit variety. "So the people who put us in here, they're magicians?"

"At least one of them is," Rain said. She looked around the red room and shrugged. "A pretty good one too. This is some serious shit."

*Is the other one secure?* Mr. Willow had asked over the phone. Like he was asking about a rabid animal. I wondered if it was impolite to ask Rain what she was, after I had refused to answer that same question from her. I decided I probably ought to work up to it.

Instead I asked, "How long have you been here?"

"I don't know. Maybe a week."

"Alone?"

Rain was silent for a long moment, and when she spoke again her voice was lower, slower. "Not at first. There was somebody else when they brought me here. A woman."

In the candlelight I saw, for just a second, a shape beside Rain: a weeping woman with blood on her clothes, holding her face in her hands. I flinched, which only made the throbbing pain in my side worse. I was only imagining it. There was nobody else in the room.

"What happened to her?"

"They took her away."

I saw that too: the woman screaming, clawing at the floor, kicking as men without faces dragged her through the door. Her screams were so clear I would have sworn they were real. They had the shape of names torn from her throat, of pleas that were so far beyond desperation they were barely even words anymore. I felt her fear as if it were my own, racing blood and pounding heart and cold sweat. The red walls pressed all around, closer and closer, and the woman's hands caught, clawlike, on the doorframe, and she was gone.

I blinked, the walls retreated, and the room faded to dull brown.

"You mean Mr. Willow? He took her away?"

Rain raised a single delicate eyebrow. Her cheekbones were sharp in the candlelight. I tried not to stare. "You met the big man, did you?" Her voice was normal again. "Not many people get to do that. Not me. I got his minions." Rain jerked her thumb toward the closed door. "That asshole out there. He's our prison guard."

"I met Mr. Willow," I said. "I didn't know he was the big man of anything."

"Is he as scary as they say? I'm picturing the mutant offspring of Charles Manson and Ted Bundy."

"He looks like a middle-aged Mormon missionary," I said, and Rain laughed. "I didn't realize he was famous."

"Everybody knows about Willow," Rain said, but then she amended, "all the monsters in Colorado, anyway. He's been around forever, but small scale. Family deal. It usually is, you know? Grandpa discovers there are monsters among us back in the day and spends his life training up all his gap-toothed redneck spawn to hunt them down. They don't usually share it around."

"Nobody's that good at keeping secrets," I protested, even though I knew she had to be right. If I was taking the logical approach, I had to accept that. Monsters were real, because I was one. Most people had no idea they existed, because I never had before. Two true things. It was an unsettling realization, to say the least, that those two truths were the new center of my world.

Rain shrugged. "Who would believe them? It's easier to keep a secret if anybody who tells the truth is considered delusional. That's the way it was with Willow's dad. He was this paranoid backwoods militia guy, you know the type, and everybody knew he was batshit. His group fell apart after something bad went down—some members of his congregation died, nobody really knows what happened. But he's been gone for years, and nobody knew his son was carrying on Daddy's mission until a few years ago." She smiled, quick and predatory. "We ran them out. That was a fun night."

Violet had said that they moved their congregation from Colorado to Nebraska. I hadn't thought to ask why. I hadn't suspected the reason could be that people objected to being grabbed off the streets and magically imprisoned in bloodstained rooms.

"But you said they got you in Colorado anyway."

"I guess the asshole decided he didn't want to stay run out." Rain stretched her legs before her and yawned. "A lot of people are going to be really pissed when they find out he's hunting in Boulder again. It's worse with humans like him, you know? The ones who just hate us because their second cousin's great-grandmother's best friend saw a scary monster in the woods are one thing. Who cares what they think? But people like Willow, they think they're doing it for our own good. He's even got people like us working for him."

"Yeah, I met some of them."

I still didn't know if Violet had been expecting me to stay, or hoping I would get away. And Lyle—I had a pretty good idea that Lyle wasn't exactly cooperating willingly, but I didn't know what hold Mr. Willow had over him and his sister. I still hurt too much from the damage Lyle had done to me to care all that much.

"What do they do to people?" I asked. Rain started to answer, but I added quickly, "I mean the ones they don't kill. Is it some kind of . . . a magic ritual or something?"

"Magic ritual?" Rain laughed again. It was a big laugh, bold and unashamed, and I was really starting to dislike it. "God, you're adorable. Yes, Breezy, it's a magic ritual. No idea what it is, though. I've only ever met one guy who survived it, and he says he can't remember. Of course, that could be all the mind-altering drugs he took to get over the trauma."

Not *what* it is, I thought. She had that wrong. *Who.* Mr. Willow and Violet had both been absolutely clear on that point. There was a *who* involved. A woman they called Mother who liked to be given gifts of bound and bleeding monsters wrapped up with a bow.

Rain went on, "What I don't get—"

She stopped, cocked her head to one side.

There were footsteps outside the room and a man's murmuring voice.

Rain crept over to the door. There was no shimmer of air when she leaned close, no sparks of light. I didn't know what I was expecting. A little more flash. Magic was supposed to be flashy.

The man said, "It's fine, it's strong enough, I swear. Yeah, I can hear both of them. Even the— Yes. I won't. Nothing's going to—" A pause. "Fine. Whatever." His voice grew quieter, and his footsteps retreated.

Rain sat down again.

"Who is that?" I asked.

"He's our prison guard."

"Is he—is he human?"

"Far as I know."

"Is he alone?"

"For now, yeah, but he'll have help when it's time to take us away." Rain leaned back on her hands and gave me a narrow look. "Don't even think about it. Even if he opens the door, we won't be able to get out. It's stupid to try anything while we're stuck in here, so don't."

"Does it work?" I asked.

"Does what work?"

"Whatever they do to people." I already regretted asking, but it was too late to take it back. "What they do when they say they can help. Does it work? You said you knew somebody who did it."

She looked at me for a long time before answering. "If you wanted to find out that bad, you should have just gone with them."

"They were a little evangelical for my tastes."

But she was still staring at me. "Whatever you're thinking, you need to get over it," she said. "We are what we are. Most of us are fine with it. There's no point in hating something that's natural. What you're asking, that's like asking a human if they can be a chimpanzee instead. Stop thinking about it. It's only the humans who think we need to be fixed." There was a nasty twist on the word *fixed*.

My instinctive thought: but I am human. I bit my lip to keep the words from escaping.

I felt a pinch in my gut, a queasy uncertainty that was more emotion than rational thought. When I let myself think of how it might go, if Mr. Willow's Mother could do what he said she could do, the possibility was so tantalizing it made my breath catch. I could get rid of these shadows, this body, this aimless flight from everything familiar. I could go home.

But right on its heels came the rest of it: Esme drooling on her towel, the knitting woman by the window, the children who played without joy, without sound. Violet touching my face and telling me to run. Lyle's apology rasping in my ear.

I needed my notebook. I needed my Real/Not Real list. I needed my observations and hypotheses. I didn't know who to believe. I didn't know what to think. Rain didn't know what I had done, didn't know I had a body count just two weeks into my new life as a monster. I wondered how she would react if she knew, if she would be less amused, more wary, or if stories like mine were common in her world.

Mr. Willow didn't know what I had done either, and he already thought I was an evil thing that needed to be destroyed.

The walls, the floor, the ceiling, all smeared in those shifting, changeable shades of red and brown. I didn't trust the judgment of anybody who could put people in a room like this. It was better to think of the walls that way: *red*, not *bloodstained.* Bloodstained didn't even do them justice. Blood soaked. Blood drenched. I didn't know how much blood that would take, or why it could keep us in. I doubted blood by the pint from the local butcher shop and a fancy textured roller from Home Depot were how they went about making a room like this.

I had no idea what time it was. There was no light visible through the boarded-up windows. I didn't think much of Rain's sit-and-wait plan, but I didn't have any better ideas. I couldn't learn anything new as long as we were stuck in here.

I couldn't lean against any of the walls without making myself sick and there was no way I was going near the stained mattress, so I lay flat on my back to ease the pain in my side and entertained a lot of creatively nasty thoughts about Lyle and his claws. Lyle, Lyle, venomous humanoid crocodile.

Not for the first time, I missed my stars. It was cold in the darkness, cold and lonely and empty and I had been dead, but it was quiet and peaceful. Nobody had ever tried to strangle me or drug me or rip me apart with their claws when I was floating in the stars.

# ᐟᐠᐟ· SEVENTEEN ·ᐟᐠᐟ

THERE WERE FOOTSTEPS in the hallway again. I sat up, and Rain rose to her feet. A key rattled and the door opened.

I was expecting somebody like Mr. Willow, with his have-you-accepted-Jesus-as-your-savior hair and warm smile, but the man in the doorway looked like he had reached the age of thirty without realizing he wasn't a frat boy anymore. No Steelers jersey, but he had blond hair in gelled spikes, a T-shirt advertising a craft beer, baggy cargo shorts, and a tattoo of a sunburst on his right calf.

He also had a shotgun. He raised it to his shoulder and pointed it at Rain. "Don't say anything."

"Why not? Don't you want to chat?"

"Shut up," the man said. "Come over here."

Rain smiled. "Come and get me."

"I don't have time for this," he said. He didn't come through the door.

"Oh, are we interrupting your busy day?" Rain said. "We're so sorry about that."

"Shut the hell up." Holding the gun with one hand, the man reached into his pocket with the other and brought out a stiff plastic zip tie. "Don't say anything. Put this on. Both hands."

He threw the tie at Rain; it dropped to the floor. She nudged it with her bare toe.

"Seriously?" She glanced at me. She was grinning. "Can you believe this guy? He thinks he's in a cop movie."

"Wrong genre," I said. My mouth was dry. I wasn't happy she had reminded the man of my presence. I tensed when he turned the gun in my direction.

"You get back," he said.

I slid along the floor until I felt the magical wall at my back.

The man turned his attention and the gun back to Rain. "Put those on and get over here. Don't talk. Don't say one word."

"Where's your backup?" Rain said, and her voice was changing again, slowing down, deeper, almost sultry, like she was flirting with him, but there was nothing flirtatious about the look in her eyes. "Aren't you supposed to wait for help before you let the animals out of their cage?"

I could see it, the cage in the old-fashioned wallpaper beneath the blood, vines and leaves turning to iron.

"Shut up! Either you come with me now, or you stay in there." He didn't say *permanently*, but only because he didn't have the appropriate sense of drama. He was shaking, nervous and scared; there was sweat trickling down the side of his face.

"I think you should come in here," Rain said.

"Stop wasting my time. Stop *talking*."

"I really think you should come in here. We have something to talk about."

He really should come in here. It was warm and red and so much better than out there.

I shook myself. I didn't want him in the room. I wanted him to leave.

The man looked just as uneasy as I felt, but when Rain said it a third time—"Come in, Brian, let's talk about why I'm here"—he stepped through the doorway.

As soon as he was inside the room, I felt it.

He was speaking to Rain, telling her to shut up again, shut up shut up shut up, but I couldn't focus on the words.

With the others, the man at my grave and Duncan Palmer in his blue Corolla, the war vets in McDonald's, the people I passed on the street, it felt like clinging vines, a tangle of shadows invisible but still somehow dark, dirty gray banners trailing behind them, a constant reminder of what they had done.

This man was nothing like that.

This man was a flood of thick black oil. His stupid hair, his angry expression, all of it vanished in the overpowering roar of the people he had killed. He had killed so many people that's all there was to him, those dark tentacles swirling like a living thing, grasping and strangling, reaching from his mouth, from his eyes, tangled about his arms and legs like ropes, dragging him along as though they were alive and he was only their puppet.

I couldn't imagine how somebody so young could have taken so many lives.

I heard twin shouts, the man and Rain, but I paid no attention. A strangled cry ripped from my throat. I flung myself at the man and tackled him around the waist. He was bigger than me, a full foot taller, but I caught him by surprise. He tripped backward, went down on his ass.

He swung the shotgun around, struck the side of my head hard enough to make white spots erupt in front of my eyes. He was shouting. Threats, curses. I couldn't understand him. I didn't care. I couldn't hear anything except the furious roar and the jackhammering of my own heart. The man rocked up on his back and kicked me, planting the sole of one shoe on the unhealed slashes from Lyle's claws. I screamed and doubled over, rolled to the side as he fired the gun.

My ears rang, and for several seconds I couldn't hear anything at all—then I heard the second shot, also wide, that time because Rain had kicked him in the face as he was climbing to his feet. She was shouting too, but her voice was so faint she could have been miles away. All I could hear was the ringing. The pain in my side was overpowering, sickening, and I was distantly aware of another, smaller pain, a new one, sharp points of heat in my shoulder and neck.

The man got his feet under him and lunged toward me,

swinging the shotgun like a bat. I ducked and grabbed his arm with both hands, digging my fingernails into his skin. He beat at my back with the gun, but I held on, and I *pulled.*

It had been so easy with the man in the car, a clean break like a bone snapping. This wasn't easy. There was too much, so many deaths, and he carried all of them, dragged them in a thick black web. I tried, I tried, but it was like falling face-first into a thicket of thorns. The pain was overwhelming.

I let go.

The man dropped like a marionette whose strings had been cut. The shotgun clattered to the floor.

Somebody was screaming, screaming without words, impossibly loud inside my head. I collapsed.

I trembled on the floor for a long time, eyes squeezed shut, unable to move.

The man's memories swallowed me in a black tsunami. His hand tight around pale wrists and ankles. Men, women. Small wrists, small ankles. Children. Some in the red room, some in a dark tunnel, an endless hungry throat. The fingers of his victims scrabbled on hard rock, clawed until they bled. The sweet scent of pine trees and the stench of blood. Gritty sand beneath my shoes. The crunch of small white bones. The startling clang of a metal door slamming, and another, and another, and laughter down a long, long tunnel.

There were too many of them, all jumbled together and confused. I couldn't separate them because he couldn't separate them anymore.

The pleas and screams faded. It felt like hours, but only moments passed. The world beyond his memories began to penetrate.

"Holy shit! What did you do?" Rain was shouting, her voice so loud it was a drumbeat inside my skull.

I tried to tell her that I didn't know, but the words came out as a pained gasp.

"That was *awesome*. What the hell are you?"

I couldn't speak. I opened my eyes, got my hands under me and pushed myself up. Rain was standing on the other side of the room, staring at me with her eyes wide, her mouth open.

"Holy shit, girl. Why aren't you dead? He shot you!"

"I don't know. He missed. I don't know."

Both blasts from the shotgun had gone wide, but I was bleeding sluggishly from pellet bites in my arm and the side of my neck. The wall behind me was pockmarked, pale wood showing through chips in the blood.

Already the pain was burrowing away. I couldn't ignore it, but I could bear it. I had spent the first seventeen years of my life never suffering anything worse than a sprained ankle and monthly cramps, but I was getting used to hurting all the time. I had never thought being dead would hurt so much more than being alive.

I breathed until I was steady, then inched across the floor toward the man.

"What are you doing?" Rain said. "Stop it. You're messed up. Relax. What are you doing?"

When I looked up at her, the shock on her face slowly gave way to a wide grin. I had attacked a man in a blind animal rage and she didn't know why, but it didn't frighten her. It delighted her.

I felt shamed and sick to my stomach. I couldn't look at Rain anymore, so I studied the man on the floor.

"How did you do that?" she asked.

"He's not dead," I said. I needed her to know that. "He's not dead. Just unconscious."

Even as I said it, I knew it wasn't strictly true. I hadn't knocked him out with a blow to the head. This was different.

His blue eyes were open, and he was breathing. I pressed my fingers to his neck; his heart was beating. There were scratches in his arm where I had dug in my fingernails. I looked at my hands, but I was covered with too much of my own blood to see any of his.

His memories were still jangling and clashing in my mind. He had come into this room alone before, without waiting for help, and that time he had been armed with a knife. A young man cowering on the mattress had bled out from twin long slashes down his arms, and his blood had seeped through the mattress and into the floor, drying in eerily red stains. For days afterward, the man had opened the door to check that his victim was still dying, and he had sat down cross-legged in the open doorway and whispered to himself: "He can't get out, he can't get out, he can't get out." It took a long time for the young man to die.

"What?" Rain said.

I was staring at the mattress. "He was going to kill you. He's— he's killed a lot of people."

Rain looked at me curiously, her beautiful amber eyes glittering in the candlelight. "I kinda figured. But how did you know?"

"It's not paint," I said, too tired for sarcasm, "and it's not ketchup."

"No, come on. You've got something else. How did you know?"

I shrugged. "I don't know."

"That," she said, "is very interesting. But I don't think you're lying to me. I think you really are that clueless."

Another shrug.

Rain reached out hesitantly, her palm open toward the wall. She recoiled with an expression of distaste. "Still there. I could have told you that. I did tell you that. Him being—" She gestured vaguely. "Didn't make any difference. Is he going to wake up?"

The man's blue eyes didn't blink, didn't contract, didn't flinch when I snapped my bloody fingers in front of his face. I could barely stand to look at him. Something about his blank stare was so much worse than the man I'd left dead in the car beside a country road. Unfinished in a way that felt like an open wound, a gash that should have been cleaned but was instead left to fester. His face was rigid, not slack; every muscle in his body had tensed as he fell. I didn't want to know what was happening behind his open eyes. I could still feel the oily cloak of his shadows, coiling and twisting like a knot of snakes. I had stripped some of those shadows away, but not all of them. He had killed so many people.

I searched through his pockets. I found the key to the room, a phone, a wallet.

Rain huffed in amusement. "Are you seriously robbing a corpse?"

"Not a corpse," I said, but I was barely paying attention to her.

He was twenty-nine years old. Not a registered organ donor. He had been sunburned the day they took his photo.

"Brian Kerr," I said. Brian, the man Mr. Willow had been speaking to on the phone, if it even mattered. "Lives in Cheyenne, Wyoming. Maybe that's where we are."

I set the wallet aside and picked up the phone, tapped the screen. No password protection. I looked at it for a few seconds before lowering it. I didn't have anybody to call. I didn't think this was a situation in which 911 would be appropriate.

"Do you have somebody you can call for help?" I asked.

Rain said, "Slide it over here."

"There's probably a GPS thing on there, to find out where we are."

Rain rolled her eyes. "Thanks, I never would have thought of that on my own." She spent a few seconds playing with the phone. "Jesus, we're in the middle of nowhere. I hate Wyoming. All the humans are crazy in Wyoming."

I crawled away from Brian Kerr's unconscious body, as close to the wall as I could get without feeling any worse than I already did.

"Do you know someone who can help?" I asked again.

Rain looked at the phone, looked at the stained mattress, looked at me.

"How many people do you think he's killed here?" she asked. "I mean, right here, rather than taking them away?"

"At least one. Somebody who took a long time to die." The young man had been pleading for help long after any normal person—any *human*—would have bled out. "Does it matter?"

"It matters what kind of blood they used," she said. She glared at the phone. "Who the hell even remembers phone numbers anymore?"

She shrugged and dialed, listened for a few moments. "Hey, it's me. Rain." A brief pause. "Yeah, ask me if I care. I've been stuck in a— Just shut up and listen for a second, okay? I need your help." She sounded chipper, cheerful even, no trace of fear in her voice. "Because you owe me. Do you remember what happened— Yes, I am. I am absolutely using that. You owe me. I know you don't want anybody to know what happened. You think everybody's all welcoming and friendly in Boulder, but if they—" Her smile was sharp. "I didn't even know you knew words like that. I ought to wash your mouth out with soap. I need a ride." Another pause. "Not that far. Just outside of Cheyenne. It's in Wyoming, asshole. The big square north of the big square you live in. No, it's not. It's not that far." She rattled off an address, repeated it patiently, and said, "Write it down. And hurry."

She hung up and set the phone on the floor beside her. She hadn't said a word about me.

"It will be a couple of hours," she said. "He's coming up from Boulder."

"He can help?"

"You stay over there. Don't get me wrong, that was kinda badass, but I don't want you near me."

"Fine. Are we getting out of here or not?"

"I think so. This room looks pretty old, but if I'm right . . .

Ghouls aren't good for anything else, but they're pretty useful for breaking through magical shit like this."

Ghouls. Awesome. Another one for the Real side of the list.

Rain nodded at the unconscious man on the floor. "Will he wake up?"

"I don't know."

"You don't know anything, do you?"

"No," I said. "I really don't."

The man didn't wake up. He didn't make a sound. He didn't blink. He was breathing, and he had a pulse, but nothing else about him changed. Not one thing.

# ·⫶⫶· EIGHTEEN ·⫶⫶·

BRIAN KERR IS still alive. He's at a hospital in Cheyenne, hooked
up to machines that monitor his heart. He breathes on his own.
They feed him through a tube. He is unresponsive to stimuli. The
news articles said he played football in college and studied commu-
nications, and he was married to Barbara Rice of Cody, Wyoming.
He told her he was helping a friend fix up an old house to sell. When
he didn't come home and didn't answer his phone, she drove out to
check on him.

An article from his hometown newspaper said: "Longtime resi-
dents of the county might remember Kerr as one of the survivors of
the Windy Ridge Boy Scout Camp animal attack fifteen years ago,

during which four boys were mauled to death by an unidentified animal."

Probably a bear, never confirmed.

That would have been how Mr. Willow found him and drew him in: I know you saw something in the woods that night. I know you know it wasn't a bear. Nobody will believe you.

The articles also said: "Due to evidence found at the scene, Kerr is now a person of interest in several open cases, including a series of disappearances spanning six states."

He's still alive.

I added him to my list anyway:

*Brian Kerr, mass murderer.*

None of the news sites mentioned that he had been found in a room painted with blood.

# ⑪ NINETEEN ⑪

"THAT WOMAN," Rain said.

She hadn't spoken for so long the sound of her voice was a surprise.

"Which woman?"

"The one that was here before you. She was looking for her kids. That's how they got her." Rain was sitting on the floor with her legs stretched out in front of her. "She thought these people took them."

The children on the playground, blank faces turning to watch as Violet and I walked by.

Rain said, "They took her away. That guy and one of his friends. Dragged her out of here. Guess she's never getting a chance to find her kids. You're not bleeding anymore."

"No." I touched my hand to my neck. The furrow left by the shotgun pellet was scabbed over, the skin already knitting itself together. It was healing much faster than Lyle's cuts on my side.

"That should have killed you," Rain said. "Point blank with a shotgun."

"He missed."

"You are so full of shit."

After a while I noticed a change in the light through the open door. Dawn had come, and somewhere in the house, beyond that barrier we couldn't cross, morning sunlight was filtering through unblocked windows.

Not long after sunrise, Rain looked up and tilted her head to the side. "Someone's here."

Her ears were sharper than mine. A full minute later I heard a car approaching. Tires crunched over gravel; the car creaked as it stopped and the engine cut out. A door slammed.

"Is that your friend?" I asked.

Rain walked to the doorway and leaned close to see down the hallway. For a few minutes we didn't hear anything else. No doorbell, no knock.

Then glass broke somewhere in the house. I jumped, startled, and Rain laughed. There was a muffled curse and footsteps in the hallway.

The word *ghoul* had made me imagine a creature with gray skin and yellow teeth and dangling rotten bits, somebody old and crooked and grotesque. But the person who came for us was a tall, skinny kid with brown hair and brown eyes. He looked human, maybe some Middle Eastern or Arab blood in his family history, no older than sixteen or seventeen.

"Took you long enough," Rain said.

"You woke me up at three in the morning and made me drive all the way to Wyoming, and you're complaining about how long it took?" the boy said. He wasn't smiling. "Who is that?"

"We don't know the dead guy. The other one is Breezy," Rain said. "At least, she says that's her name. I have my doubts. Breezy, Zeke. Zeke, Breezy. Don't let her touch you."

"Why not?" The kid wasn't particularly alarmed by the warning.

Rain pointed at the unconscious man on the floor. "She did that," she said.

I pressed my hand over the aching gashes in my side and tried to look harmless. "It was an accident," I lied. "He's not dead."

Zeke gave me a quick look, then reached out tentatively to touch the doorframe. "What did they use for this?"

"The blood of a hundred virgins," Rain said. "Who knows? Who cares? What are you— Don't!"

He stepped through the doorway, made a face like he was smelling something gross, and stepped back out. He was only in the room for a second, but it was long enough for me to feel his brief, shifting shadow. He was a killer.

"That was stupid," Rain snapped. "You could have been stuck in here with us."

"No, I couldn't."

"You don't know that."

"You wouldn't have called me if you thought it would work on me."

"Maybe I called you because I don't know anybody else stupid enough to come. Can you break it?"

Instead of answering, Zeke ran his fingers gingerly over the wood of the doorframe, touching it lightly, like he expected it to be damp and sticky rather than long dried.

"Maybe," Zeke said. He turned and disappeared into the house.

Rain called after him, "Where are you going?"

A storm door clapped shut elsewhere in the house.

Rain rolled her eyes. "I hate ghouls."

"Know a lot of them?" I asked. What I really wanted to know was why the only person she could call for help was a teenage boy, but I was pretty sure she wouldn't answer.

She shrugged. "No. Still hate them."

The storm door opened again; the hinges were squeaky. When Zeke came back, he was carrying an ax.

"Do I even want to know why you—" Rain stopped. "No. I don't want to know why you have an ax. I can guess and it's revolting. Isn't that messy? No, don't tell me."

"Shut up and stand back."

Rain didn't move until Zeke raised the ax above his head and swung. She stepped back quickly, and he struck the frame at the height of the latch. The ax made a solid *thunk* and chips of wood spat out. Zeke chopped at the frame again and again, hitting all the way around the door until the wood was reduced to a mess of shattered splinters.

He broke away some dangling slivers, tossed them aside. "Well?"

Rain reached for the doorway, pushing her fingers tentatively into the open space. When she didn't meet any resistance, she stepped forward. "Finally. Let's get out of here."

"Why would that even work?" I said. The rest of the room was still painted with blood. We weren't any less surrounded than we had been a minute ago.

"Why are you asking me?" Rain said. "I don't do human magic. You could have asked our friend here, but you knocked him out before you got the chance."

"What do we do about him?" I said. Brian Kerr's blue eyes stared, unblinking, at the ceiling.

Rain was already walking down the hallway. "He's your mess. I don't care what you do with him."

"What happened to him?" Zeke stood in the doorway, ax resting on his shoulder.

"Will you believe me if I tell you I have no idea?" I said.

Zeke took a couple of steps closer. "He's not dead."

"Uh, I know. He's breathing."

Zeke looked at me. "That doesn't mean anything. You're breathing too." He frowned, uncertain. "You have noticed, right? That you're—"

"A reanimated corpse? Yes, I've noticed." I crossed my arms over my chest, suddenly, sharply self-conscious. "But almost nobody else has, and it only took you ten seconds. How did you know?"

"I can tell," Zeke said.

"That's a totally helpful answer. How? Do I smell or something?"

"A little bit. What happened to you?"

"I don't remember," I said.

That was good enough for him. Zeke turned and walked out of the room. "You coming?"

I stepped through the ruined doorway. No resistance, no pressure, no magic. It was like nothing had ever been stopping me at all. Magic was already making my head hurt and I didn't even know anything about it yet.

I was morbidly curious about the kind of house a man who kidnapped monsters might live in. I was hoping for cobwebs and draped black curtains and jars filled with pickled body parts. Cages of all sizes. Weapons, lined up and polished on display.

But it was only a house. One level, two bedrooms, one bathroom. The kitchen was painfully ordinary. There were red-checked curtains on the windows, dishes in the sink, mail piled on the table. There was coffee in the pot on the counter, a mug beside it, the faint stale scent of yesterday's brew hanging in the air. In the living room there were photographs on the mantel. I recognized Brian Kerr, younger, posing with a bunch of white guys beneath a doorway marked with Greek letters.

There was a picture of Mr. Willow too, smiling blandly, his arm hooked over a boy in a baseball uniform. I shuddered and turned away.

"Check this out."

Rain was on the other side of the kitchen, standing before what would have been the formal dining room. But that wasn't what it was being used for.

The room was filled with stuff. Not junk, but personal things. Clothes and coats and backpacks and shoes. Kids' schoolbags and jackets, big purses that must have come from old ladies, briefcases and laptop bags. At least three suitcases that I could see. A bright green ski jacket. A ten-gallon Stetson sitting atop a pair of cowboy boots, belt and shining Texas flag buckle curled on the floor beside them. A small pink bike with streamers on the handles and training wheels. A backpack with a sleeping pad strapped to it, an empty water bottle hanging by a clip. A stuffed green turtle with a chewed ear.

My throat was tight. My stomach turned queasily.

These were the belongings they had taken from the people they abducted. I knew it before I saw my own things, the stolen little boy's backpack and stolen skateboard tossed carelessly to the floor. Brian Kerr's memories weren't as vivid as they had been when I first took them from him, but they were still there, just as the memories of the dead family in North Dakota still lingered at the back of my mind, and the memory of a baseball bat stained with blood and the smell of peanut butter. Once I have a murderer's memories in my mind, I have them for good.

And I remembered the people Brian Kerr had taken those things from.

Rain darted forward for a black sweatshirt, pulled it over her head, and stepped away, like she was afraid something would grab her if she gave it a chance.

"That is messed up," she said.

I retrieved my backpack and skateboard, brought them back to the kitchen table to check the contents. My NASA notebook was still there, pen stuck in the spiral, and the handful of bills and change I had accepted from generous strangers. In the bottom of the pack was the plastic bag with the clothes I had been wearing when I died. My other clothes were there as well, the ones I had stripped off and shoved into the washer at Mr. Willow's farmhouse. They smelled faintly of detergent. Somebody, probably Violet, had folded my jeans and shirt and put them in the pack, along with my damp shoes in a plastic grocery bag.

Rain and Zeke were poking around the house, opening doors and peering into closets, so I went looking for the bathroom. I stripped off Violet's dress, ran water in the sink to scrub the blood off my hands and body. I dressed again in the too-long jeans and Wonder Woman T-shirt, and I wrapped the scarf around my neck to hide the bruises. I was going to leave the ruined dress in a heap on the floor, but I changed my mind and stuffed them into the pack. Everything I knew about magic came from *Harry Potter* and Sunny's repeated viewings of *Wizards of Waverly Place*, but I remembered the young man who had bled out on the mattress, taking so very long to die. That was enough for me to suspect that leaving a large quantity of my blood lying around might not be the best idea.

I left the bathroom and walked into the middle of an argument.

"We have to tell someone," Rain was saying. "You don't get it. You weren't here—"

"So tell someone," Zeke said. "Tell whoever you want. I don't care. Just leave me out of it."

"Stop being such a coward. What do you think she's going to do?"

"I don't care. I'm not going."

"Going where?"

They both looked at me, taking in my changed clothes, the backpack over one shoulder. I held tight to the wheels of the skateboard. Sunlight slanted through the kitchen door in a bright triangle; there was a broken window beside the door, a scattering of glass on the floor. I pushed down the urge to run past them and get outside, keep running until I found a road, until the house disappeared over the horizon.

"We have to tell people about these men," Rain said. "Tell them what they're doing. I can go, but I want you to come with me. You met them too."

I could see the dining room behind Rain, but I didn't want to look at it. There was a yellow baseball cap on the floor, dirty, bill dented in a line down the center. A crying little girl had worn it over her braids. Her skin had been more green than pink, her tongue oddly long when she screamed, and her eyes were bright, unnatural spots of light. Brian Kerr had killed her.

I nodded numbly. "Yeah. I can do that."

Zeke started to say something, stopped, and Rain let out an exasperated sigh. "What the hell is your problem?"

After a moment, Zeke said, "I don't think it's a good idea for her to go to a magician." His eyes flicked toward me when he said *her*, and he said *magician* the way most people would say *maggot*.

Rain laughed. She reached out to muss his hair; Zeke flinched away. "What's the matter? Afraid you'll be grounded for visiting the big bad witch in the woods?"

Zeke crossed his arms over his chest. It made him look like a little kid being scolded by an angry teacher. "It's not a good idea."

"Why isn't it a good idea?" I asked. They ignored me.

Rain's smile turned mean. "I can't believe you're scared of Ingrid. She helped you."

"She's human. She's a magician."

"Just because you're racist against humans doesn't mean they're all bad," Rain said. She reached for Zeke's arm, and this time he shoved her back against the counter.

"Touch me again and I will break your arm," he said.

Rain held both of her hands up, palms out, a mocking surrender. "That's why everybody loves ghouls so much. All those good manners and social graces. We'll go without you, if you're going to be like that. Just take us back to Boulder. I'll find somebody else to drive us."

Zeke shook his head firmly. "No." He looked at me, looked away quickly.

"No, what? No, you're not going to drive us to Boulder?"

"I'm not—" Whatever Zeke was going to say, he changed his mind midsentence. "Fine. Whatever. Let's go talk to the crazy hippie witch. It's your funeral."

"That's okay," I said quietly. "I never got one the first time around."

"I *knew* it," Rain said. "I knew you weren't breathing."

Zeke said to me, "That's why you shouldn't go to Ingrid. You're—"

"I'm what?"

"Interesting," he said. "She'll think you're interesting."

It was the same thing Rain had said earlier. Interesting like a two-headed calf, like a bug under a microscope, like an infectious disease.

"Oh, that's great." Rain let out a barking laugh. "He's worried about you. How sweet. That is messed up even for a ghoul. Ingrid won't hurt you. She's not like that. This asshole doesn't know her like I do."

Zeke only shook his head.

I didn't think I was going to like being the kind of interesting everybody kept telling me I was.

Mr. Willow had said of the unseen Mother: she will be so happy to see you.

But interesting also implied this woman might know something about what I was. I didn't have any place I could go, didn't have anybody I could go to. All I had was a lot of questions. I could think of a few things I might want to ask a witch. That's a very human thing to do, I told myself. Ask questions, poke at a mystery, look for the truth. "Trying to learn everything we can about the universe we live in is the most fundamental human endeavor," Karen Garrow had said in one of her science shows, and her voice had been filled with awe.

I could do that. I could be fundamentally human and try to understand what was going on. It wasn't much of a plan, but it was all I had.

"Okay," I said. "Yeah. Let's go."

Zeke turned and stomped out the door, ax in hand.

"Well, come on," Rain said. "I still don't want you touching me, but I'm not going to miss it when you finally put two and two together and start thinking about his diet. I need the laugh."

# ⫸ TWENTY ⫷

I THOUGHT ABOUT it in the thirty seconds it took for me to walk from the house to the truck, which was a black, beat-up piece of junk that didn't look like it had very many miles left in it. On the windows of the bed topper somebody had written *wash me* in the opaque dirt, and somebody else had replied *bite me*.

I was digging in my backpack for my heart-shaped sunglasses and I was thinking: right, okay, ghouls are real too. I'm pretty sure I learned all about them in one of my old Goosebumps books. Something about graveyards. Lurking in graveyards. I remembered that much.

"Oh," I said.

I stopped ten feet from the truck.

Rain snickered.

"What's your problem?" Zeke said through the open door.

"Um," I said, and Rain's snicker turned into a full laugh.

Zeke started the truck and put it into gear. "You don't smell appetizing," he said. "You're not that dead."

"That is not as reassuring as you think it is," I said.

"Are you coming or not?"

We were in the middle of nowhere. There was yellow prairie grass in every direction, a few distant houses along a dirt road, and dusty blue mountains on the horizon, still tipped with snow. The house sat alone at the end of a long driveway, without even a barn or a shed to keep it company. There was a soft-top Jeep parked outside. Not the best vehicle to use if you had to truss up people you'd kidnapped and drive them around, but maybe Brian Kerr had a system. Unless somebody drove right up to the house, they wouldn't see the broken window. They wouldn't have any reason to look inside and find the red bedroom with the boarded-up windows and the man lying on the floor like a discarded doll.

The sun was crawling higher and the day was already warm, the air dry and sharp.

I got into the truck.

# ⁕ TWENTY-ONE ⁕

WE DROVE EAST first, then south toward Colorado. The land was empty and dry, marked by evidence of civilization in narrow strips along roads and exits. We passed through the thin outskirts of Cheyenne and turned onto the interstate. The truck was old and noisy and it sounded like it would rattle apart if Zeke pushed it faster than sixty-five. Shook like it too, a deep vibration I could feel in my teeth and my bones.

My side hurt constantly, no matter how I shifted or braced myself. I reached beneath my shirt to check if I was bleeding again. My fingers came away tacky with blood. I didn't know why this injury wasn't healing like the others, but I was perfectly happy to blame Lyle.

Zeke was driving with one hand on the wheel, one elbow resting on the door, head propped up like he was having trouble staying awake. He was leaning away from Rain, careful not to bump her when he shifted gears.

Rain said, "If you fall asleep and kill us, I'm going to be pissed."

He didn't look at her. "It won't kill me, and she's already kind of dead. That leaves you, and I don't care what happens to you."

It was the first thing anybody had said since we left the house. Their argument about the witch settled, they didn't seem to have a lot to say to each other. I was getting the impression they maybe didn't like each other very much.

I watched the passing landscape through the window. Fields of grass turning brown for summer, wire fences and cows, pickup trucks rolling along the frontage roads. The day felt different from my nighttime ride across Nebraska. More exposed, less welcoming.

"All the stuff in that house," I began.

I regretted breaking the silence as soon as the words were out. I didn't want to think about the scared, screaming little girl with the braids and the yellow ball cap, or the young man gasping and gurgling as he slowly, slowly died. I didn't feel guilty about Brian Kerr. I only wished I hadn't left him alive.

"What about it?" Rain said, when I didn't go on.

"It all belonged to people like—like us?"

"Monsters," she said.

"And there are lots of different kinds of—" I didn't want to say it. "Monsters?"

Rain raised one eyebrow. "Breezy, you can go ahead and ask if vampires are real. We won't judge you."

"Are they?" I asked.

"Not that I know of," she said. "Never met one."

"I have," Zeke said.

"Really?" Rain looked surprised. "You've met a real vampire?"

"Yeah, once."

"I thought they were an urban legend, like the phone call coming from inside the house," Rain said thoughtfully. "Are they anything like the stories? All suave and sexy with vague European accents and bespoke suits?"

"No. They're kind of gross."

"The kid who eats human corpses for dinner is calling something else *gross*."

"Well, they are," Zeke said. "They're all hairy and pale. They live underground." Rain wasn't looking at him, so she didn't see the slight twitch of his lips. He was messing with her. Lying through his mostly human teeth. That made me like him a little bit more, even if he had told me I smelled like death.

"What about mermaids?" When they both looked at me, I explained, "My sister swore she saw a mermaid in Lake Michigan once."

I hadn't thought of that day in years, but now I remembered it vividly: the hot summer sun, the cold lap of water, and Sunny running along the shore, shouting about the ugly green person eating fish in the lake. We had laughed at her at the time, even though she was red faced and shaky, her lips trembling, her eyes damp. Dad had taken her hand and led her back up the beach, even after she had shaken her head and wiped her nose and insisted she didn't want to go. They didn't find anything, and by the time they came back Dad had promised Sunny ice cream and she was laughing like she had never been scared at all.

"Mermaids," Rain said. "In Lake Michigan. I hope you got your sister's head checked out."

But Zeke said, "There are a lot of people living in the Great Lakes. She's lucky they didn't grab her. They can be nasty. And they're cannibals."

"Pot, kettle," Rain said.

Zeke ignored her. "That's how they fight. Winner eats loser. People bet on the fights."

"The first rule of cannibal mermaid fight club is don't talk about cannibal mermaid fight club." Rain laughed at Zeke's confused look. "You have absolutely no idea what I'm talking about. You are so full of it. You've never seen a mermaid."

Zeke only shrugged. "They smell like fish."

Neither of them minded me asking questions on the theme of "real or not real?" so I kept at it, if only for a way to pass the time. "Ghosts?" confirmed what I had already figured out from my encounter on the country road; they were real, certainly, but they didn't have a whole lot going on. "Werewolves?" led Rain into a long, elaborate story about a pair of brothers she had once known, or slept with, or who had been sleeping with each other, it wasn't entirely clear, only that it featured a smokejumper and a park ranger and I believed about one-tenth of it.

"How about this one," I said, after the smokejumper and the park ranger drove off into the sunset together. "What would you call somebody who looks perfectly normal but can spontaneously grow huge claws and run really fast?"

"Is that what happened to you, with all those scratches?" Rain asked.

"Yeah. What was he?"

"Was he hairy? Scaly? Smell like a trash dump? Red eyes?"

"No. He was just a guy, at least until the claws came out."

"No idea," Rain said. "Lots of things have claws. You're gonna have to give us more than that."

But I didn't have anything more, only the marks Lyle had left. "What about somebody with glowing green eyes and a scream that can make people's ears bleed?"

"Who the hell have you been hanging out with?" Rain said. "You need better friends. Are we talking about a woman?"

"Yes."

"She could be a banshee," Zeke said.

Rain nodded. "Sounds like it, but there aren't many of them around."

One less, now, if what Violet had been telling the truth about what Mr. Willow could do.

I made the mistake of asking about fairies and they spent twenty minutes arguing about what counted as a fairy and how they were different from sprites or elves or whatever, and whether it was even worth knowing the differences if nobody had ever seen half of the things that qualified. I was going to have to add an Unknown column to my Real/Not Real list.

"Unicorns?" I said, after the fairy discussion had subsided, unresolved.

Rain snorted a laugh, and Zeke said, "No."

"He would know," Rain added. "I hear they like 'em young and pure."

My next question was there on my tongue. Closer to angels, Mr. Willow had said about Esme. Esme with her animal growl and her bib and her empty stare. I wondered if she had claws too, or if Mr. Willow's help had taken them away. Closer to demons.

I didn't ask. I couldn't even get a handle on monsters in this world yet. Other realms were more than I was prepared to deal with.

Instead I said, "Dragons?"

"Dragons?" Rain repeated.

I sighed. "This might all be worth it if dragons were real."

# ⫶∥⫶ TWENTY-TWO ⫶∥⫶

LATER, MUCH LATER, I did ask. By then my Real/Not Real list was a little longer, and the Unknown list on the next page was longer than both of them combined.

I asked, "Are demons real?"

Zeke and I were walking through the Gold Hill Cemetery outside Boulder. It was a warm morning, cloudless and clear, just like every other Colorado summer day. The cemetery was on a hill, steeper than you would think made sense for burying coffins, surrounded by a wire fence with a gate that looked like it hadn't been closed in decades. The trees above the cemetery had been burned black by a forest fire a few years ago, but everything close to the

ground was overgrown with rich green grass and bright wildflowers. Every step we took stirred up an explosion of grasshoppers.

We found the headstone we were looking for tucked away in
a cluster of rustling aspens. *Beloved Mother, Who Hath Suffered.
Died 1973.* No name. No date of birth. Possessive and dismissive,
carved in stone.

Zeke had gathered up a bunch of wildflowers to put on the
grave. I thought it was sweet, but I didn't want to admit that out
loud, so I said, "You know there's nobody there, right? They buried
an empty box. They only wanted everybody to think she was dead."

I liked that there was one place in the old cemetery where I
could stand and know there was nobody below me.

Zeke threw one of the flowers at me. It hit me in the nose, but I
caught it before it fell. Purple lupine, and I only knew that because
when Sunny was little she loved this picture book about a woman
who traveled all over the world, had a lifetime of adventures, and
in her old age planted flowers to make the world more beautiful. I
must have read that book to Sunny about a dozen times, and we all
had to endure her brief but fervent backyard gardening phase that
followed.

I twirled the flower between my fingers. "Are they? Are demons
real?"

"Is this the unicorn thing again?" Zeke asked.

"Just so you know, I still don't believe you about unicorns," I
said, because I knew it would make him roll his eyes, which was
almost as good as a laugh. "I will always believe unicorns are real.
They're pretty and sparkly and their horns are made of pure joy, but

they only appear for people who aren't jerks. That's why you'll never meet one."

"Neither will you," Zeke said.

I stuck my tongue out, the most mature comeback I could manage. "Tell me about demons. You know, demons from hell that possess people. Black eyes and pea soup and crab walks, the whole deal. Are they real?"

"No such thing. They're just a stupid human story," Zeke said. It was what I expected him to say, but he surprised me by continuing. "There's no one monster that's like that, but there are a lot that humans would probably call demons. Including you."

"And you."

"But they're just people. They're not different. They're not from somewhere else."

"Not from hell, you mean."

"Wherever." Zeke dismissed it with a quick shrug; the word had no meaning to him. Monsters are the least superstitious people I've ever met. "It's just a story. Humans always like to blame everything on invisible monsters from an invisible world."

Zeke turned away from the grave and started walking again, not down toward the car but up the hill, farther into the cemetery. When we had first set foot through the gate, half an hour ago, I had asked him if he felt anything, and he had shrugged and said, "It's quiet. Peaceful."

"What about angels?" I asked.

"Same thing. What's the difference?"

It was the difference between people who were cruel and people who were kind, between stories about evil and stories about good, but maybe in his mind that wasn't much of a difference at all.

"How do you know?" I asked.

"Because that's how humans are," he said. He said it the way a marine biologist might say, *Because that's how giant squids are*, curious and knowledgeable, but observing an alien species from the outside.

There was a little voice in the back of my mind, an angry stage whisper that said: I am human. I know how we are.

But I knew the difference between the truth and a lie, even inside my own head.

And I knew he was right. I was asking because there was a part of me that still wanted to assign away blame. A part that still wanted to believe all of this, the magic and the monsters, it was all something apart, something not merely hidden but separate from the world I had known before.

Zeke was quiet a moment before he said, "You don't believe in that stuff, do you?"

"No," I said.

I didn't have to think about it. Heaven or hell, clouds and harps or fire and brimstone. I knew which list those kinds of afterlife belonged on.

"I know it's not real," I said. "And if anybody should know, it's me."

I watched the Gold Hill grasshoppers flinging themselves this way and that, all around the overgrown gravestones and charred trees. Violet had said the darkness was inside me. She was wrong.

"Not bigger, but brighter," I said to myself. At Zeke's look, I explained, "It's something Sally Ride said once. She was the first American woman to go into space. Not the first woman ever. That was Valentina Tereshkova in 1963. It took the Americans twenty more years to get a woman up there. That was Sally Ride."

"Is she one of your dead astronauts?" he asked.

"They're not *my* dead astronauts," I said. So maybe being dead myself hadn't stopped me from talking about my dead heroes all the time, but at least Zeke didn't tell me it was morbid like Melanie used to. "And, no. I mean, yes, she's dead, but she died of cancer, in her sixties. Not in space. But somebody asked her once in an interview about what it was like, and she said, 'The stars don't look bigger, but they do look brighter.'"

I looked up at the blue sky and squinted in the brilliant sun. Zeke had never asked. I had never told anybody before.

"That's all I remember about that whole year," I said. "It was dark and cold and empty. But there were stars. It was too lonely to be heaven, and there wouldn't be stars in hell."

# ⑾ TWENTY-THREE ⑾

WE DROVE INTO Boulder from the north. Busy midday traffic surrounded us, a sprawl of stores and parking lots and restaurants strung along busy streets, buses lurching from stop to stop, cyclists hunched over handlebars in the bike lanes.

At a stoplight, Zeke took out his phone, made a call, and left a short message: "Taking Rain to Ingrid's, won't be long."

After he hung up, Rain said, "I can't believe you. Nothing's going to happen. Ingrid's not stupid enough to do anything to you."

Zeke was watching the road, not looking at us. "It's not me I'm worried about," he said.

Rain opened her mouth, seemed to think better of it, and kept quiet.

We turned west and left the city behind. Climbed into the mountains, past the dam and reservoir at Nederland, straight through town and out the other side. I grew more nervous with every mile. Mr. Willow and Brian Kerr had left me wary of people who lived in remote locations.

About twenty minutes outside Nederland, Zeke turned off the highway and onto a narrow dirt road that skirted the edge of a thick pine forest, following a broad valley ringed by snow-spotted mountains. We turned again, this time onto a driveway that climbed through the trees before winding down a low ridge and into a gentle bowl of a valley. Tall shaggy animals grazed in a pasture. Llamas or alpacas. I didn't know the difference. They ignored us.

The driveway led to a house and a red barn surrounded by a wooden fence. A speckled gray horse nosed at tufts of grass in a corral. The house itself was small and old, a genuine log cabin of rich ruddy wood, with a stone chimney at one end and a long porch stretched across the front.

It was a beautiful scene, sunny and bright beneath the deep blue sky, the mountains so close and so clear. It could have been from a postcard: *Greetings from Colorful Colorado! Wish you were here!*

All I could think about was how far I would have to run to get away.

The gate was open, but Zeke stopped before pulling through.

"You're not even going up to the house?" Rain asked.

"No."

"What the hell did you do to piss her off?"

"Nothing. I said I'd bring you here. You're here."

The house looked so pretty and idyllic, that quaint cabin huddled down in the blue mountains and green pastures. There was a hummingbird feeder hanging on the porch and a wind chime on the opposite side, both swaying slightly in a breeze not quite strong enough to make the bells ring.

If I had to imagine what a witch's house would look like, that wouldn't have been it. There definitely wouldn't have been alpacas.

"Look, don't listen to this idiot," Rain said to me. "Ingrid's fine. She's like a liaison between all the different people around here. Monsters like us, magicians like her, people who aren't either but know about both, right?"

"Right," I said. So now there were human-monster liaisons too. It would probably be weird to ask for her résumé.

"And all she wants is information."

"That's not all she wants."

Rain elbowed Zeke in the side without looking at him. "Yes, it is. But she has to keep things fair. She doesn't want to owe anybody. So you tell her what you know about Willow and his people, and she'll let you ask her something in return. That's how it works."

"It's bullshit," Zeke said. "She just made that up and people are stupid enough to go along with it."

"Oh my god, shut up," Rain said. "You're too much of a pussy to even drive through the gate. Nobody cares what you think. Seriously." She poked my shoulder and indicated the door. "Let's go.

Don't worry about it."

"What kind of something do I get to ask?" I could think of two or three or five hundred questions I might have.

"Something important. That's what you have, so that's what you get."

"That's it?" It sounded suspiciously like the sort of arrangement a fairy-tale king would be tricked into agreeing to right before losing his entire kingdom to a conniving sorceress.

"She won't hurt you," Rain said. "No matter what this idiot says. She's not like that."

"She is with some people," Zeke said.

Rain made a frustrated sound. "Why are you being such an ass? She's not— There she is." She nudged me in the side again. "Go on, get out."

The woman who stepped onto the porch was dressed in jeans and a blue T-shirt, with wire-rimmed glasses perched on her nose and her long gray hair pulled into a braid over her shoulder. She lifted one hand in a wave and started walking toward us. Rain headed down the driveway to greet her. I moved to follow, but Zeke stopped me with touch on my arm.

"Don't give her anything that belongs to you." His voice was low, too quiet for Rain to hear.

"Like what? I don't have anything."

"Whatever she asks for, don't give her anything. Hair or skin or—or whatever."

"She's going to ask for my hair?" I said, skeptical. "That's not creepy or anything. Why?"

"Because you're"—he gestured at my face—"whatever you are, and she's a magician." The *duh, obviously* was implied by his tone. "She'll ask for something. Don't give it to her."

"Not even information?"

"What? No, that's fine. You can talk to her."

"Okay. No locks of hair. Only talking."

"And don't accept anything she offers," Zeke said. "Nothing. Even if it seems harmless. Even if she says she can't help you otherwise. Do you understand?"

Rain and the woman met on the driveway, and they embraced.

"Yes," I said, "but why?"

"She can't do anything to you if you're just talking to her," Zeke said, still speaking quietly and quickly. "It's not . . ." He searched for the right word. "It's not *binding*. She just lets people think it is because they're too stupid to know better. But if you give her anything, or take something from her—"

"What? What can she do?"

"I don't know," he admitted. "But if I were you, I wouldn't want to find out. Don't trust her."

Ingrid hooked her arm through Rain's and together they walked up the driveway. In spite of her gray hair, Ingrid's skin was smooth, crinkling only in lines around her eyes.

"Does your brother know you're here?" she asked.

"Yes," Zeke said.

"You'll have to tell him I said hi." Ingrid turned her steel-gray eyes to me. Her voice was rich and deep, and she spoke with a faint accent. German, maybe, but she had been in the United States for a long time. "What have you brought me, Rain?"

"This is Breezy," Rain said. "Breezy, this is Ingrid Schultz."

I nodded. "Nice to meet you."

Ingrid slipped her arm free of Rain's. I tensed as she approached. She was a tall woman, a full head taller than me, and every instinct in my body was telling me to make myself small and unnoticeable. She didn't do anything so obvious as sniff or walk around me in a circle, but there was something sharp and assessing in her gaze.

Her friendly smile vanished. She stepped back. "You should come inside. This might take a while. Not you," she said to Zeke. "You stay out here."

She returned to the house. Rain glanced at me, shrugged, and together we followed.

# ᐈ TWENTY-FOUR ᐈ

"PLEASE TAKE A SEAT," said Ingrid. She gestured to a sagging sofa. "Would you like something to drink?"

"No, thank you," I said.

"Are you sure? Iced tea?"

"I'm sure." After the concoction Mr. Willow had made me drink, I wasn't going to be accepting beverages from strangers any time soon.

"I would love some iced tea," Rain said. "I'll help you get it."

They went into the kitchen, leaving me alone.

Ingrid's living room was small and cluttered, almost claustrophobic, with heavy curtains on the windows, busy patterns on folded quilts, a coat rack fat with winter parkas. A trunk served as a coffee table; it was stained with condensation rings and stacked with issues of *The New Yorker* and *The Economist*. There was a black woodstove at one end of the room, firewood piled beside it. In a corner leaned a bookshelf jammed with hardbacks and photo albums on all shelves except one, which was crowded with dusty jars and bowls of what looked like potpourri. I leaned in to smell an open bowl.

I was only a few inches away before I realized the bowl wasn't filled with dried flowers at all. They were beetle shells, shiny and black behind the curve of the glass.

The floorboards creaked as Rain and Ingrid returned. Rain dropped into an armchair by the window, and Ingrid sat on the sofa.

"Have a seat." She patted the cushion beside her.

I stepped around the wooden trunk and perched on the edge of the sofa, as far as I could be from her without making it obvious. I expected her to ask me about myself, where I had come from or where I was going, and I was piecing together another patchwork girl in my mind, a weak story I didn't expect her to believe.

But Ingrid didn't care about any of that.

"Now," she said, "tell me what you are."

"Dead," I said. "Sort of."

Rain coughed through her swallow of iced tea.

"Fascinating. How long have you been dead?" Ingrid asked, a small smile playing on her lips.

"What's the date today?" I asked.

"June twenty-seventh."

"A year and seventeen days. You can't tell just by looking at me?"

"Should I be seeing an aura? A magical pulse? No. There is nothing so obvious as that."

It had been obvious to Zeke, but at least she wasn't telling me I smelled dead.

"Have you been aware all this time?" Ingrid asked.

"Not exactly." I didn't want to tell her about my stars.

"Do you remember how you died?"

"No." The bruises around my neck were hidden under the scarf.

She didn't believe me. "Not at all?"

According to the news reports, nobody had seen me leave the party. Nobody had seen anybody suspicious hanging around. No older guys, no drug dealers, no vagrants. Nobody who looked like they didn't belong with a bunch of high school kids engaging in relatively harmless underage drinking. No strange cars or vans lurking on neighborhood streets. No calls on my phone. Nobody had seen anything. There were statistics about missing teenagers at the end of some of the articles. I hadn't realized before how many people disappeared every year and never returned. No bodies, no tracks, nothing. They just vanished.

I remembered slipping on the damp grass with Melanie as we walked toward Nate's house. I remembered the loud music, the bass line heavy in my chest, and laughter as the front door opened, the hot crowded living room and bright light from the kitchen, the blue margarita mix splattered on white tile thanks to somebody who had turned on the blender without its lid. I remembered the open glass doors to the yard, Christmas lights on the trees and hedges, and Melanie telling me that Jania had done that, obviously, not Nate, because Nate would never decorate for a party but he would let his girlfriend string up lights if she wanted to. I remembered the taste of beer, cold at first and lukewarm later, the smooth feel of the plastic cup, warm bodies jostling my bare shoulders. I remembered Melanie snort-laughing at something I said, and the way she tugged her hair over her shoulder and twisted it up, the small hairs at the back of her neck damp with sweat. I remembered the harsh light of the bathroom and my own reflection in the mirror, the red mark on my face and a sting I felt deeper than my skin, and the dizzy feeling of being just beyond tipsy, the muddle of disappointment and embarrassment, tears gathering in my eyes and—

"No," I said. I curled my fingers into fists. "I don't. I imagine it was a pretty traumatic experience."

I waited, expecting more questions, but Ingrid only looked at me, sipped her tea and looked. I grew more and more uncomfortable as the minutes ticked away. Beneath the fresh air flowing through the open windows and the spicy scent of the herbs growing in pots, there was an old, stale smell in the room, something dusty and faint. It reminded me of playing hide-and-seek with Meadow in our grandmother's attic.

I turned away from Ingrid's steady gaze and glanced around the room, but I looked back after a moment. If this was meant to be a trade for information, I wanted to know what she was going to offer.

I asked, "Do you know what I am?"

"Do you?" she replied.

In her chair by the window, Rain laughed. "She doesn't know much."

"I ruled out zombie," I said. "I'm not craving any brains and nothing has rotted off yet."

Ingrid was unamused. "This is not a game."

"I always thought that when people died they stayed dead," I said. I didn't know what she wanted me to say. "Except in comics. Nobody except Uncle Ben stays dead in comics."

She set her glass down. "They do, usually. Your situation is unusual, but not entirely unheard of. Normally one finds creatures like you in epidemics or war zones, where there is a great deal of death, and even then it is exceedingly rare. Did Rain explain to you how this works?"

I glanced at Rain. "She said it's a trade. Information for information."

"Do you have something to offer?"

"Yes," I said.

"Something valuable?"

I hesitated. Thought about the room painted in blood, the discarded belongings, the church on the prairie. "Something dangerous."

"Very well." Ingrid stood to light two candles by the window. A heady, sweet scent filled the room. "I believe I can help you understand a little about what you are, with Rain's help, if she's willing?"

"Sure," said Rain.

Ingrid sat again and said to me, "You're here because you were murdered. That's how unnatural things like you come to exist."

Now I was an *unnatural thing*. So much for Rain's chimps-and-humans comparison. I wondered if *unnatural thing* was a step up or a step down from *freaky bitch*.

Ingrid went on, "Nobody who dies a natural death, or a peaceful death, comes back as a revenant. Do you know what that means?"

"Not really."

"*Revenant* is a word that has both quite a lot of meaning and very little. It only means that you've returned."

"Accurate," I said. I refrained from telling her I had figured that out on my own. "What does that mean? Have you met somebody like me before?"

"I haven't, no," she said. "Few people have. You are a very rare creature."

"But . . . why? Why did I come back?"

"Is that really what you want to know?"

"Uh, yes. That's really what I want to know. Did I—" I wasn't even sure what to ask. "Did I do something? Did somebody else do something?"

Ingrid looked disappointed. "There are no good answers to those questions. Not that you would understand. It is no small feat of magic to bring the dead back to life."

"But somebody knows how to do it? Do *you* know how to do it? To make something like me—"

"A monster," Rain said.

I glared at her. "People get killed all the time and don't come back. Something must have happened."

"Indeed, something must have." Ingrid leaned back in the sofa. "Can you bleed?"

"Can I— What?"

"Bleed," Ingrid said. "If I cut you, will you bleed?"

"Oh. Uh, yes."

"I would like some of your blood."

I started to ask her why, stopped and shook my head. "No."

"No?"

"No."

"What did the ghoul tell you I was going to do with it?"

Rain snickered. "I'm sure it was good, whatever he said."

I said nothing. The scent of the candles was stinging my eyes.

"He's a frightened child with a limited view of the world and, more important, he doesn't know the first thing about how magic works. His kind rarely do. I only need a few drops," Ingrid said. "Surely you can spare that much?"

"No," I said.

"I can't fully answer your question without it. That would be like asking a doctor to diagnose an illness without an X-ray."

Exactly what Zeke had said she would say.

"No."

Rain said, "Told you she would be like this."

Ingrid sighed. "Very well. We'll try this a different way. Rain?"

"Sure," Rain said.

Ingrid set her glass down and reached for my hand. I started to pull away, but she caught my fingers and held them. Her grip was firm. She held my hand, examining my fingers and probing the phalanges beneath the skin. A chill crept over me, raising goose bumps all along my arms.

"You will remember, eventually," she said. "You will remember how you came to be this way. You will remember the moment you died and did not die."

"You will remember," Rain said. Her low seductive voice was back, slow as a hot summer's night, deep as a well. "You'll remember eventually."

The slick cool grass, Melanie's laugh, hot stinging skin. One by one the sensations returned.

"You may think the memories are gone," Ingrid went on, after what seemed an impossible length of time. "And you may take comfort in that. You may tell yourself you have not changed. But it is a mistake to think of yourself as the same person you were before."

"I'm not—"

Ingrid squeezed my fingers and I stopped, sealed my lips together.

I waited, waited, trying not to meet her eyes, trying to count my breaths. I lost focus every time I made it to nine or ten. The slick cool grass, Melanie's laugh, hot stinging skin. The whole of that night was spooling out before me, bright, loud with details I had forgotten, whirling through my mind with frantic energy.

"You'll do well pretending to be human, for a while," Ingrid said.

"You're pretending to be human," Rain echoed quietly, no more than a murmur.

I am human, I thought. I couldn't say it.

"But it won't last. In time you will choose to be more monster than human. You will shed the pretense of care, the charade of empathy. When you make that choice, there is no way back."

"There is no way back," Rain said.

"What do you crave?" Ingrid asked.

I was dizzy, unstable, and disoriented. Rain was still speaking, but I couldn't understand her anymore, the words were flowing and falling and meaningless. Ingrid must have given me something after all, even though I had heeded Zeke's warning. There was something in the air, in those pungent candles, in her touch and in Rain's voice, some earthy rich drug like Mr. Willow's herbs and insects. I closed my eyes. I tasted blood. Blood and iron and grit, and I tasted peanut butter too, and Sunday roast and potatoes. I saw a knife penetrating my abdomen and the muzzle flare of a gun. I saw the baseball bat that had been my birthday present swinging down at my face and felt the rough scrape of solid rock beneath my fingers as I scrambled through an absolute darkness and no, no, no, these were the wrong memories, the wrong echoes, these belonged to people who had been dead and gone for years, buried and rotted away long before I had become what I was. I had no right to these memories. The killers, the killers were mine, but the victims belonged only to themselves.

"What do you crave?" Ingrid asked, and Rain said, "You know what you want to do."

The impossible memories evaporated like mist in the morning sun, and I was alone. I was alone in the backyard of an empty house, alone on a dark roadside, alone in the red room, but every time I lifted my hand, every time I reached out, another person appeared, and they flinched, and they fell. First the ones I knew, the men I had already killed, then more, people I had never seen before, men and women with black shadows clinging to the insides of their skin, anchored to the blunt teeth at the backs of their mouths, every single one of them a murderer, every single one irresistible. I touched them one by one, featherlight and intimate, and one by one they died, falling in lifeless heaps as I walked across cities, across mountains and plains, across neighborhoods of houses lit from within with cowering yellow light. There was blood on my hands, blood in my mouth, blood running in rivulets around my feet, and every time it dried and flaked away, I found another mur-derer. I walked until I became a plague of vengeance in a human mask and the city began to look like my city, the neighborhoods like those I had always known, and I was walking down a street I knew, approaching a house I had seen before. A single light shone in an upstairs window. A shadow moved behind the glass. Furtive, scared. A dead boy.

I opened my eyes.

I was slumped into the corner of Ingrid's sofa. My neck was stiff, my side throbbing where Lyle had cut me, my fingers cold. The candles had burned down and softened. The light in the room was golden, the breeze cooler.

It had been just after noon when I first stepped into Ingrid's house. Now it was early evening. I had lost hours in the space between her words.

"What," I said. My mouth was dry, my lips chapped. My heart

raced and I tried to pull my hand free, but Ingrid held tight. "What did you do to me?"

"Your ability to lie to yourself won't last," she said. "Blood? Pain? Revenge? Is that what you want?"

"No. No. I don't want anything." Panic was rising like a thunderstorm. I couldn't think clearly. She wouldn't let me go. Rain was gone. Ingrid and I were alone and I didn't know what she had done. "I don't— What are you doing? Let me go."

"Revenge," she said, as though I had answered. "You crave it more than anything. You won't be able to stop yourself."

"Stop. What did you do to me?" I saw myself insensible and openmouthed, as empty as Brian Kerr on the floor of a blood-painted room, and just as vulnerable. "What did you do?"

"I didn't have to do anything. It is your nature now," she said. "It is instinct. You will start with those you choose to believe are guilty, or dangerous, but you won't stop there. It will become easier and easier to convince yourself that others deserve it too, and soon you won't concern yourself with reasons at all."

"No. Let me go."

"There is only one way to prevent it. There is only one person whose death can have any real meaning to you. It can set you free. The person who did this to you, the one who ended your life—"

"Stop. Let me go!"

I didn't realize I was shouting until I felt the tear of it in my throat. The entire forest fell silent and held its breath.

I wrenched my hand away and stood so quickly I knocked my shin into the edge of the trunk, felt my recently healed knee twinge in protest. Outside birds chattered again and a breeze stirred through the aspen trees. The shadows were long. It would be dark soon.

I had refused to give Ingrid what she asked for, but she had taken something anyway.

I relaxed my hands from fists at my sides. "I don't want to hear any more. I'm leaving."

"You should stay here. There is more for us to discuss. You don't want to know what will happen to you?"

"No."

"You don't want to know what you will do?"

"No. I don't want to know."

"Are you sure?" Ingrid crossed her legs and sat back, folded her hands over her knee. Even though she was sitting and I was standing, I felt small and quaking before her. "This is the best part. You are a fascinating creature."

"No," I said. "I want to leave."

"Whether you hear it or not has no effect on how true it is," she said. "You have no choice anymore. Your death has made you into this thing, and there is nothing you can do about it. If you give me but a drop I can tell you—"

"I don't care. I'm leaving."

"Sit down."

"No. I said no. I don't want to hear it. I don't need to know."

"You can keep your ignorance, if you want, but you still owe me your information in trade."

She was right. I had agreed. As much as I wanted to run from that house and never look back, I wanted even more to go without Ingrid believing I had reneged on our deal. It may not have been magically binding, but I didn't trust her.

I sat again, but not on the sofa. I didn't want to be close enough for her to touch. I settled into the armchair by the window.

"What do you want to know?"

"What do you want to tell me?" she replied.

I thought it over before answering. I didn't know what she was going to do with the information I offered. Before meeting her, before she had stolen an entire afternoon, I would have thought that anybody, with any intentions at all, would be better than Mr. Willow. But Ingrid unsettled me nearly as much as he did.

"Lies are not as valuable as the truth," Ingrid said drily.

"I'm not going to lie," I told her, and I meant it. Picking and choosing bits of the truth was not quite the same thing as lying. "I'm just trying to figure out where to start. It's been a weird few days."

"Tell me," she said.

I told her some of it, but not everything. I didn't tell her about the men I had killed, but I told her about hitchhiking across the country and meeting a kid at a truck stop who picked me out as somebody, *something*, unusual. I didn't tell her his name. I told her how I had found my way to Mr. Willow's church, but I also told her I wasn't sure exactly where it was. Mr. Willow was there with Violet and Lyle, and I had no interest in protecting them, but helpless Esme was also at the house, and the children and the woman with the knitting needles. I didn't trust Ingrid to distinguish between prisoner and captor.

I did tell her that it was more of a cover than a real church, and she snorted, unsurprised.

"Yes," she said. "He did that here as well. It was his father's idea. A man can get away with all manner of irrational nonsense if everybody believes he's doing it for God."

I also told her what I had done to Brian Kerr. Rain would tell her anyway, and I wasn't opposed to Ingrid knowing I could be dangerous too.

I didn't tell her about the stolen memories.

"We had thought, when we drove Willow and his congregation away, that they would stay gone," Ingrid said, when I was finished. "He won't like that you and Rain have escaped his grasp. He'll send somebody after you."

"Can he really do what he thinks he's doing?" I asked. "Those people I saw, they looked—some of them looked like they were brain damaged, to be honest, but is it possible they used to be monsters and aren't anymore? One of the girls said she was—said it had worked for her. Is that even possible?"

Ingrid's lips parted, the beginning of an answer, but she paused, and she thought about it for a long while. "I don't know," she said finally. "He wouldn't be the first to try, but Edward Willow was never a very skilled magician. I find it hard to believe he could do it without help, and any creature that could help would be doing so for its own purposes."

Stone and iron and laughter in the darkness. *She will be so happy to see you.* I suppressed a shudder.

Ingrid went on. "But if your estimate of how many people they've taken is accurate, he has a lot of power at his disposal. Anything is possible. He must be stopped."

On that, at least, we were in agreement. "What are you going to do?"

"It's not my decision to make." She stood up. "I will share what you have told me with the community. We drove him away before, and we will do it again if necessary. I won't keep you any longer."

Just like that, our conversation was over.

Ingrid waited until we were outside to say, "You should have listened to how this will end for you."

A familiar house on the dark street, a single light burning, a shadow in the window. I pressed my fingers against the scarf around my neck, digging into the hidden bruises, the ones that never healed, and for a moment I felt the hands that had put them there. I had listened. Whatever she had done to me, however she had put that vision of the future in my head, I knew exactly what she was telling me.

I stepped down from the porch. The sun was setting, draping the valley and forest in shadow, but the tops of the hills were still bright. Zeke's truck was parked outside the fence; I had expected him to be gone. By the barn Rain was talking with a man who laughed loudly at whatever she was saying.

"You are not what you used to be," Ingrid said. "You can't go on pretending nothing has changed."

"Oh, I know that," I told her. I kept my voice light, my tone flippant. "Do you really think that's what I'm doing? Give me a little bit of credit. I'm just not convinced you or anybody else knows anything either. It was nice talking to you. Have a good night."

# ⫶⫶ TWENTY-FIVE ⫶⫶

AS I LEFT the house, Rain wandered over from the barn to meet me. She introduced me to Stuart, Ingrid's son, who smiled too widely and held on to my hand a shade too long.

I pulled my hand away, rubbed it surreptitiously on my jeans. Ingrid had never killed anyone, but her son had, and unlike most of the killers I had met since I woke up, Stuart looked exactly sketchy enough to be a murderer.

"Guess that must've gotten boring for you," I said to Rain, "just sitting there."

"It wasn't so bad. I can entertain myself. You get what you came for?"

I didn't want to ask, not with Ingrid's creepy son standing right there, but I had to know. "Did you know she was going to do that?"

"Do what? She wasn't doing anything to you. You were just talking."

I didn't like the way Rain was smiling. "Right. Okay. Can we go?"

"You can do whatever you want. I'm going to stick around for a while." She waved at Zeke, still waiting by the truck. "I'm sure I'm heartbroken to miss that fun sleepover."

"You could stay too," Stuart said. He had the oiliest smile I had ever seen. "Ma won't mind. We've got room."

"No, thanks," I said, and I walked away. Walked, even though I wanted to run.

Zeke pushed away from the truck as I approached. "You're not staying?"

"No," I said. Rain and Stuart were heading into the house, and warm yellow light shone through the windows. "I don't want to be around anybody as old as my dad who smiles at me like that."

"Yeah, Stuart is a creep," he said. "He has a thing for monsters."

"A *thing?* You mean like a fetish?" I scrubbed my hand on my jeans again. "Gross. You could have warned me."

"I said we shouldn't come here," he pointed out.

"Yeah, yeah. You were right. Can you drive me back to Boulder?" I wasn't quite sure yet where I would go from there, but I did know I didn't want to spend the night in the mountains.

"Sure. Get in."

I waited until we had left Ingrid's property before I said, "He's a murderer too. That Stuart guy. He's not just a pervert."

"How do you know?" There was hesitation in Zeke's voice, as though he wasn't sure he wanted to know the answer.

"I can tell," I said. "It's one of my superpowers. It's that and healing like Wolverine."

"For everyone?"

"Yes."

He was quiet after that. I drew my legs up on the seat and leaned against the door. We left the dirt road and turned onto the paved highway again, wound down through the trees, through Nederland, past the reservoir, into the high steep gash of Boulder Canyon.

The silence was starting to bother me. "You're not going to ask me what Ingrid said?"

"No."

"You're not curious?"

"Not really."

"She thinks I'm going become a vengeful murderer who kills everybody I meet while laughing maniacally and bathing in their blood."

I rested my head against the cool glass. The mountains were dark now that the sun had set, and the headlights of passing cars flashed through the windshield. Now that I was thinking about it clearly, I could see the problems in what she had said. I wasn't going to start hunting down innocent people. I hadn't been able to hurt Lyle, not even in self-defense, because he wasn't a murderer. But Ingrid wanted me to think I could. Ingrid thought I was *fascinating*.

An entire afternoon gone. It made me feel cold all over, naked and exposed, not knowing what she had done. Had she sat there the whole time, holding my hand, waiting and watching while my mind whirled and spun? Or had she taken a break, got herself some tea, read a few articles in *The Economist*, gone outside to chat with Rain and Stuart, leaving me there slumped on the couch?

"Or something like that," I said.

"Is that all?" Zeke asked.

"You think it should have been worse?"

"Do you feel like murdering everybody you meet?"

"No," I said. Not everybody. "She asked for some of my blood."

Zeke looked at me sharply. "Did you—"

"I didn't give her anything. You said not to."

"You were in there a long time."

"I didn't give her anything. Why does it matter, anyway? What did she want to do with it?"

"I don't know," Zeke said. "Magic. Nothing good."

I sighed and closed my eyes for a moment. I couldn't sleep, but I was tired, worn out, and stretched too thin. I hated not being able to sleep.

"She didn't even answer all of my questions."

She hadn't told me *why*. Why was I different, why did I come back, why was I like this, the one thing I really wanted to know, and she had brushed it aside. I wasn't even sure if I could believe that it was question without an answer. Somebody had to know something.

I could still hear the man whispering as he dug into my grave: *Oh, you're perfect, you're beautiful, you're perfect.* He must have known what he would find when he started digging.

It hadn't occurred to me before, but now I had to wonder if maybe I had killed the one person who could answer my questions.

"I don't think I like magicians very much," I said. Zeke started to speak, but I interrupted him. "I know. You told me so. I'll remember next time."

"Ingrid's not even one of the bad ones. There are worse."

"But you still don't like her."

"I don't think she always knows the difference between helping people and using people."

"Rain doesn't seem to mind."

Zeke glanced at me. "Rain always knows when she's using people."

"Ingrid's never killed anybody. Not like her creepy son."

"Good for her."

I looked across the cab of the truck at Zeke. He looked normal, as far as I could tell. Human. No obvious monster traits. He caught me staring at him and turned away.

"Who was it?" I asked. I immediately regretted it. I winced and said quickly, "No, don't answer that. Don't. I don't want to know."

The shadows around him were brittle, frail, like leafless branches in winter.

"Just the once," I guessed.

He didn't answer, but he didn't deny it either.

"That's reassuring," I said. "Considering. But now I'm kind of wondering where you get your food from, and at the same time trying really hard not to wonder at all."

"You don't—"

"Oh, don't worry," I said. "'You don't smell appetizing.'"

Zeke grinned, fleeting and not very nice, but still a smile. I had been starting to think he didn't know how.

I had said it to tease him, but it was also true, in a way. There was no excitement, no yearning. Zeke had killed before, but he hadn't liked it. Not like the man by my grave, and not like Duncan Palmer. Not like Ingrid's son, whose shadows had mostly felt like slick pride. The more killers I met, the better I was getting at feeling out the differences.

Zeke relaxed after that, and so did I. It's amazing what mutual denial of supernatural ill intent can do to ease the tension.

"Where were you going?" Zeke asked. "Before they found you."

"Nowhere. I don't know. I haven't decided."

Zeke didn't say anything for a moment, then he said, "I have to work tonight, but you can stay at our place, if you want."

"Your parents won't mind?" I asked.

"It's just me and my brother."

"Your brother won't mind?"

"I don't know. He might."

"And if he does?"

A shrug. "We get dinner for a week?"

"Oh my god," I said, but I couldn't help but laugh. "You can't make jokes about eating dead people if you actually eat dead people."

"You're sure it's a joke?"

I was, about as sure as I could be, but I only said, "Shut up. And thanks, I guess. For the dramatic rescue too."

"It wasn't that dramatic," Zeke said.

"You used an ax. That makes it dramatic."

We spilled out of the canyon and into the city. Streetlights and houses sprung up along the street, and the roads filled with nighttime traffic around the intersections.

"Anyway, I appreciate it," I said. "But if I catch you sharpening your knives, I'm going to change my mind."

"You won't," Zeke said. "Our knives are always sharp."

# ⑈ TWENTY-SIX ⑈

HOME FOR ZEKE and his brother was a small brick house on Boulder's west side. One level, a squat worn rectangle, with an overgrown yard badly in need of mowing. The street was quiet. Light shone from the front windows of the neighbors' houses and silhouettes moved behind curtains, people making dinner and watching TV, but Zeke's house was dark.

He let me in, flipped on the light, and said, "I have to go. I'm going to be late for work."

I was curious about what kind of job a ghoul might have. "Where do you work?"

Zeke made a face. "I, uh, clean places. You know, like office buildings, after hours?"

"That is not nearly as exciting as I was expecting," I said. "I was kind of hoping you worked in a morgue or something."

"Yeah, I wish. I would tell you not to touch anything, but we don't have anything worth stealing. You can sleep on the couch, I guess."

I dropped my skateboard and backpack on the floor. "Thanks."

Zeke had his hand on the door, but he hesitated. "Don't go into the basement. Even if you—just don't."

"Why not?"

"Because I told you not to. Jake will be home in a couple of hours," he said, and he left.

I watched him back out of the driveway and waited until he turned the corner at the end of the street.

Then I shamelessly began to snoop around.

I had never been in a monster's house before.

The house was small and old, but it was clean. The living room, the kitchen, the bathroom's eye-searing green fixtures straight out of the seventies, the bedroom with its hospital-neat twin beds, all of it was unbelievably clean, the kind of clean that came from being dusted regularly, mopped, polished, scrubbed with toothbrushes in the crevices. No dust in the vents, no bugs in the light fixtures.

There was nothing in the refrigerator except spotless shelves and the strong smell of bleach. I was so relieved not to find Tupperware full of mysterious meat I almost laughed out loud. The drawers were empty except one, which held five knives—sharp, as promised—and all I found in the cabinets were some glasses and a half-empty bottle of bourbon.

Everything they owned could fit into a couple of boxes. I didn't know if that was strange or not. If somebody had asked me a week ago, when I was a lonely aimless hitchhiker without a pulse, I wouldn't have even suspected that monsters would bother to have houses. Houses and jobs and phones and cars, witchy liaisons and magical communities, brothers expected home from work. It all felt so ordinary.

One door in the living room led to the garage, another to what I assumed was the basement. I reached for the knob, ready to ignore Zeke's warning, but I stopped when I heard something clank downstairs.

Water pipes, I told myself. Old plumbing.

I left the door closed.

There was a laptop on the kitchen table, a clunky older model covered with cheerful Hello Kitty decals and silver sticker letters spelling out *Kristy :)*. I turned it on and leaned back in the chair, winced at the press of wood against my injured side. I heard the noise in the basement again and looked at the closed door, looked away when the computer booted. The desktop background matched the stickers and decals. Poor Kristy. She shouldn't have left her laptop unattended.

I was in the news again. Nebraska state troopers had been called to the scene of a suspicious death two days ago. Duncan Palmer of Minneapolis, Minnesota, was found in his car on a rural road north of I-80. There were no obvious signs of foul play.

The enterprising small town reporter had dug up Palmer's past as a murder suspect, and discovering that was like the tumblers of a lock falling into place. I read through everything I could find. I stared for a long time at the school photo of the little boy Palmer had killed. Timothy Rosoff. He was chubby and gap-toothed and grinning, with a ridiculous cowlick sticking up from the back of his head. I smelled peanut butter, and for the first time it didn't make me nauseous. It made me feel vindictive, almost proud.

I looked for news about Brian Kerr too, hoping for the same flash of certainty, but there was nothing.

Nothing from home either. The nameless man I'd killed by my grave wasn't even in the news anymore.

The excitement I felt piecing together Duncan Palmer's crime didn't last. I dragged my backpack over to the table, pulled out my notebook, and opened it to the second page. I had always hated my handwriting, resented how curly and big and girly it was, and I hated it even more now.

> 1. Sleeping pills
>
> 2. Drowning
>
> 3. Rat poison
>
> 4. Gunshot
>
> 5. Electrocution
>
> 6. Hanging
>
> 7. Stabbing
>
> 8. Skated face-first into tree

I added:

> 9. Eviscerated by Lyle

Good band name, I thought.

One more and I would have a perfect ten.

I pulled the chair away from the table and angled it toward the kitchen light, pulled up my T-shirt and tucked it beneath my chin. The wound was red and scabbed, hot to the touch. It looked infected. I didn't even know if that was possible. I hadn't bothered cleaning any of my other injuries. My dad always said the most important thing to do for an open wound was keep it clean.

I needed to see what was under the scabs. I selected a knife from the kitchen drawer.

Before I could sit again, I heard another sound from behind the basement door. Not a metallic clank, but the creak of wood.

Somebody was on the stairs.

I glanced over my shoulder.

The basement door was open.

My heart jumped.

Only a crack, but it was open. It had been closed before. I was sure of it.

I was ten feet from the door, maybe twelve. I tried to guess how many steps it would take me to get there, how fast I could move, whether I could shut the door before—before what? Zeke had warned me not to go into the basement. How to Survive a Horror Movie 101: Never go into the basement. The rule had to apply double when you were alone in a monster's house, even if the monster in question was an awkward teenage boy who had only left you alone because he had to go clean toilets in an office building.

But the door was open.

And, I thought, if this is a horror movie, I'm on Team Monster already.

I saw the flash of an eye through the gap. It was low to the ground, gone before I could blink. Claws scrabbled noisily down the stairs.

I made myself start breathing again. I didn't put down the knife.

Six steps to the basement door. I pulled it open and fumbled for the light switch. The stairs made a ninety degree turn halfway down. On the landing there was a broom and a blue plastic bucket filled with cleaning supplies. Sponges, rags, furniture polish, spray bottle of Lysol. And—I knew it—a toothbrush. Beside the bucket was a stack of picture books. *Where the Wild Things Are* was on the top. That had been my favorite when I was a kid.

I crept down the stairs. They creaked beneath my weight; I paused every few treads to listen. I stopped when I reached the landing halfway down. I could see the edge of a woven rug on the concrete floor at the bottom, but not much else. The air was musty and cool.

"Hello?" I said.

There was a faint scratching below.

"Hey. I'm not going to hurt you." My voice wavered. I wondered if I should be hiding the knife behind my back. "I just want to, um. Say hi."

A shadow moved at the base of the steps. It was compact and low, creeping close the ground.

The shadow became a small skinny *thing*. More animal than

humanoid, with a narrow head and big ears. Long, long limbs that ended in long, long claws stretched forward to grasp at the rug, picking at the threads like a cat might knead a blanket. It turned its head—sniffing the air, I thought with a fresh spark of worry, scenting *me*—and pulled itself forward. Long teeth jutted from the jaw.

But it was the eyes that got my attention. Big and round and yellow and eerily bright—

And frightened.

It was scared of me, the stranger in its house.

My own fear vanished. What I felt in its place was more like pity with a helping of guilt.

"Hi," I said. I kept my voice low, easy. Moving slowly, I sat on the step and picked the top book from the stack. "Are these your books? I love this book. Would you like me to read it to you? Is that why they're here? That has to be why they're here, right?"

I was speaking too quickly; my voice shook. The thing didn't move, didn't make a sound.

I opened the book and started to read about the night Max wore his wolf suit. The thing settled into the darkness as no more than a shape with big yellow eyes. If it blinked, I didn't see it. I had read that same book to Sunny a hundred times when she was little. She had insisted on dressing up as a wolf with a crown two Halloweens in a row. Mom and Dad had discovered fairly early that I was so proud of my reading skills they could delegate bedtime stories to me whenever they wanted. Mom and Dad would lurk outside the door, smiling fondly, and sometimes Meadow would listen too, always pretending not to care. Sunny had loved bedtime stories long after she could read for herself, but she had lost interest a few years ago. She still read all the time, had won the local library summer reading contest for three years, but if she ever missed me reading to her, she had never mentioned it.

When I finished the book, the thing at the bottom of the stairs made a quiet noise, a disgruntled little huff that wasn't quite a word.

"That's the end," I said. "You know it always ends the same way."

I didn't want to think about Sunny and Mom and Dad anymore. I shouldn't have come down here. I had thought it would be better, to make that little creature less scared of me, but it didn't help at all.

The thing blinked at me, just once, and slunk away into the darkness. I heard claws tapping faintly on the cement floor, the soft rustle of something that might have been paper or straw, and the basement was silent.

# ⫴ T W E N T Y - S E V E N ⫴

I RETURNED TO the kitchen with its bright lights to clean the wounds Lyle had given me. I positioned the tip of the knife over the longest claw mark and pressed down to make a dent in the scab.

My hand was shaking. I stared at the blade. I had done this before. It was item number seven on my list of possible ways to die. By the time I got to seven, I was pretty sure nothing I could do to myself would be permanent. By the time I got to seven, I was already contemplating more extreme options—incineration, decapitation—and knowing they too wouldn't work. The wound from number seven had faded to a scar, a fine white line just below my navel. It had bled a lot. It had hurt even more.

I pushed the knife into the wound again. It broke through the skin with a bright spark of pain. I watched the blood trickle down my side.

I pressed the tip of the knife into another spot, clean unharmed skin, made another puncture. Watched it bleed again. Again, then deeper, and deeper still, puncturing a matchstick scatter of small cuts around the slashes Lyle had made. The sting of breaking skin gave way to a different kind of ache. My breath was short and shallow and my lungs burned. I was going to ruin my stolen jeans. I didn't know how to wash bloodstains out of clothes. I ought to learn.

A key scraped in the front door. I jumped to my feet as a man came in.

"Hi," I said. I was still holding my shirt up. The knife in my hand was bloody.

The man locked the door, lifted the curtain on the front window to glance out, then turned to me and said, "Hi. I'm Jake Horn. Zeke's brother."

I waved a little, stopped when I realized I was waving the bloody knife. "Hi. I'm Breezy. I'm the reanimated corpse your brother found in Wyoming."

"He told me. He said you needed help." Jake hesitated, then took a few steps closer, but cautiously. "What are you doing?"

"I'm, um. This is awkward."

I lowered the knife. My face grew hot. I was standing in his kitchen with a bloody knife in one hand, half a dozen stab wounds on my side, and no good explanation. I thought maybe I should put the knife down, but I didn't want to spread blood all over the counter.

"I'm just trying to clean it," I said finally. It sounded even stupider out loud than it did inside my head. "It's healing, but not like it should. I thought . . . maybe I should clean it."

Jake stared at me. "That doesn't hurt?"

"Yeah, it hurts. It hurts a lot."

"It's stopped bleeding," Jake said. He looked curious rather than revolted, but he stayed carefully out of knife-jabbing range.

"I heal fast. I don't know why."

"Magic."

I rolled my eyes. "Wow, thanks, that's so helpful. I never would have figured that one out on my own, all this magic happening to me."

Jake looked at me for a few more seconds. He looked a lot like his brother, but unlike Zeke, he had no trouble meeting my eyes. He turned and disappeared down the hallway for about a minute. He came back with a silver scalpel.

"Try that instead of a kitchen knife," Jake said. He leaned against the counter. "It's not happening *to* you. You are the source of the magic."

"I don't know what that means. It feels like it's happening to me." I set the knife down, picked up the glinting scalpel. "I'm not going to ask why you keep a scalpel in your bedroom."

"Somebody tried to kill you, right?"

I tugged down my scarf and lifted my chin to show off the bruises. "He succeeded."

"If he had really succeeded," Jake said, amused, "you wouldn't be sitting here, bleeding all over my kitchen."

"I'm barely bleeding at all anymore." I would be again, as soon as I got to work with the scalpel, but I hesitated. "I still don't understand."

"That's where magic comes from."

"From being murdered?"

"From death," he said. "From any kind of death. That's how magicians get their magic."

"By killing people?" My voice rose with alarm. "Seriously? I thought—I don't know. I thought they were born with it. Like it's genetic or something." I wasn't going to admit I had only assumed that because that's how it worked in *Harry Potter*. I felt a pang of sadness that *Harry Potter* had been lying to me all along.

"Nah, humans aren't born with magic," Jake said. Unlike Rain, he didn't seem to be making fun of me for what I didn't know. I decided I liked him just for that. "They get it from the death of any living thing. Most use animals or insects."

The mixture Mr. Willow had used to knock me out, and the bowl of dead beetles in Ingrid's house, not to mention the blood-soaked room, they made a lot more sense with that context, but they weren't all that came to mind.

"A lot of birds died the day I came back," I said. "I mean, like, thousands of birds. Was that— Obviously it was related, right?"

Jake's eyebrows went up in surprise. "That was you? In Chicago?"

I shifted uncomfortably. "You heard about it?"

"Everybody heard about it. When something like that happens, well, it's kind of hard to ignore. Usually it means a magician has seriously fucked up."

I tugged at the scarf and tried to hide how my hands were trembling. "Does that mean somebody did this to me on purpose?"

"Not necessarily," Jake said. "He didn't have to know what he was doing, or even to be doing it to you specifically. Magic is messy. It's unpredictable. Even when it works, it doesn't usually work how the magician wants it to. And sometimes it's a complete accident."

"You mean I'm an *accident?*"

"It's possible. Nobody's taken credit for the birds. Or blame, I guess. Nobody has any idea who was involved."

"Not at all?"

"Do you?"

I didn't know his name, but I knew how angry he felt when he stood outside a house on a winter prairie. *Oh, you're perfect, you're beautiful,* that's what he had said when he leaned over my grave. I knew he had decided to shoot the children and the husband first to get them out of the way. I knew the thrill he had felt pushing a knife into the woman's heart. How he had carefully wiped his shoes on the doormat before leaving.

I knew he was dead, because I had killed him.

But if nobody else had put it together yet, I wasn't going to do it for them. My brave new monster-filled world was hard enough to navigate without me revealing myself as a murderer to everybody I met.

"No, nothing," I said, the words as casual and dismissive as I could manage. "I don't know how any of this works. What about plants? Does killing them make magic? Plants are living things."

Jake laughed. "You know, I have no idea. Maybe it takes a lot of plants to do anything worthwhile."

"Like if a magician started a forest fire."

"If it would work, I'm sure somebody's tried it," Jake said. "I really don't know. We're sort of immune to most magic, so I only know what other people have told me."

"Immune?" I repeated, then I understood. "Oh. So that's why Zeke could get into that room when Rain and I couldn't even touch the walls. Have you always been . . ." I hesitated. There was no polite way to ask. "Were you born like this? A, uh, ghoul?"

Jake was surprised by the question. "Well, yeah."

"Oh. How does that even work?"

"Do you need me to give you the talk about what happens when a mommy and a daddy like each other very much?"

"I really don't, thanks. So, people—I mean, humans—humans aren't born magical, but they can do magic if they kill stuff."

"Right."

"And some things—I mean, people, sorry—some people are born not human, because their parents weren't human, and that's just . . . just biology."

"More or less."

"And I'm not either one of those things."

"Nope," said Jake. "You're a little different."

"Okay. I think I get it. Uh, thanks."

"What for?"

I looked down at the scalpel. My hand was still shaking. "You're the first person I've met who's actually tried to explain anything to me. Rain and Ingrid just kind of assumed that I already knew all of that. I asked Ingrid why I was, you know, like this, but she just said I wouldn't understand."

"That's her way of saying she doesn't know either."

"She could have just told me that."

"She doesn't like to admit she doesn't know things. Do you want help?"

For a second I thought he meant help in the big picture, the cosmic picture, help with life and death and afterlife and questions and answers and the fact that nothing made any sense at all anymore, and my knee-jerk reaction was to insist I didn't need anything.

But he was only talking about my injuries. He held out his hand for the scalpel.

I didn't pass it over.

Jake smiled slightly. "Don't worry. You don't smell appetizing."

"That's exactly what your brother said, and it's even worse the second time. You know that implies other people do smell appetizing, right?"

"Only the ones who are all the way dead," Jake said. "Do you want help or not?"

I gave him the scalpel. Without a couple of mirrors and some rapidly acquired contortionist skills, I was never going to be able to do it myself. Jake patted the counter beside the sink and told me to jump up so he could see better. He prodded the wounds with the scalpel; I hissed and clenched my teeth.

"I know you heard me when I said it hurts."

"Sorry." Jake didn't sound sorry; he sounded interested. "It's weird. It's healing unevenly."

"I'm sure they cover that in the *Undead Medical Emergency Handbook*, but I lost my copy. Do you know what you're doing?"

"Sure."

"Lots of practice with first aid?"

"Yes, actually," he said. "My brother is a dumbass."

He didn't say it meanly. He said it fondly, and for a moment I missed my sisters so much my chest hurt.

Jake pressed the scalpel in, more surely this time. Blood seeped out and I stopped watching.

"How did you meet Rain?" Jake asked calmly, like he wasn't starting a bloody excavation into my side.

"We got locked up together. I didn't get to pick my roommate."

"You didn't know her before that?"

"No. Why?"

"No reason," Jake said, in that voice people use when they have a lot of reasons but would prefer not to share. "What did she say to Zeke? To get him to help her," he added, when I glanced at him.

"I don't know." I thought back to the one side of the phone conversation I had heard. "She said he owed her for something."

"Did she threaten him?" He looked up at me, and from that close, I could see that the pupils of his eyes weren't quite round. It was subtle, no more than a slight oval distortion, but it was there.

"I don't know. Maybe. I don't know what she was talking about. He didn't tell you?"

"He told me what you guys found in that house," Jake said.

"This is going to hurt."

It did hurt, but more than that, if felt unbelievably weird when he pried the scalpel into the cut and pressed his fingers in to draw something out. Sodden scraps of cloth: pieces of Violet's dress driven into the wounds by Lyle's claws.

"That's disgusting," I said.

Jake dropped the soggy mess into the sink and grabbed a towel, dampened it and began cleaning the wound. When he was done, he pressed the towel to my side and told me to hold it in place.

"I guess you don't need stitches," he said.

"No, it'll close on its own," I said, a little breathless. "Thanks."

I dropped from the counter and sat at the table while Jake washed his hands.

"I'm not sure it would even work," I said.

He glanced over his shoulder. "What?"

"Chopping me up into little pieces in revenge for threatening your little brother, or whatever it is you were thinking."

"That's not exactly what I had in mind."

"Well. Good. But it probably wouldn't work anyway."

"Because none of the other things you tried worked?" Jake dried his hands on his jeans—apparently they only had one towel, and I was bleeding into it—and sat down beside me. He nodded at my NASA notebook lying open on the table. "The sleeping pills were a really stupid idea."

"I *know*." I tilted my head back and stared at the ceiling. It was better than looking at my own blood, better than looking at the list. "Dumbest idea ever. But let's not talk about what does or doesn't happen in my digestive system anymore."

"I'm surprised the electrocution didn't have any effect. Electricity kills a lot of things, even things that almost nothing else can hurt."

"Not me," I said. "I mean, yeah, it hurt, but it only stunned me for a couple of minutes."

"Gunshot?"

I had a puckered scar the size of a nickel on my chest. I hadn't been brave enough to aim it at my head. "I figured by then it wasn't going to work."

"But you kept doing it anyway?"

"They say that's one definition of insanity."

I lifted the towel away from the wound. It was already knitting together. I didn't want to talk about my many failed attempts at making my death permanent. At some point it had become more habit than earnest experimentation. I was already growing tired of my new collection of scars.

"It's been that way since you . . ."

"Woke up? Came back? Un-died? Yeah."

"Do you remember how it happened?" he asked.

No. I remember nothing. That's what I had told Ingrid and Rain. Nothing nothing nothing.

It was so easy to lie, but for the first time, I didn't want to. I hadn't realized, during all the days I spent wandering through Chicago, hitchhiking across the country, how lonely it was to put so much effort into lying about who I was. The patchwork girl made up of my friends and their friends, embellished by people's careless assumptions and expectations, she was unraveling, and I didn't want to piece her back together.

"I remember going to a party," I said. "I am a dead teenage cliché. I remember the stupid music and the beer and my best friend. . . ." I touched my cheek as though I could still feel the warm sting of Melanie's hand. "She slapped me. That's almost the last thing I remember. That doesn't seem fair, does it? My last memory of my entire life is my best friend since kindergarten slapping me."

"Did you have a fight?" Jake asked.

"No." I took a breath. There was an uncomfortable knot in my stomach. "I kissed her. I, uh. It seemed like a good idea at the time. She didn't think so."

I wasn't sure what kind of reaction I was expecting, but Jake didn't look alarmed or disgusted. He was smiling. It was a sad smile. "I got a black eye and a bloody nose when I tried that."

"Yeah? What happened?"

He shrugged. "Nothing. He apologized and went to get some ice. We told our parents I fell out of a tree."

"Did he ever forgive you?"

"I don't know. What does your family think happened to you?"

I accepted the change of topic. "I'm missing. They had fliers and volunteers and a neighborhood search and everything. Yard signs. You've never seen anybody do yard signs like the concerned citizens of Evanston do yard signs. I would probably be on a milk carton if they still did that. Do they still do that?" I gestured at the laptop; the screen had gone dark. "There's a web page. My friends made it. It was the one year anniversary a few weeks ago. They posted all these things about . . . nothing important. Stupid stuff."

I had read through the entire page, every post and comment, all the way back to when it first started. There was a picture at the top of the page: me and Melanie together at a diner we used to visit on Friday afternoons. I remembered that day; Maria had taken the picture. She had been sitting across the table from us, complaining about how soggy her fries were and trying to get the waiter's attention. Melanie had whispered to me that Maria didn't care about her fries, she just wanted to flirt with the waiter, and I had sat up on my knees to look over the side of the booth to get a look at him. He wasn't anything special, a thin-faced college boy wearing the stupid restaurant uniform and a fake smile, everything about his demeanor saying that he knew the high school kids making a mess in his section would skimp on the tips. He barely even glanced at Maria when she finally got him to come over. She huffed and rolled her eyes, then immediately switched her attention to taking pictures of everybody around her. She told me and Melanie to smile, and Melanie had hooked her arm around my neck and we both put on big, stupid grins for the camera. It wasn't Maria's waiter who brought her fresh fries to our table but somebody we knew from school. He appeared beside our table and said, "Hi, Breezy," not even glancing at Maria when he set the basket of fries in front of her. I said, "Hi, Ricky," polite reflex, and he had hovered awkwardly until Melanie cracked up with her familiar, snorting laugh and said, "We don't need anything else, not unless you want to recite some poetry for us." He flushed red and slunk away.

If I thought about it, closed my eyes, and remembered, I could still feel the heat of Melanie's arm around my neck, across the back of my shoulders, and count the seconds she let it linger.

The online comments in the beginning had all been suggestions, speculation, worries. Predictions that other girls would go missing soon. Thoughts about how to organize. There had been search parties. They put up posters. They spread rumors. The cops brought out the canine units. The dogs never had a chance. I wasn't decaying, so there was no corpse smell for them to follow. But I wasn't myself anymore either. I was *too degraded.*

All that effort, all that searching, and nobody once looked in the backyard of that foreclosed house just a few blocks from my home. I was only buried beneath eighteen inches of soil. A whole year, and nobody had noticed. People must have come through that house, potential buyers standing at the glass door, looking across the cracked cement porch and brown grass, talking about how much space there was for entertaining, for kids to play, it just needed a little bit of work, a little bit of landscaping. They must have looked right over me, right over the disturbed ground where somebody had dug a grave, but not a very deep one.

The more recent comments on the page had been memories, pictures, insults, rumors. Ran away with an older boyfriend, maybe she promised to love him long time, get it, it's just a joke, don't be so easily offended. Not saying she was a slut but, come on, you know how she was. She should have been more careful. Shouldn't have been drinking and wearing those clothes. Like anybody was surprised. Didn't her parents feel stupid for not knowing what she was like?

Reading through those comments felt like invading the edges of somebody else's life, another version of me who had done things I never had, suffered the hatred of people I had never even met, an imaginary girl overshadowing the real one.

"I don't think they're looking for me anymore," I said.

"Why didn't you go home?" Jake asked.

"I did," I said. "Right after I woke up. Nobody was home. So I left. What was I supposed to tell them anyway?"

He didn't try to answer. He only said, "I'm sorry."

I looked away, and Jake stood and walked out of the room. A minute later he came back with a folded-up blanket and a pillow. He set them on one end of the sofa, then stepped over to the front window and looked through the curtains again.

"Why do you keep doing that?" I said.

"Habit. I've got work in the morning, so I'm going to—"

There was a quiet scratching behind the basement door.

"I have a confession to make," I said. "Zeke told me not to go down into the basement."

"But you did anyway?" Jake walked over to the door, pounded on it a few times. The scratching stopped, and the stairs creaked. "So you met Steve?"

"It has a name?" I said, incredulous. "Its name is *Steve*? What is it?"

"I don't know if it really has a name," Jake said. "It's a brownie. They don't talk. But Zeke felt sorry for it because our landlady just kept calling it 'that horrible thing,' so he gave it a name."

"Your landlady knows about it? Is it like a pet?"

"It's not a wild animal. It came with the house," Jake explained. "We don't know for sure, but we think our landlady's mother brought it with her when she moved here. After she died, it refused to leave. But it didn't want anybody else moving in either. It doesn't like humans."

"What did it do?"

"Scared them away," Jake said. "Little things, mostly, but after it pushed one man down the stairs, word got around."

"He was badly hurt?"

"He broke his neck. He died." Jake looked at me, waiting for my reaction.

The big-eyed creature might have been alarming to look at, but it was hard to imagine it trying to kill people between its bedtime stories. It was so little and quiet and scared.

"It didn't try to hurt me," I said. "It didn't do anything."

"You're not human."

"Yes, I—" I stopped.

I wanted to argue with him, but I couldn't. The protest was dust on my tongue.

Jake pretended not to notice. "So now our landlady doesn't rent to humans anymore. It'll leave you alone as long as you don't go downstairs."

"I won't. For real this time." But it wasn't the thing in the basement that interested me. It was the fact that a human might know enough about monsters to rent only to people the homicidal house elf in the basement wouldn't hurt. I had so many questions. "Is that the kind of thing a landlord can put on craigslist? Is it in the lease?

Is your landlady human?"

"She is, yeah," Jake said. "There are some humans who know just enough about us to know they don't want to know more. Look, I have to work in the morning, so I'm going to sleep."

I didn't want him to go; I wanted him to stay up and answer all my questions about monster-human relations in property management. But he did look pretty tired, so I only said, "Good night. Thanks for letting me stay here."

Jake disappeared into the bedroom and closed the door.

I didn't feel right using his computer and poking around his house while he was in the other room, so I went out into the backyard. I kicked off my shoes and stepped onto the lawn. The grass was scratchy and dry. I lay down, hooked my hands behind my head, looked at the sky.

Every time I thought I was getting a grasp on the rules of this new world I had awoken into, they shifted again. Violet and Mr. Willow insisted there was an obvious boundary between the worlds, a line with good humans on one side and evil creatures on the other. But even if I didn't trust Rain's motives or Ingrid's explanations, they certainly didn't rank above Willow and Brian Kerr on the potential evil scale. And assuming they weren't secretly planning to make a meal of me in the middle of the night, Zeke and Jake had been nothing but kind. I didn't know who to believe. They all wanted me to be afraid of something—monsters, humans, magic—but all I wanted was for things to start making sense again.

Maybe there was something wrong with the fear center of my brain. Maybe it had been damaged when I died. Maybe a worm got in there during all that time I was in the ground and chewed up one important knot of neurons, the knot responsible for warning the rest of me not to get into cars with murderers or accept help from psychotic cult preachers or go home with monsters who eat human corpses.

In quiet moments, when I held my breath and listened, I imagined I could hear the worms still digging around, breaking connections any normal person's brain should be able to make.

I had never known this world existed. I hadn't asked for any part of it. I didn't want it.

But you can't go back to not knowing something once you've been thrown into the middle of it.

The air was cool, crisp, and the night was peaceful. I watched the stars, and I thought about monsters and magic and murderers, and it wasn't like sleeping, but it was as close as I could get.

# ⋅⋅⋅ TWENTY-EIGHT ⋅⋅⋅

BEFORE I DISCOVERED what I had become, before I learned how much time had passed while I floated in the stars, before I made a list of all the ways I had tried and failed to kill myself, before I had a body count and an endless supply of murderers' memories chasing around my head, I woke up in an unmarked grave, and I killed a man.

And I went home.

Barefoot and chilly on the empty streets, spitting mud from my mouth and scrubbing dirt from my eyes, I went home.

There's a story about Yuri Gagarin, the first human to travel into space, and what he said when he came back to Earth. April 12,

1961. The Vostok 1 capsule and its pilot were only gone for 108 minutes, but those 108 minutes took them into space for one complete orbit, the farthest from Earth anybody had ever ventured.

When Gagarin landed, so the story goes, a farmer and her daughter saw him parachute to the ground in his orange flight suit and his helmet, and the woman asked him, "Have you come from outer space?"

He wasn't wearing a space suit, although that would make the story better. The Soviets didn't put their cosmonauts into space suits until after 1971, when Soyuz 11 suffered catastrophic decompression before reentry and its three crewmen became the first and only humans in history—so far—to die in true space rather than on the launch pad or in the upper atmosphere.

But before that, a man fell from the sky, and when the farmer asked if he came from outer space, he replied, "As a matter of fact, I have!" He told her he must find a telephone to call Moscow and let them know he was home. That's how the story goes. It's a foolish story, a silly story, but it's the kind of story we want to believe of humankind's first space explorer, that young man with the big bright smile who might have been the boy next door if only he hadn't been the one to leave the earth instead.

I was thinking about Yuri Gagarin as I walked home and blood flowed through my brain again.

"Hi, Mom and Dad. Sorry I'm late. Have I been gone long?" That's what I would say. I had no idea how long I had been lying in that grave. It felt like eternity. It felt like no time at all.

They would ask me where I had been. They would say, "We

thought you were dead."

And I would reply, "As a matter of fact, I have been!"

Dogs snarled as I passed and threw themselves hysterically against their fences. Dead birds littered the ground in small sad lumps. Twice I caught myself wiping invisible blood from my fingers and cringing at piercing screams I couldn't hear.

I was confused and disoriented, but the neighborhood was familiar. I wasn't very far from home. Close enough that if I had asked to borrow the car, Dad would have told me to walk instead.

Our house looked much the same, but there was a flower bed in the yard that hadn't been there before, and one of the sick old trees was gone. Dad had been talking about having somebody chop it down forever, but I never thought he would do it. There was a hole where the stump would have been.

There were no lights on. I had lost my keys and my phone. I crossed the lawn, avoiding the scattered dead birds, and punched in the code to let myself in through the garage. Mom's car was there, but Dad's was gone.

This is what I told myself when I went inside:

It was the same night as the party.

Somebody had played a prank on me. A joke.

My family didn't know anything was wrong. In the morning I would call my friends and they would laugh themselves sick. I would laugh too. My father would frown. Meadow would roll her eyes. Sunny would ask me if it was scary being buried, even as a joke. Mom would help me plot my revenge.

I should go downstairs and shower and get to bed. Tomorrow I would laugh and everything would be fine.

For a few minutes, I tried to believe.

Then I saw the note on the counter. It was addressed to Greta, one of my mother's postdocs. Mom's handwriting on a plain white sheet. Greta kept an eye on our house when we went out of town. Brought in the mail, watered the plants. I picked up the note, read it twice, set it down.

On the calendar on the refrigerator, there was a red line drawn through a week at the beginning of June. In big looping letters, Sunny had written, "To the lake!" My mother's aunt gave us a new calendar every year. It had been African mammals before; now it was tropical birds.

They had gone to the lake cottage without me.

My hands began shaking and I couldn't control my breath. There was a police detective's business card clipped to a magnet next to the calendar. We weren't the kind of family that ever needed to call the police. Our house had never been broken into, our cars never vandalized, our safety never threatened. The card was half-hidden behind a coupon for an oil change, like it had been there so long they had stopped looking at it every day.

I checked the bedrooms to be sure. The house was empty. I went into the study and turned on my mother's computer.

Mom had dozens of articles bookmarked, from the *Evanston RoundTable*, the *Review*, even the *Tribune*. They all told the same story. Seventeen-year-old Breezy Lin of Evanston had gone to a party with friends, but she never made it home. Police had found my phone and keys at Nate Havers's house. They had talked to my parents, Melanie, Maria, Tatiana, and all the people I knew at school, my friends at the skate park on Lake Shore Drive, teachers and guidance counselors, everyone. There had been community meetings, bake sales, organized searches. Nate's parents had given a statement: they had no idea there would be underage drinking at their son's party, they were helping in any way they could, etc., etc.

I had been missing for a year.

I kept reading. The articles helpfully informed me I was a good kid with good grades and no history of trouble, but I was also friends with a group of teenagers who had a tendency to get a little wild. My friends must have loved that. Pride more than indignation, that's how they would react, as long as nobody's college chances suffered. They would have relished telling the cops and counselors all about my mostly imaginary reputation.

The police never admitted to having any leads. The most recent article was from several months ago. Either the news had stopped caring or Mom had stopped collecting.

I went into Mom's personal email—she never changed her password—and found the emails she exchanged with her sister Colleen. Mom explained they were leaving town for the week because Meadow had been having trouble in school and Sunny was depressed and they all needed to get away. Every day was difficult. Breezy was supposed to be graduating, getting ready for college, growing up. Mom didn't know how to have hope anymore.

She wrote that she still froze every time the phone rang. She didn't know what my father was thinking. Aunt Colleen told her that she couldn't give up, that her daughters needed her now.

Breezy needs me, Mom had written. She needs us.

I could hear her voice as I read, resigned, torn with exhaustion. One of the news articles in the *RoundTable* reported that Dr. Erin Donahue had cried openly at a meeting as she stood before the community and pleaded for information about her daughter's whereabouts. My mother never cried. Not in private, not in public. Not even when her own mother had died at the end of a long, slow sickness. Mom got angry instead of sad. Her voice rose, her skin turned pink, her hands shook, and after the storm passed she would laugh and say, "Well, I'm Irish. I'm allowed to have a temper." She didn't cry.

I read the words, but they slipped over the surface of my mind, painless and slick. I felt sorry for her, this mother, this weeping, unfamiliar woman who was mourning a lost daughter who might have been anyone, a whole person made of more than blood and dirt and ice.

I left the computer on and went through the house again. In my parent's room I found a prescription for sleeping pills on my father's side of the bed and a book about grief on my mother's. Across the hall in Sunny's room, her soccer uniform was thrown over her chair, freshly washed but not folded; I was relieved to see she was still playing. Meadow's room had changed the most. She had replaced her black bedspread and black curtains with pale blues and greens, her pictures of blood-red roses and tormented angels with simple line drawings of faraway monuments: the Coliseum, the Great Wall, the Sphinx.

I went down to my own room last. I imagined myself opening

the door and finding myself lying there in bed, a sleepy confused version of me who would blink at the light, shove her messy hair out of her face and ask, "Who are you?"

My schoolbooks were arranged in a neat stack on my desk, my laptop closed and unplugged beside them. The cops would have taken it, looked through my photos and emails, laughed about the tameness of the porn, saying, wow, that girl was either confused or greedy, but she could have gone for something a little more hard-core and made our jobs more interesting.

There was a faint depression in the comforter where somebody had sat at the edge of the bed.

I sat in that same spot and pressed my hands together between my knees. It was Mom who came down to my room, probably, but maybe Dad too. Never together. Mom would come late at night, or early in the morning before anybody was awake, open the door quietly, shut it behind her. Meadow and Sunny would know she did it, but they would never say anything.

Sitting there on my bed, I thought: I can lie.

"I can't remember," I could say. "I don't remember anything after the party. I don't know what happened." I could lie to the police, to the doctors, to my parents. I could lie to my sisters. "I don't remember leaving the party. I just woke up and came home. I didn't even know how much time had passed."

And they would nod. Their expressions would be sympathetic and relieved. They would take me to the hospital. A nurse would examine me. She would ask delicate questions and she wouldn't believe my answers.

The police would want to know about the dead man by my grave.

"I don't know him," I would say. "I've never seen him before. I don't know anything about him. I didn't kill him."

They would ask if I knew he was a murderer. I would lie, lie, lie.

I inhaled and exhaled. Closed my mouth and stopped breathing. I waited for the burn in my lungs, the pressure in my chest building into pain, but it never came. What came instead was the memory of blood on my hands, whimpering winter wind, a family dinner ended by bullets and knives.

I jumped up from my bed and stumbled into the bathroom. I retched until my throat was raw and my gut ached. I felt hollow, my insides scraped out. I rose to rinse my mouth, and that's when I saw the bruises around my neck.

Handprints, a butterfly matched set, livid and purple. I fit my own hands to the marks and tried to remember what it had felt like, being strangled.

I didn't leave that night. I stayed in the silent, empty house for five days.

During the day I hid in my room behind the closed door. When Greta came over, I listened to the floorboards creaking, water running, doors opening and closing. At night I went out again. I left my own skateboard leaning against the wall in the entryway and stole another from an open garage several streets away. I spent the nights skating around, past familiar houses and streets, unnoticed. I didn't speak to anybody. I avoided all contact, all conversation. Some people made me nervous in a way I couldn't define, but I scurried away from them like a cockroach hiding when the kitchen light comes on. I didn't think to examine the sensation at first.

The first time I truly paid attention to somebody who felt different was at a stoplight in Morton Grove. It was late at night. I stopped to wait for the light to change. Green to yellow to red, and the white walk sign appeared. A single stopped car. The driver's face was a pale smudge through the glass. But his shadow—

His shadow was breathtaking.

I first felt it from the sidewalk, but it was only a tickle, a spider-creep brush on the back of my neck. Ten feet away and it unfurled like a black sail, a balloon of gauzy silk. I wobbled on my skateboard, put one foot down to catch myself, and stopped in front of the car. The headlights drowned me from the waist down. Through the windshield the driver's face was unremarkable. Round and soft, a middle-aged man carrying his years in his jowls, balding, ordinary.

I knew him. I didn't know his name, but I knew him. I had never met him before, but I knew him. Our lives had never intersected before that moment, but I knew without a doubt one true thing about him: he was a killer.

He tapped the horn. The light was green and he was shaking his head at me, inching the car forward. Startled, I ran back to the sidewalk. The man drove away, and with him went his shadow.

I stood on that corner for a long time as the lights cycled through their rhythm of stops and starts. Being so close to that man, meeting his eyes through the windshield, seeing the bland impatience there, it left me with a jittery feeling, a nauseous clamor of nerves I didn't understand.

It wasn't until I was back in my basement with the blinds closed did I remember where I had felt it before: the man at my grave. The one I had killed with a touch, before I even knew what I was doing. He had felt like that, in those first panicked moments after I woke up.

I began looking for killers.

Short of walking down the street and hoping a murderer was waiting in line at Starbucks, I wasn't entirely sure how to go about finding them, not until I remembered Joya Allen.

Joya Allen had been a casual friend of mine in middle school, but for high school she went to Saint A's and I didn't see her much anymore. During our junior year of high school she killed her stepfather in a car accident. She hadn't been reckless or drunk; she'd lost control of her mother's BMW on the icy street and hit the man in their own driveway. The impact slammed him against the front of the house and broke his spine. It was officially an accident, but there were rumors. Joya had never liked her stepfather very much. He was overbearing, intrusive. Handsey with her friends. They were only rumors.

I didn't know the limits of my newfound sense. I didn't know if guilt mattered, if intent mattered, if accidental deaths were the same as cold-blooded murders. I didn't know anything. I certainly didn't know any convicted murderers. But I did know where Joya Allen lived.

I went to her house one night and lurked like a stalker in the hedge separating her yard from her neighbor's. I didn't know which bedroom was hers, but it didn't matter. That close to the house, close enough I could have tossed a handful of pebbles up to the second story windows, I felt a dark mist of guilt flowing outward, as encompassing as fog from the lake, spreading from a single point in an upstairs bedroom.

My fingers itched. I clenched my hands into fists at my sides.

I pictured myself walking over to the door and finding a key under the mat.

Waiting until I was sure everybody was asleep. Slipping inside.

Creeping up the stairs, soft steps on soft carpet.

Standing over Joya as she muttered in her sleep. She would be dreaming of the man she had killed. Remembering how she felt in the moment she made the decision to hit the gas, anger and hatred and disgust and fear. The thump of car striking flesh, a crunch, remembering, and reliving.

I would place my hand on Joya's warm forehead.

I would feel for the shadow of her guilt, and I would *pull*.

I wondered if it would be easier to kill the second time. The possibility made me nervous in a way I didn't like. I didn't want to hurt Joya.

I left her house without looking back.

But I paid more attention after that. There were more killers around than I expected, but I kept my distance, and kept my hands to myself. I always returned to my house before dawn. I drew the curtains and hid from the sun, a silent ghost in my own home.

Silent, but not alone. The man I had killed was my constant companion. A real estate agent found his body a few days after I woke up. I read about it in the news, but those bloodless articles felt distant and impersonal compared to what I had taken from him. His memories, snapped into my mind at the moment of his death, had faded from immediacy, but I still had them. I will always have them. When I lay in the dark and could not quiet my mind, he and I crept together through a small house in the drifting snow, peered through the windows, and thrilled when the woman walked into view.

I didn't want to understand. I wanted him out of my head and his disgusting memories gone. When he intruded and I caught myself yearning, planning, *wanting*, I flung myself out of bed and ran into the bathroom. I searched through the drawers until I found a pair of scissors, a package of disposable razors, a metal nail file. I hoped the pain might drive him away, but the sight of my own blood rising from the cuts on my legs only made the memories stronger. Children slumped over their dinners. The husband, the interloper, dead on the floor. And her, clutching at the stab wounds in her chest, dying.

After the blood stopped flowing and the cuts began to heal, I took my father's sleeping pills from his bedroom and swallowed them all.

It didn't work. Number one on my list of failures.

I went to the lake and tried to drown. I stole rat poison from a neighbor's garage. Failure, failure. I made a list to keep track. I took a kitchen knife from the wooden block on the counter and filled the bathtub, climbed in and trembled, blade in hand, until the water was pink and cold and my skin was pruned. Failure.

According to the calendar my family was due back from the cottage on Sunday.

I cleaned the shower and the bathroom, wiped everything dry and put the towels in the washer. I erased all the evidence I had been there. I looked for cash in my room, in Meadow's and Sunny's, but decided not to take it. I took only a pen and the space camp notebook from my desk. I balled up the dirty clothes I had been wearing when I died and stuffed them into a plastic bag. I didn't know what else to do with them.

I left before dawn. I swung the plastic bag over my shoulder, dropped the stolen skateboard to the asphalt, and I left.

# ⫸ TWENTY-NINE ⫷

I WAS STILL on the lawn when Zeke came home. Watching the stars and tracking the satellites as they passed overhead, wondering which of them might be the ISS. Before, in my previous life, my normal life, I would have been imagining how I might describe that night later, in an interview, when somebody asked me, "When did you first know you wanted to go into space?" And I would say, "I always knew," and I would talk about lying on the grass and watching the space station in orbit.

The truck pulled into the driveway; the front door opened and shut. I felt the grasping shadows that whispered *killer*. A minute or two later I heard voices through the open bedroom window. Jake was angry about Zeke's field trip to Wyoming, angry about Rain, angry about the visit to Ingrid's, and probably angry about me too, but he didn't really get around to that before a door slammed and the argument ended.

The kitchen door squeaked open. "What are you doing out here?"

Trying not to eavesdrop. "Looking at the stars," I said.

The southeastern sky was washed out by Denver's yellow glow, and the dark shoulders of the mountains loomed in the west, but there were still more stars than I ever saw at home.

I rolled my head to the side to look at Zeke. "Are you in trouble for helping us?"

Zeke let the door swing shut behind him and sat on the edge of the concrete patio. "Jake's just being an asshole."

I thought maybe Jake had good reason to be upset, but I wasn't about to complain about being rescued from that red room.

"It's okay for him to do any stupid thing, but if I—" Zeke stopped abruptly, kicked idly at the crisp grass. "What are you even doing out here? It's the middle of the night."

"I don't sleep."

"Why not?"

"I mean, I can't sleep. I haven't slept since I woke up from being dead."

"Huh. Weird."

"That's one word for it. Can I ask you something?"

"I guess," Zeke said warily.

"Can you die?"

"Uh, yeah. We die. Not as easily as humans."

"What does that mean? Extreme old age? Ghoul cancer?"

"No," he said. "Somebody pretty much always kills us."

The way he said it, so flat and accepting, it was worse than anger or fear would have been. Habit, Jake had said, when he compulsively checked through the front window.

"Who?" I asked. "People like that guy in Wyoming?"

"Yeah. Humans," Zeke said, like it was obvious. Maybe it should have been.

"Is that what happened to your parents?"

A pause, then, "Yeah."

"I'm sorry."

"It was a few years ago."

I didn't think a few years would make any difference when it came to losing your parents. "How old were you?"

"Twelve. Jake was seventeen. Eighteen. It happened right after his birthday."

"My sister Sunny is twelve," I said, mostly to myself. "Thirteen, now. I missed her birthday."

"Is she your only sister?" Zeke asked.

"No. There are three of us. Meadow is in the middle. We—" The word caught in my throat. For a second it hurt to speak. "It's just the two of them now."

A few years ago, when I started high school, Mom and Dad had called a family meeting. They had never done that before. My sisters and I joined them in the dining room. Mom and Dad assured us nothing bad had happened, but they wanted to talk to us about the plans they were making in case something ever did. Our mother's older sister, Kathleen, had agreed to take us in. Meadow and I exchanged a skeptical glance across the table. Kathleen's second husband hated kids in general and us in particular. But that was what the adults had decided. Aunt Colleen was a photographer and always traveling, and Dad hadn't seen his family in China since he left for the United States at eighteen. Kathleen was the best option. Mom went over our college funds, their life insurance, their wills. Dad assured us they weren't sick or taking up skydiving. They just wanted to be prepared. We listened, but the words washed over us without impact, because who ever believes their parents are going to die? Even Sunny laughed when Dad said we would have to fight among ourselves over who got his best bathrobe, the soft gray one we all coveted on cold winter mornings. Meadow added that we would also fight over who got Grandma's china set because none of us wanted to be stuck with something so ugly. It was hideous, with big pink flowers and faded green leaves, smears of brown paint meant to be branches, and gold edging like fat worms. Mom shook her head and said she would ask the lawyer about arranging for the china to be mysteriously dropped off a moving truck during probate.

None of their plans had required me to take care of my sisters on my own. To become responsible, to get a job, to pay the bills and solve the problems, to be the adult. It had never even come up.

"Can I ask another question?" I said.

"Can I stop you?" Zeke replied.

"Unlikely. My third grade teacher, Mr. Schrader, told my

parents I wasn't allowed to raise my hand in class anymore because I was bothering the other students."

"Were you?"

"Mr. Schrader was a jerk." He was the same teacher who had called me a liar in front of the class when I couldn't share any Chinese words as part of Culture Day because my dad had never taught me any. "Ingrid said everybody knows stories about things—people like me."

"Okay?"

"I don't know those stories." I sat up, drew my knees to my chest, and hugged my arms around my legs. "I tried looking it up, but they don't cover this stuff on Wikipedia. All Google gave me was a bunch of Dungeons and Dragons character profiles and this random French TV show. Nothing helpful."

"Humans don't know anything," Zeke said.

"Yeah, we suck. I'm serious. Do you know something? Have you ever heard of anything like me?"

"There was this guy we used to know, this human. Jake and I sort of lived with him one winter." Zeke leaned forward, rested his chin on his knees, mirroring my position. It made him look young and vulnerable. "He was in Vietnam, you know, back in the sixties or whenever. I guess they—attacked a village. Killed everybody who lived there." He sounded honestly baffled when he added, "I don't understand human wars."

"Neither do we," I said.

"After they took out this village, people from their unit, what's it called?"

"Platoon."

"Right. From their platoon. They started to die. They would go off into the jungle and something would get them. They couldn't stop it. They only saw it once."

A faint shiver wormed down my spine. "It was one of the people from the village? Somebody they killed."

"A kid, yeah. A little boy."

"But only the one kid," I said. "Millions of people died in Vietnam. Why did that one kid come back? Why was he special?"

Zeke only shrugged.

"Does anybody know?"

"I don't know. Magicians don't exactly share their secrets with people like us."

"Ingrid thinks I'm going to be like that kid. Start killing a whole bunch of people."

"Ingrid can't tell you what you're going to do. Magic can't do that."

"You just said you don't know how magic works."

"I know that much," he said.

It could have been reassuring, but I wasn't in the mood to be reassured. I especially wasn't in the mood to be reassured by the vague and ill-defined rules of what magic could and couldn't do.

"One more question." If Zeke really wanted me to stop, he would have gone inside already. "Why did you help Rain when she asked? I know you didn't want to," I said, before he could deny it. "Whatever it was made your brother angry enough to threaten to cut me into little pieces if I was part of it."

"Jake said that?" Zeke said, surprised.

"Well, no. He didn't say anything, but he was holding a scalpel when he didn't say it."

"He wouldn't do that."

"So what was it? I get the impression she's not a friend of yours and, to be honest, she creeps me out."

"She's a nightmare," Zeke said.

I started to answer, hesitated, turned the word over in my mind. "You don't mean a bad dream, or, like, a really unpleasant person."

"No. I mean she's a nightmare."

"I don't know what that means," I said.

"I don't know how to explain it. That's what she is. She can do things to people's minds just by talking to them. Make them think they're in danger or lost or whatever. Give them real nightmares."

My skin crawled with an uncomfortable realization. "Do they have to be asleep?"

"No. She can do waking nightmares too."

Rain, in the red room, speaking in that sultry low voice, and the images that rose unbidden in my mind. The screaming woman—a mother separated from her children—the blank-faced men dragging her away. Telling Brian Kerr to come into the room, and how quickly I had wanted to agree. They had her mouth taped shut before I woke up. They knew what she could do.

And again, at Ingrid's house, repeating what Ingrid was saying, and how clearly and how vividly I had seen what she wanted me to see.

I hadn't questioned it at the time. I hadn't wondered where the thoughts were coming from, or why Ingrid wanted Rain there at all. I had been so focused on figuring out what I could do to other people I hadn't suspected what she was doing to me.

"She can make you think anything? Anything at all?" I said.

"I don't think so," Zeke said. "I think she can only use something you're already scared of. Like, if you've never been scared of spiders, she can't make you think giant spiders are going to eat you. But if you're scared of heights she can make you think you're going to die falling off the bed."

What was I scared of? If they had asked, I wouldn't have had a good answer. But Rain didn't need to ask. She had plucked it from my mind and turned it back on me, she and Ingrid together.

I took a breath—reflexive, unnecessary—to steady my voice. "Okay, that makes every conversation I've had with her a hundred times more disturbing, but it doesn't exactly answer my question. Are you avoiding answering? If you don't want to tell me why you helped her, it's fine. I'm just curious."

"It's not that. It's just . . . We haven't been here very long. When we first got here, we . . . we didn't really know anybody. We didn't know who to trust. We met Ingrid and her son."

"The pervert."

"He and Rain have a thing—"

"I so don't want to know the details."

"You really don't. Anyway, they helped us, I guess." Zeke didn't sound like he had appreciated the help. "Found a place to live, told us who we could trust, who we couldn't, you know. It was, um, more than we expected."

"Why?"

"Nobody likes ghouls."

"Is that it? Rain and her creepy boyfriend helped you, and you owed her?"

"A little, yeah. A couple months later she came by one day and said she was calling in a favor. Family emergency. It didn't sound like a big deal, so Jake went with her. They were gone all night, and when he came back he had—"

A long pause.

"Food," Zeke said.

It took me a second to understand he didn't mean takeout from the local Thai place.

"Rain's never killed anybody," I said.

He said nothing.

"Neither has Jake. He definitely hasn't."

Zeke was relieved, but he tried to hide it. It wasn't hard to guess what kind of secrets he had been imagining Jake was keeping from him.

"But if Rain can do what you say she can, she wouldn't have to do it herself, would she?" I said. "She could, you know, scare somebody else into doing it. On purpose or on accident."

"I guess."

"Does it work on you? What she can do?"

Zeke was quiet for a moment before answering. "We can tell when she's trying to do it."

That sounded like a qualified yes, but it also sounded like he didn't want to talk about it. I let it drop. I said, "Oh, by the way, I met Steve."

"I told you not to go into the basement."

"When has that ever worked? I'm a girl in a horror movie. I have to go into the basement."

"Is that what you think this is?" Zeke asked.

"I woke up buried in somebody's backyard. I'm dead, but I can't die. I'm a *monster*. What else am I supposed to think?"

"I don't know."

"That's super helpful."

"I don't know how else things can be." Zeke's voice was quiet.

All at once I wanted the conversation to be over. I didn't understand why he was talking to me anyway. Maybe he was bored or lonely, but it didn't matter. It was just another day, another stupid monster for him, but I didn't want to hear that this was normal, this was ordinary, this was how people lived, people who had been there all along, never mind that I had never been smart enough or sharp enough to see them. I wanted him to go away and leave me alone.

"You don't have to stay up to entertain me," I said.

Zeke gave me a quick look. "Yeah, okay." He stood up and offered a quiet "Good night" as he went inside.

I missed him as soon as he was gone. Alone was worse. I hadn't noticed, when I had been running away across the country, because I hadn't wanted to notice. But now that there were people who knew what I was and didn't seem to care, the thought of endless empty days and nights of solitude stretching into the future was too painful to consider.

I was going to need a hobby. Learn to knit. Get a library card.

Join a Warcraft guild. Take up vigilantism. There are so many more hours in a day when you don't spend a third of them sleeping.

I was going to have to learn how to pass the time, if I was going to stay like this forever.

# ·⑾· THIRTY ·⑾·

IN THE MORNING I was reading the news from Cheyenne when Jake shuffled into the living room. Zeke was asleep on the couch; he hadn't stirred when I came in as the sky started to turn pink. Jake picked up the blanket from the floor and dropped it over Zeke, tucked it over his shoulder.

"You could have made him take the floor," he said. He yawned and ran his hand through his hair.

I shrugged. "It's fine."

Jake sat down and glanced at the computer. "What's that?"

I turned it so he could see the article I was reading. They had found Brian Kerr. I explained, "He's the one who takes the monsters . . . wherever they take them. To try to change them."

I said *wherever*, but I was thinking *whoever*.

There was the figure of a woman lurking at the edge of all my thoughts, the Mother to whom Mr. Willow was bringing his tributes. Ingrid had said it might be a creature, a monster, but in my mind she was tall and grim and featureless, a terrible silent shape with arms opened in a gathering embrace. I hadn't told anybody what I knew about her yet. Not Rain, not Ingrid, and I wasn't going to tell Jake either. She was the linchpin at the center of Mr. Willow's world. I was keeping her to myself.

I kept telling myself it was because I wanted more information. It felt so clean and rational to think of it that way. Information. Facts, data. I couldn't trust secondary evidence. I had been telling myself that all night. A responsible researcher would go to the source.

The article about Brian Kerr didn't have much information: The paramedics and state police had been called to the house after Kerr's wife found him unconscious on the premises. Nothing about the room full of belongings. Nothing about the blood. There was a picture of him perched on a wooden fence and smiling, majestic mountains in the background. He looked normal, nonthreatening, but the sight of his face put a knot in my stomach. I scratched my fingernails softly against my jeans and imagined a phantom pain, the splinter-sharp agony of scrabbling helplessly along a long stone tunnel.

There were too many of Brian Kerr's memories trapped in my head.

So I turned the conversation to something that had bothered me since the night before, when I finally realized how Rain had been manipulating my thoughts in the red room.

I asked, "Does Rain have kids?"

Jake hesitated, which was all the answer I needed.

"She does," I said. "Doesn't she?"

"Why do you want to know?"

"Zeke told me that you helped her with a family emergency. And she did her nightmare thing on you, made you think something bad would happen if you told anybody. That was about her kids, wasn't it?"

"Is that true?" Zeke pushed the blanket down and sat up; his voice was rough with sleep. "Jake?"

"That's not what happened," Jake said.

"A boy and a girl. Maybe seven or eight years old?"

Jake shook his head. "I have no idea how you know that. I know she didn't tell you. She doesn't want anybody to know."

Maybe not, but she had wanted to find out, without asking, if I had seen them. That's why she had made up that other woman and put her into my mind. It might have worked too—I might have been overcome with sympathy, eager to share that I had seen the kids at the church—if only I hadn't been so wrapped in myself, so convinced that being this thing that I was, this inhuman monster, meant being so unique and isolated that the idea of mothers and children and families all in it together hadn't even occurred to me.

"She didn't tell me. But she does, right?"

"Yeah. I don't know how old they are. They're not human. Rain's a lot older than she looks."

"What are you talking about? Since when does Rain have kids?" Zeke asked.

"It's not—"

"That's what that was about?" Zeke said. "When you went with her that day?"

"Yeah, but it's not—"

"You know what she is. And you still—"

"Zeke." The angrier Zeke got, the more tired Jake looked. "It didn't happen like that. The kids needed help."

"Why didn't you tell me?" Zeke asked.

Jake glanced at me before answering. I couldn't read that look at all, but I had a feeling they would be having a very different conversation if I wasn't in the room.

"They were staying with their grandfather, their human grandfather. He didn't know what they are."

"Why would she leave them with a *human*?" Zeke asked, disgusted.

"I don't know. She didn't tell me, okay? All she said was that her kids had called her and she needed to go pick them up right away. By the time we got there . . ." Jake rubbed his hand over his face. "The kids were defending themselves."

"What did—"

"I'm not going to tell you what he did." Jake voice was sharp.

Zeke shut his mouth.

"It doesn't matter. It was technically suicide, but it was messy enough that the cops would ask questions. So we cleaned it up and got them out of there. That's all. I don't know where she took them after that. She said she was going to find somebody else to look after them, but I don't know who."

Two little kids with the power to manipulate thoughts, separated from their mother, protecting themselves, and your friendly neighborhood ghoul on call to help clean up the crime scene. I was selfishly glad Jake didn't share any details, but I understood now why he had been so angry at Rain for getting Zeke to help her.

"You should have told me," Zeke said.

"I thought—" Jake sighed. "You're right. I should have."

"I need to talk to Rain," I said. "Can you call her?"

"Why?"

"Wherever she took them, it wasn't as safe as she thought. I think she went looking for Mr. Willow's people because they have her kids," I said. "She kind of told me when we were stuck in that room, but I didn't realize she was talking about herself."

"You know where they are?" Jake asked.

"I know where they were a few days ago."

Zeke pulled the blanket up to his chin and slumped into the couch. "She's at Ingrid's. I'm not calling."

Jake went to get his phone.

I didn't tell them that it might be too late for Rain's children. I wasn't planning on telling her either. Not until she told me what I wanted to know first.

# ⫸ THIRTY-ONE ⫷

RAIN REFUSED TO come to Jake and Zeke's house. She listened to my proposed trade—information about her children for information about Willow—and accepted with a reasonable minimum of cursing and threats of bodily harm.

"Meet me downtown," she said. "Pearl Street, in front of the bookstore. Be there in about an hour. There's someone you have to meet."

"Who is it?"

"The guy who put me in touch with our Wyoming friend," she said. "I told you about him, remember? He's one of the lucky survivors. Speaking of which, you see the Cheyenne news this morning? How does it feel to be famous?"

I said, "I'll be there," and hung up.

She hadn't said to come alone, and I didn't know how to find Pearl Street anyway. It only took a little bit of wheedling to convince Zeke to come with me. Jake left for work after making Zeke swear about a dozen times, a dozen different ways, not to do anything stupid and definitely not to go anywhere with Rain or any of her friends or any monster-hunting humans we might come across. Zeke rolled his eyes, but he promised.

It was midmorning on a warm, sunny Saturday, the sky cloudless and deep blue, and Pearl Street was crowded with people: couples walking with cups of coffee in hand, kids playing, buskers plucking songs on their guitars. After the strangeness of the past several days, everything felt off, artificial, as though the entire city had been lowered around us like a movie set during the night.

Rain was leaning against a storefront when we arrived, hands tucked into the pockets of her black hoodie. "You know Ritter?" she asked Zeke. "Climber guy, lives in his van, not too fond of showers?"

"Human?"

"Yeah, but he's harmless. Totally chill. He works at a bagel shop."

"That's a stellar character reference," I said.

"Considering the people you've been hanging out with, you have no room to judge. How'd you like their ugly little roommate?"

"Oh, Steve? We're cool. We understand each other."

If I was expecting Rain to be different—some external evidence of fear or relief, a glimmer of maternal instinct, or even guilt for putting her children in danger again—I was disappointed. She looked and acted exactly as she had the day before. We might have been making plans to go see a movie rather than discussing the fate of her missing children.

Rain's friend was sitting on a low wall in front of a bookstore and café. He lifted a hand in greeting when he spotted her, started to smile, grimaced instead.

"What did you bring him for?" he said.

Zeke stared right back and didn't say anything.

Rain leaned over to kiss the man's cheek. "Not my idea. Don't worry, I won't let him bite. Ritter, this is Breezy. Breezy, Ritter. She's the one I told you about."

"You're the one that put Brian Kerr in the hospital," Ritter said.

He was closer to thirty than twenty, with dirty-blond hair pulled back in a limp ponytail and a scraggly beard coaxed into twin loose twists. He was wearing ratty jeans and flip-flops and a red T-shirt that said I SKI♥LAND in block letters. He held a ukulele in his hands and the case was open on the ground in front of him, a few dollar bills and change scattered over the velvet lining. He had never killed anybody.

"I guess so," I said warily. "How did you hear about that already?"

"News travels," Ritter said. "I'm not the only one around here who's had a problem with those assholes. Trust me, I'm not going to judge you for it. That man has done some serious shit. If you messed him up, I want to buy you a drink." He squinted in the sun. "Or I would, if you weren't like twelve."

"My age is kind of a divide-by-zero number at this point. How do you know them?"

Ritter gave me a wry smile. "I used to be one of them."

He didn't say *one of them* like he was talking about a group of kids he used to know, like he would say he used to be in a band or on a team, or even the shamefaced way he might say, "I used to be a Young Republican." He said it like it was something he had lost, something mournful from long ago.

"You mean you were . . ." I didn't know how to ask. "Different?"

"They don't go after normal kids," Ritter said. "I used to be able to see ghosts."

"Are you sure they were ghosts?" Zeke asked.

Ritter twitched his shoulders. "Yeah, I'm sure. I used to call them my 'glowy people.' My stepmom thought I was making things up to screw with her."

"When did you start seeing them?" Zeke said.

"Uh, I don't remember," Ritter said, frowning. "I could always see them. I was never scared of them or anything. They don't do anything, right? They just float around. There was one on the street outside our house. I was like eight before I realized nobody else could see it."

"But you could always see them?" Zeke said. "Even when you were a baby?"

"What does it matter?" Rain asked.

Ritter brushed his fingers over the strings of the ukulele. He was looking more uncomfortable with every question. "I think so. I don't exactly remember, you know? Why?"

"Something happened when you were born," Zeke said.

Ritter's fingers fell still on the instrument. "How do you know that?"

"Your mother died."

"Jesus, could you be more tactless?" Rain kicked at Zeke's feet. He stepped out of reach.

"Nah, he's right," Ritter said. "It's fine. How did you know?"

"Humans can't see ghosts without a reason. That takes magic, and magic means somebody died."

Ritter snapped his fingers and pointed at Zeke. "See, that, that's what I didn't know before. I know it now, sure, but they never told me that. Pastor Willow and all his people. He never told me there was an explanation. He never told us shit."

"How did you meet them?" I asked.

"I got in trouble when I was a kid. Got caught, you know." Ritter held his fingers to his lips to mime smoking a joint. "My dad and stepmom decided I should start going to this youth group thing, at this church our neighbors went to. This place over on Baseline. I don't know if it's still there. This was, I dunno, ten years ago. I thought it would be talking about Jesus and playing basketball and going camping and whatever, and if I got my grades up, they'd forget about it and stop making me go. It was mostly fine, too, a little woo-woo and everything. No prayers or shit. I doubt any of them ever even read the Bible. They had this house where we could hang out without any adults. That made it fun. But there was this one guy, this older kid, he was really intense about it." Ritter plucked at the ukulele strings again, a quick progression. The notes vibrated brightly and faded. "Intense about everything, like he didn't want any of us having fun."

"Brian Kerr," I said.

Ritter nodded. "It was only the second or third time I went when he told me he knew I was different. I didn't plan to tell anybody. I was a dumb shit, but I wasn't stupid enough to announce to a bunch of Jesus freaks I saw dead people. But they were saying, like, everybody experiences things they can't explain, the world's full of mysteries, maybe you know about them, blah blah blah, and I thought, maybe they'd understand? And one day Brian came up to me and said, 'We can make it go away.' I told him I didn't know what the hell of he was talking about, so he got one of the younger girls to talk to me. She was always saying things like, 'It doesn't mean you're a bad person, it just means you have something bad attached to you, you have a darkness inside you,' other crap like that."

Violet's lines hadn't changed much since then.

Ritter went on, "I didn't listen at first because, whatever, my ghosts didn't hurt anybody. But she was really convincing. I started to think, oh shit, she's right, this isn't normal, there is something seriously wrong with me. So I said okay. They could fix me."

"What did they do?" I asked.

"They took it away," Ritter said.

"How?"

Ritter looked at me for a long, long moment. "I don't remember."

In Brian Kerr's memories, there were towering pine trees, the scent of the forest, a yawning dark hole in the side of a mountain, and fear. His fear. He had been dragging other people to their deaths, but he was as scared of what waited in that darkness as they were. No matter how many times he walked away alive, he was still afraid.

"But it worked?" I said. "Whatever they did, it worked?"

Ritter glanced down, tapped the wooden body of the ukulele, shrugged and laughed a little, humorless and tired. "Yeah. I guess. I miss them, you know? The ghosts. They never hurt me. I kind of liked them. That one outside our house, I couldn't tell who it was, but I used to pretend it was a kid like me who died riding his bike or something, and I'd talk to him like he could hear. I wouldn't mind seeing them again."

He was quiet after that. All around us was the lazy commotion of a crowded street on a Saturday morning, but nobody gave us a second look. I felt the tendril tug of a killer, somebody besides Zeke, but I couldn't pick out who it was before the sensation was gone.

"That girl you met," I said. "That was Violet?"

"Yeah. Redhead. Sweet little kid, but creepy too."

"I need to talk to her."

"No way," Ritter said, shaking his head. "Bad idea. All that stuff about being cursed and releasing your soul from evil and all that bullshit, she believes it. She believes everything that bastard tells her."

Maybe she had ten years ago, but I wasn't sure it was true anymore. Violet had let me go, or tried to. Even Lyle, who I could barely think about without shuddering, had apologized as he snapped my bones and tore my skin. Something was broken at the center of Mr. Willow's congregation. His foot soldiers were not as loyal as he believed them to be.

"I want to talk to her anyway. You know how to get in touch

with them, don't you? Who did you call for Rain?"

"This kid Danny. Danny Mendoza. He's all right. They told him they couldn't help him, but they kept him around anyway. Working for them, you know, doing whatever."

Truck Stop Danny, the trying-too-hard Goth who could see a girl across a parking lot and know she was a monster and send her right into Mr. Willow's hands. No wonder they kept him around.

Zeke asked, "Why would he do that?"

Ritter shrugged. "He's not into their shit, man, but it's not like he has anywhere else to go."

"You have to call him again," I said.

Ritter was already shaking his head. "No. Not a chance. I am done with those people."

"You did it before."

"Because I thought—" He stopped, looked at Rain, frowned in confusion. "You said you needed— What did you need?"

"It doesn't matter," Rain said. "You don't care. You didn't care before, and you don't care now. You know it's none of your business."

Ritter was holding the neck of the ukulele so tight I thought it would snap. "But I—"

"It's only a favor," Rain said. All of her easy friendliness was gone. She was looking right at Ritter, and her eyes were like embers. "A little favor. I'll owe you one. No big deal. Just call the guy."

Zeke glanced at me, but I didn't need the warning. I knew what she was doing.

"I don't think," Ritter began, but he was reaching into his pocket for his phone. "What am I supposed to say to him?"

Rain looked at me, and I said quietly, "Violet's the one I need to talk to."

"Find out how Breezy can talk to that Violet girl. That's all."

Ritter looked at the phone like he wasn't sure what to do with it. "That's all? I don't want to go back. I don't—I can't—"

"You don't have to go back. They'll never know you were involved."

His face was pale except for two flushed smudges on his cheeks. He made the call.

Rain leaned close to listen to the conversation, and she murmured in Ritter's ear to guide his replies. It might have been intimate, almost romantic, if only he didn't look so scared. He spoke for a minute or two, then looked up and held the phone out to me.

"He wants to talk to you."

I accepted the phone. "Yeah?"

"You're an idiot." Truck Stop Danny. He sounded younger over the phone. "What the hell do you think you're doing?"

"What do you care what I'm doing? I should be dead now, thanks to you."

"I didn't think you'd actually be stupid enough to go to them."

"Then why did you even try?"

"Because it's a hundred bucks for me for every stupid one," he said. "And I need to eat. Not my fault you fell for that shelter-from-the-storm bullshit."

"But I learned so many interesting things from the experience."

"You know they're looking for you. You and the nightmare. They know she's hanging around Boulder a lot."

"They're here?" My skin crawled. I couldn't stop myself from looking up and down the street, as though I might spot Mr. Willow lurking right there among the shoppers and students.

"Just the crazy chick right now," Danny said. "The pastor and his attack dog are dealing with the cops in Wyoming."

"Violet's here? Where is she?"

Danny didn't answer right away.

"You know where she is," I said. "Tell me."

"You should get out of there," Danny said. "Leave town. Forget about them."

"I will. After I talk to Violet."

"You didn't get enough of her already?"

"Why don't you want to tell me? You didn't have any trouble sending me to her before."

Danny sighed loudly. "You know what? You're right. You're not my problem. I am done with this shit."

"Good for you. Tell me how to find Violet."

"Willow's got a place in town. His dad's house. He never sold it." Danny gave me an address, told me how to find it, grunted in confirmation when I repeated it back to him.

"That's it?"

"Don't call me again. Thanks to you I'm out of a job."

"Wait! One more thing."

"What?"

"How did you know? When you saw me at that truck stop. How did you know what I was?"

"I can see," he said.

"What do you mean? What can you see?"

Danny didn't say anything for several seconds. "I can see what's under your skin."

He hung up.

I handed the phone back to Ritter. He was still collecting himself, shaky and pale. He pocketed the phone, put his ukulele in its case without gathering up the money.

"You get what you need?"

I nodded.

"Then you're going to leave me alone. And you." He clicked the case shut, stood up, and looked at Rain. "Next time you call, I'm not answering. Don't ever come near me again."

Rain stood too, but she said nothing.

Ritter turned to me. "You shouldn't be helping her either. You're going to get yourself killed."

"It's too late for that," I said. "Thanks."

What I didn't say was that I wasn't doing any of it to help Rain. I wasn't proud of it, but my knowledge of her kids' whereabouts was the only thing I had to trade for a way to get in touch with Violet again. I told myself I was playing by the rules of this new world I had woken up into. Valuable information for dangerous information.

I almost didn't feel bad about it.

Then I thought about those kids on the playground, the *creak-creak* of the merry-go-round as they pushed each other in circles, and I couldn't meet Rain's eyes.

# ·ıı· THIRTY-TWO ·ıı·

"THERE'S NO WAY I'm going with you," Rain said after Ritter was gone. "I'm done here. Tell me what you know."

"I didn't invite you," I said. I sat down on the brick wall to dig through my backpack.

"I would say you should take him, even if he is useless." Rain jerked her thumb toward Zeke. "But that would be kind of like bringing a cockroach casserole to a picnic. Sure, it might send everybody screaming, but they'd only come back with an exterminator."

"I think you think that metaphor makes more sense than it actually does," I said. I handed Danny's blue flier to her. Church of the Prairie. NEED HELP? Map and address at the bottom of the page. "This is where I saw them. There's a woman with them. I don't know who she is, or what she is. I didn't talk to her."

Rain unfolded the page and looked it over. For the first time, I saw a flicker of worry in her eyes, quickly shuttered.

All she said was, "See you around." She walked away.

I zipped up my backpack and slipped my arms into the straps. "You're not going to try to talk me out of it?"

Zeke was looking at the ground by my feet. "Would it do any good?"

"No. Probably not."

"You want me to go with you?"

He knew a lot more about monsters than I did. He could walk through magical barriers. He had killed somebody before. He had a car. Absolutely. Yes. If Danny was lying, if I had misjudged Violet, if this didn't go how I expected, I wanted him with me.

But I shook my head. "You promised Jake you wouldn't."

"He'll get over it."

"Maybe, but first he'll blame me," I said. "I'll be fine."

Zeke started to say something, changed his mind. He tossed his phone to me. "In case you need help again."

"Thanks."

"Yeah, whatever. Be careful."

He walked away, hands shoved into his pockets. He hadn't asked me what I was going to do.

There were only a handful of numbers in the phone, most identified by letters rather than names. *J* was the one he used most often, so I guessed that's who I was supposed to call if I needed help.

I was sure Jake would love that.

The directions Danny had given me led me down the bike path along Broadway to south Boulder. I skated in the sun, dodging joggers and cyclists, until I found the right street. I identified the house but kept my distance. It was small but well kept. Clean white paint, green shutters, trimmed lawn. There were no cars parked in the driveway. I didn't see any signs of life, so I spent a little while skating around the neighborhood, doing my best to look bored and harmless. I passed the house three or four times and nothing changed. I didn't have any plan for what I could do if Violet didn't show up. I wasn't even sure what I was going to do if she did.

The next time I turned onto the street, there was a car parked in front of the house. Nebraska plates. I couldn't remember if it was one of the cars I had seen outside the farmhouse.

I stopped on the other side of the street rolled the skateboard back and forth, back and forth, the wheels rumbling softly on the asphalt, and I waited.

The front door opened. Violet walked out to the car and lifted a couple of plastic grocery bags from the backseat. She was wearing jeans and a pink T-shirt rather than the flowery dress, and her red hair was pulled back into a ponytail. She turned to go into the house again, but when she reached the door she stopped, and she turned. She met my eyes across the street.

I picked up the skateboard and walked over to her.

"Is anybody else here?" I asked.

"No. Nobody. Danny called me. He told me you were looking for me."

"And you're still here alone?"

"It's just me, I promise," Violet said. "Lyle and Edward are in Cheyenne. They found Brian."

"I know. I saw the news."

"Edward went to the hospital. He said Brian is dying. There's nothing the doctors can do." I couldn't tell if she was upset or relieved. "The nightmare didn't do that."

"No. That was me."

We stood there in uncomfortable silence, Violet in the shade, me in the sun.

She inhaled carefully. "What you did to Brian . . . can you do that to anybody?"

"Oh." I almost wanted to laugh. "I get it. That's why you're here alone."

It didn't matter if I had a plan or not, because Violet had one of her own.

When I was in tenth grade this kid named Anthony Chung brought a gun to school. It wasn't the gun that shocked everybody; he wasn't the first and he wouldn't be the last. What surprised everybody, what they couldn't get their heads around, was that it was Anthony Chung who did it. Anthony Chung, cross-country star, Science Olympiad team captain, honors student, no older siblings in gangs, no delinquent friends. He was well liked. He wasn't a bully and nobody bullied him. Everybody kept asking, "Where did a good kid like that even get a gun?" It didn't belong to his parents. Mom and Dad had asked me and Melanie one day after school, "You wouldn't know where to find a gun, would you?" We promised we didn't. I was thinking about all the friends I knew whose parents kept guns in their bedside drawers, in their coat closets, under their beds, and wondering why everybody was more worried about where Anthony had gotten the gun rather than why he had it in the first place.

I looked up and down the street. Nobody was watching. Bees hummed lazily around a bed of white and yellow daisies beneath the front window. The sun was hot on my head and shoulders.

"Where would a good kid like you even get a gun?" I murmured.

"What?"

A fat bumblebee settled on a blossom. Violet's green eyes were so wary, so scared.

"Why don't you ask what you really want to ask?" I said.

"What are you?"

"No. Not that."

Violet hesitated, then said, "Let's go inside."

# ᛞ THIRTY-THREE ᛞ

VIOLET LED ME through the living room and into the kitchen. The house was neat but dusty. The only books on the shelves were Bibles and Christian self-help books, and the only decorations were inspirational posters of sunrises and footprints in wet sand, with phrases like TRUST IN FAITH and NEVER GIVE UP printed in a bold font. There were small angels embroidered onto the pillows on the sofa. Looked like they had put some effort into their cover story of being a church group, if only in their interior design choices. It didn't look like a place Mr. Willow's family or anybody else had ever lived.

There were no photographs.

Violet gestured for me to take a seat at the table.

"I saw you once," I said. I didn't continue until she sat across from me. "In this video a friend of mine got from her church. An exorcism video. That was you, wasn't it?"

"That was never supposed to get out." Violet's voice was calm, but her eyes tightened with an old pain. "I thought they were trying to help. They *were* trying to help."

"Why? Why would they think you needed an exorcist?"

"It's not important."

"It's important to me," I said. "Tell me or I'm leaving."

Violet's lips twisted, not quite a smile. She didn't call my bluff. "I killed my brother."

"No, you didn't." I was certain of it, but she shook her head.

"I did. I did. You don't understand."

"So tell me."

"His name was Teddy. He was two years older than me, and he was everything to our family. He was so good and so bright. We all loved him. He was our light. But he was sick." Violet's broken smile drained away. "There was something wrong with his heart. He collapsed one day playing with his friends. The doctors did all kinds of tests. They said he could still live a long, happy life if he was careful. And Teddy, he had always loved riding his bike and player soccer, but he was so good about it. He just laughed and said he would have to find another hobby, like making pottery."

She stopped to draw in a few rough breaths. I waited.

"After my parents brought him home from the hospital, I came home from school and Teddy was watching TV. He was supposed to be resting. And . . . you know when you're out in the sun and a cloud comes in, but you didn't see it coming, you didn't know the weather was changing, all you know is the light is gone and the colors are gone and you're cold when you should be warm?" Violet spoke rapidly, her breath catching between words. "I started crying. I was having a fit. I was out of control. I was always bad, I always had tantrums when I didn't get my way, and my parents tried to make me stop, but I didn't care. I was screaming so much it hurt them. My mother was bleeding from her ears and Teddy was covering his head with his pillow and I was doing that to them, but I didn't care. I didn't stop. It took both of my parents to carry me up to my room and . . ."

"What?"

Violet looked down, scraped her fingertips over the table. "When they went back downstairs, Teddy was dead. His heart just stopped. He was supposed to be okay. The doctors said he would be okay, but he died. My parents—they said it wasn't my fault, they didn't understand, but they took me to their priest. Father Matt and . . . you saw the video. You know what happened."

The priest had died too. I asked, "Your parents aren't like you?"

"I'm adopted. They didn't know anything about my birth mother. They were so afraid of me. Of what I could do. They didn't know what else to think."

"But they were wrong. You weren't possessed."

"They believed in possession. That was something they could understand. People can only see the world as they know it. It wasn't their fault."

"You're a banshee, right?"

She flinched as though the word itself could hurt her. "I'm not anything anymore."

"I thought banshees wailed *because* somebody was dying, not the other way around. You weren't—"

"But I was! Don't you understand?" The look Violet gave me was bleak. "Teddy should have lived. He was going to live, but I killed him. He could have had his whole life, but now he never will, because of me. Father Matt was only trying to help me and now he can't help anybody else. I did that."

"No, you didn't," I said again, but still she didn't hear me.

"They knew what they had to do." She said it so earnestly, with so much guilt, I wondered who she was trying to convince.

"How did you meet Mr. Willow?" I asked.

"After Father Matt died, they heard about a man who helped kids who were troubled. Spiritually troubled."

"How old were you?"

"Eleven," she said.

"You've been with Mr. Willow since you were eleven?" I couldn't keep the shock from my voice. "Your parents sent an eleven-year-old girl to a stranger?"

"I still talk to my parents sometimes. They know I'm okay." Violet sat forward and spread her hands on the table. "Edward's the one who helped me understand what I was doing."

"But you weren't doing anything. You were only trying to warn them."

Violet didn't seem to hear me. "Magic is unnatural. We're unnatural. It's wrong to be like this. We *kill* people. Don't you understand?

There are people everywhere in danger. They don't know we exist. They don't know what we can do. How can you bear it?"

I thought about the little girl in the baseball cap crying as Brian led her into the darkness. About Jake checking through the front window for unnamed dangers on the street and the fact that in spite of their dietary requirements he and his brother had only ever killed one person between them. About all the empty shells of people in the house in Nebraska. About Rain's children, protecting themselves from their grandfather, a man who didn't need magic to be a monster.

"How can *you* bear it?" I retorted. "Did you know all along he was kidnapping and killing people?"

"He's not—"

"Are they all like me? People who are just looking for a place to stay? For some help? That's why you pay Danny to trick them?"

"You don't understand. It's not like—"

"Do you even care if they've ever hurt anybody? Do you care if they have families? Do you ask them if they want to go home? Do you even give them a chance to live their lives and never hurt anybody?"

"We're not like—"

"Yes, you *are*," I said, my voice rising. I caught myself, took a breath to keep from shouting. "I know everything Brian did. What all of you did. Don't lie to me about it."

Violet pressed her lips together. She still wasn't looking at me.

"What I don't know is how many ended up like that girl at the house. Like Esme."

"Edward says it only happens like that when they . . ."

"What?"

"When they're not accepting," Violet said quietly. "When they fight it."

She knotted her hands together on the table. Her face was pale, her shoulders slumped.

"You really believe that?" I asked.

Violet didn't answer.

"Did Esme want it?"

She said, very softly, "No."

"She came to you for help," I guessed, "and you did that to her."

Violet was quiet for a long moment. "Esme and Lyle never hurt anybody."

"Never? You want to see my scars?"

"Before," Violet said. "When they came to us. They were being hunted, and they were just trying to get back to their family. Esme is the bravest girl I've ever met. She only wanted . . ." There were tears in Violet's eyes, a rough catch in her voice. "Before I met her, I didn't even know that people like . . . like that, I didn't know we could have families. I didn't know there were people who protected each other. Edward always said, he said they were all outcasts, because nobody wanted them. But Esme told me he was wrong."

"So what you're saying," I said, my voice shaking with anger, "is that you were totally okay helping Mr. Willow murder people until you realized somebody might actually miss them."

She wiped a tear from her eye. "She was going to show me. She was going to take me home to their family."

I sat back in the chair. I could still feel a twinge in my side where Lyle's gashes had healed. I was tired of talking around the point. I didn't want to feel sorry for her, for the scared little girl she had been, the one who had only ever wanted a family that wouldn't send her away for being different in a way they refused to understand.

"I have one more question," I said.

Violet nodded.

"Why is he doing this? Why did Mr. Willow wake up one day and decide to start hunting down monsters?" She opened her mouth, but I went on, "And don't tell me it's because we're irredeemably evil. I haven't even met very many monsters yet and I already know that's bullshit. *You* know it's bullshit. Did he used to be one too?"

"No!" Violet looked shocked. "He does it to protect people. He knows—he's known since he was a child what damage monsters can do, and the humans who let them live. Monsters destroyed his family. And it used to be that he had to kill them, when his father was in charge, but now he wants to help them." To her credit, Violet lowered her gaze and amended, "Or he used to. He's lost his way. I've tried to talk to him, to make him understand that what he did to Esme was wrong, but he won't listen."

"So you want to stop him. Fine. Why don't you do it yourself? You don't need my help."

Violet shook her head. "No. No. I could never do that to him."

"Why not?"

"I *can't*," Violet said, miserable. "I can't. He's done too much for me. It's because of him I'm not a monster anymore. I can't."

Too grateful to act herself, or too brainwashed, but I didn't think it really mattered. She was disillusioned now, but there was still a frightened eleven-year-old girl inside Violet, abandoned by her parents and taken in by a man who promised to make her better. There was no way to reason with that scared little girl.

"Get Lyle to do it," I said. "It's his sister who got messed up."

"He thinks we might be able to help her," Violet said. "Edward told him it might be possible. That there might be a way to ask for a . . . favor."

"Is there?"

"I don't know. We don't know."

"So that's where I come in," I said.

"It's different for you," Violet said. "You're not like us. It wasn't an accident that you came to us. Don't you see? You're a gift. You're exactly what we need."

It was the worst thing she could have said. It was precisely what I expected. Violet and I weren't that different from each other. We both divided the world into *killers* and *everybody else,* and she knew which side of that line I was on.

"Katie—whoever you are—"

"You don't need to know my name."

"You can help us."

"Say what you want."

"You know what I mean."

"I want you to say it to my face."

Violet couldn't meet my eyes. "He'll come here if I ask. You don't have to—it can be like Brian. Whatever you did to him. That's enough."

"So you can sit by his hospital bed and hold his hand and tell him how sorry you are?"

"No! I don't—"

"What do I get out of this?"

"What?"

"You want to hire a contract killer, you have to offer something in return. I don't work for free."

Violet's mouth dropped open. "You want money?"

"No," I said. "That's not what I want."

"But what—" She stopped.

"I want you to take me where you take the rest of them," I said.

In Brian Kerr's memories I heard the clang of metal on metal and a low, low laugh rolling along a throat of stone. She waited at the end of a dark tunnel. The shiver of fear might have been my own, or it might have been an echo of his. He had never gone all the way to the end. He was human. He never had to. His job was to take the others and wait for them to emerge changed, or broken, or not at all.

Violet was shaking her head. "You don't know what she'll do."

She was right. I had no idea what would happen. But I had to find out. Wherever I went next, whatever I chose to do with the rest of my afterlife, I couldn't begin without knowing. I had to see for myself.

"Take me to her and I'll do what you want."

Violet didn't try to talk me out of it. She said, "You'll have to ride in the trunk."

# ⑾ THIRTY-FOUR ⑾

VIOLET WASN'T JOKING. She made me ride in the trunk.

"I can't let you see how to get there," she said. "Nobody can know where it is."

So into the trunk I went. It smelled of rubber and oil, and the gritty carpet was sticky in places, like a bottle of soda had exploded and nobody had bothered to clean it up. I hoped it was soda. I lay on my back, backpack and skateboard jammed in beside me, and for once in my life I was grateful to be barely five foot three. The space was airless and hot.

I rolled with each turn and tried not to think about the squashing-each-other game my sisters and I had played when we were younger. Still played, sometimes, because we were just that mature, when all three of us were stuck in the backseat, and whoever was in the middle smashed the others against the doors every time the car turned.

I closed my eyes and stopped breathing until the rumble of the car chased away the memory of Sunny's delighted laughter and Meadow's annoyed grumbling. It was getting harder to make myself stop thinking of them.

I couldn't guess how far we were going or what direction we were traveling, but I did notice when the speed dropped and the asphalt gave way to washboard dirt. About ten minutes on the dirt road and I learned something new about my existence among the living dead: I could still get carsick.

When we finally stopped, the trunk popped open and Violet said, "They're not here yet. It'll be a while. You might as well get out."

She had called Lyle and Mr. Willow before we left the house. She hadn't sounded very convincing when she told them she had found me in Boulder and it would be best to "get it over with" before I escaped again, but it had worked. They were on their way from Wyoming.

I climbed out of the trunk and took a few gulping breaths. We were parked on a dirt road so narrow it barely deserved the name, a rutted and rocky lane that disappeared into the woods in both directions. Narrow pines and white-barked aspens gathered close on both sides, branches reaching overhead, and steep hills rose above the forest.

"Where are we?" I asked.

"Nobody knows this place," Violet said, which wasn't any kind of answer.

The forest smelled clean and rich: warm sun on pine trees, fresh dry air, a faint hint of vanilla. Green grass and white flowers grew from the blanket of fallen needles beneath the trees. Overhead a white contrail tracked across the cloudless sky. The afternoon was beautiful and green and calm. I listened but heard only the gentle trickle of a stream nearby. No cars, no voices.

No birds.

No insects.

No squirrels chattering and chasing on tree trunks.

We were alone.

It should have been peaceful, but the silence was too complete. Violet looked nauseated and pale. There was more in those woods than I could see.

"What's out here?" I asked.

Violet took a shaky breath. "I'll show you."

She slammed the trunk and started walking. The dirt road narrowed until it was no more than a trail cutting through thick underbrush. Leafy branches swayed as Violet passed; I stayed a few steps back to keep from being slapped. We crossed the creek by hopping from stone to stone. My foot slipped on the second step and plunged into the water. It was colder than I expected, and with the cold came a memory that didn't belong to me: Brian Kerr had splashed through this same creek, walked this trail in wet shoes, dodged these whiplike branches countless times.

Violet stopped, half turned toward me. "Are you okay?"

"Fine," I said. My shoe squelched. "Can I ask you something?"

"What is it?" she said reluctantly.

"Those kids that were at the church, on the playground. Did they come out of this more like you or more like Esme?"

Violet turned away. "We don't know yet."

"How can you not know?"

"It takes children a little while to . . ." She walked a few steps while she sought the right word. "Recover."

There was a dull ache in my throat. "What do you mean?"

"It can be frightening for them."

"Was it bad for you? When you were a kid?"

Violet only walked faster.

"Do you even care?" I demanded.

I couldn't stop thinking about the girl with the yellow baseball cap. Her body was somewhere in the darkness. Her hat had fallen off as she fought and tried to run, and Brian Kerr had picked it up. I remembered that much. I didn't remember why.

"Did you even ask what was happening to all the kids who came after you? The ones Mr. Willow doesn't like as much as you? The ones he doesn't want to keep as a pretty house pet?"

Violet spun around. Her hands were clenched in fists at her sides, and there were bright red spots of anger in her cheeks. "You don't know what you're talking about."

A knot of guilt tightened in my chest. That had been cruel. I shouldn't have said that. I should have remembered the little girl with the green eyes playing with her stuffed rabbit before her parents and their priest tied her to a bed.

"You were only eleven," I said. "He lied to you."

"Shut up."

I shut up.

We passed the remains of a small cabin, a brown square of roughhewn logs and the base of a toppled stone chimney. There was a fire ring in the center and faded beer cans tossed in the corners. Beyond the ruined cabin, the trail sloped upward and the ground turned to gravel beneath our feet. We were walking over a tailings pile that had washed down from an old mine.

There was a sturdy metal gate over the entrance to the mine, bolted into the stone and covered with signs. DANGER, KEEP OUT, warnings about the legal implications and minimum fines for trespassing, all rusted at the corners and pockmarked with bullet holes. The lock was new, but the gate was old and distorted, as though somebody had tried to pry their way in.

Or smash their way out.

Brian Kerr had stood before that iron gate with a key in his sweaty hands. He had missed the lock because he was shaking so much. He had been terrified of this place, the first time he came here and every time afterward, and his fear burned through me like a fever.

"What's in there?" Wrong question. I cleared my throat. "Who's in there?"

*She'll be so happy to see you.*

Violet only shook her head.

I sat on a fallen log below the tailings pile, picked up a handful of gravel, and let it fall though my fingers. It was warm on the surface, cooler a couple of inches down.

"Can I ask you something? Just one more question?"

"I don't think you should talk to me anymore," Violet said.

"Do you believe him? Do you really believe that being like this makes us evil? That it makes us something we have to fix?"

"Yes," she said without hesitation.

"Even the little kids? Even the people who have never hurt anyone?"

Violet stood facing the mine, her back to me, her arms crossed over her chest.

"You're not a child," she said, "and you have hurt people."

"I know I have. I'm not talking about me."

"You don't understand anything."

I was quiet a moment before answering, "Maybe not, but I think I'm beginning to."

In the still, hot afternoon, I could feel the mine breathing silently, inhaling and exhaling with a slow, slow rhythm.

# THIRTY-FIVE

THE SUN WAS sinking low and the shadows growing long when Violet broke the silence.

"They're coming."

She was looking down the trail. I didn't hear anything.

"You should get ready," she said.

I lay down and closed my eyes. Time to play dead. It wasn't funny even inside my head.

A few minutes passed before I heard Lyle's voice and Mr. Willow's answer. Footsteps crunched on the forest floor. I felt the cobweb of Mr. Willow's guilt, curled up and tucked away as it had been when we first met.

"Did it give you much trouble?" Mr. Willow asked. His voice was calm, disinterested. He might have been asking about a stray dog Violet caught digging in the garbage.

"No," Violet said. "She came to me willingly."

The gravel was rough and warm beneath my cheek. A shadow fell over me, but he wasn't close enough to touch. Not yet.

"And you're ready?"

"Yes." It was Lyle who answered. His voice broke.

Mr. Willow noticed. "I'm very proud of you, Lyle, but this is an important responsibility. I want you to be sure."

I wanted to see Lyle's face, but I couldn't risk opening my eyes. I didn't know what he knew about Violet's intentions. She claimed he would go along with our plan to stop Mr. Willow—to kill him—but I wasn't convinced. I could too easily remember how powerless I had been fighting against Lyle, how strong and fast he was, how much damage he had inflicted while obeying Mr. Willow's commands.

"I am sure," Lyle said. His voice was anything but steady. "I've been waiting for this for a long time, Pastor."

"I'm glad to hear that. I really am." Mr. Willow sounded like a kindergarten teacher praising a slow student's progress. "But you have to remember why we're here. We don't do this for ourselves. We do this for the creatures who need our help."

"Like my sister," said Lyle.

"Yes," said Mr. Willow, after a beat. "There will always be people like Esme who need our help."

"Even if they don't want it."

Damn it. Stop talking, Lyle. Just get Mr. Willow close enough for me to touch.

"It will be dark soon," Violet said.

But Lyle wouldn't let it go. "Even if they don't want it, right?"

"What is this about, Lyle?" Mr. Willow said. "You know what this creature is capable of. You saw what it did to our friend Brian. Why are you so full of doubt today?"

"He's not," Violet said too quickly.

"I'm not." I didn't have to see Lyle to know he was lying. "Give me the keys."

"This is not a task to be undertaken if you are feeling uncertain," Mr. Willow said.

"I'm not. I'll take her. Where are the keys?"

"I am more concerned about your well-being than I am about this creature," said Mr. Willow. He was almost convincing. "We don't have to do this tonight."

Violet said, "But she might escape again. We can't risk it. Edward. Can't you take her yourself?"

It wasn't going to work. Mr. Willow was keeping his distance. Maybe he didn't know what I was, but he knew what I could do. We had been stupid to think it would be so easy.

I opened my eyes. "I think we should do it tonight."

Mr. Willow turned to me in surprise. "Violet, what have you done?" he said.

"I'm sorry." There were tears in her eyes.

I stood, unsteady on the gravel. Mr. Willow took a step back. I was just far enough up the slope to be the same height as him.

"Brian was like a son to me," he said.

"I never thought I'd feel sorry for a mass murderer," I said, "but that almost makes me feel sorry for him."

I took one step toward him. Just one, then I lunged.

I wasn't fast enough. I caught the fabric of his shirt, but he spun away and I tripped, off-balance on the sliding gravel. Willow kicked out as I fell, caught me on the side of my face with his heel. Bright pain flashed through my jaw and his shirt slipped from my grasp.

It took me a second to recover, get back on my feet, but Lyle was faster. He sprang after Mr. Willow, who was already running. Branches and underbrush crashed as they raced away from the mine. The touch of Mr. Willow's shadow slipped away like a blanket sliding from a bed.

Violet grabbed my elbow to help me up. "We have to stop him!"

"Just let . . ." I blinked to clear my vision, worked my jaw slowly. It wasn't broken again. "Let Lyle catch him."

"We can't." Violet shook my arm; the jostling made my head hurt. "We can't. We can't, he'll never forgive himself. We *can't*. We have to stop him."

She gave up on me and ran after them. I followed, unsteady and dizzy. I caught up to Violet just as she reached the remains of the old cabin. She had stopped in the middle of the trail, but I didn't see why until I was standing beside her.

Mr. Willow and Lyle were circling each other slowly beside the old cabin. Lyle lashed out at Willow, and Willow stumbled backward, but he didn't fall.

"She didn't want it!" Lyle screamed. He sounded young and

scared, completely out of control. "She didn't want it! She didn't want it!"

He lashed out again, so fast the motion of his hands was a blur, and blood blossomed on Willow's shoulder. He made a choked sound of surprise and threw up his hands to ward off the second blow. Lyle slashed him across the palms, and Mr. Willow yelped in pain.

That's what it took to get Violet moving. She flung herself at Lyle and grabbed his arm. He shoved her aside, and she fell, but she was up again in an instant.

"Stop!" she cried. She reached for his arm again, and that time she held on. "Lyle, stop!"

It was enough to make him pause. There was blood dropping from his claws, staining his fingers red, but his face was pale, his expression terrified. He looked at Violet, looked at Willow, looked at Violet again. Waiting for her to say something else, to tell him what to do.

Before them Mr. Willow doubled over and gasped for breath. The arm of his shirt was shredded and soaked with blood. He straightened up, touched the wound gingerly, grimaced, and wiped the blood on his trousers. He glanced quickly at Lyle, at Violet hanging on his arm, at me keeping my distance from the fight. Searching for a way to escape.

Lyle shook off Violet's grip and strode forward. Mr. Willow stepped back, but he didn't run. He was surprisingly steady on his feet, considering how much those wounds had to hurt.

"Lyle," he said calmly, as though he were placating a wild

animal. He put both hands up. Lyle had torn gashes across his palms and blood trickled down his wrists. "You don't have to—"

"Give me the keys," Lyle said.

Willow blinked. "The—"

"The keys. Give me the keys or I'll rip your throat out."

Willow leaned over to rest his hands on his knees, but he wasn't gasping for breath now. He was laughing. It was a raw, rasping sound, and he shook his head from side to side as his shoulders trembled. He was laughing, and when he stood upright again, there were bloody handprints on both legs. He reached into his pocket and brought out a cluster of keys. His smile was hideous.

"What are you going to do?" Mr. Willow asked, the question wheezing painfully from his chest. "You want the keys? What are you going to do? *What are you going to do?*"

Lyle gaped at him and said nothing.

"Here they are." Willow shook the keys, like dangling a toy in front of a dog. "Do you want them? Is that what you want? Go to her. Is that what you want?"

"I want—" I expected Lyle to shout, to rage, but he choked on his words, and his answer was as small and hesitant as a child's. "I want Esme to be like she was."

Mr. Willow laughed again, that terrible gasping laugh. "And you think she'll give that to you?"

"Give me—"

"You think you can ask for that? For a favor? For *kindness*?" Mr. Willow's face was pale and damp with sweat. All of his calm, his careful poise, it had fled, and left in its place was a ragged, bleeding man on the edge of hysteria. Blood trickled down his arms in red rivulets. He threw the keys to Lyle, who made no move to catch them. "Take them. Go to her. Go to Mother. Ask her to give you your sister back. Ask her if it's not too late. If you're lucky, she'll let you limp out of there an empty shell who can't even remember how stupid and arrogant you've been. You and your wretched sister can—"

A roar ripped from Lyle's throat and echoed through the forest. He leaped at Mr. Willow, a growling blur of motion. Willow jumped backward, but he wasn't fast enough. Lyle struck him across the chest. The blow lifted Willow off his feet and flung him into the trunk of a tree. He hit with a dull crunch and slumped to the ground. Fresh blood bloomed from wounds on his chest and his abdomen.

Lyle was on him instantly, crouched over him like a wild animal, claws raised to strike.

*"Lyle!"*

Violet's scream was so loud and so piercing it ripped through the forest. It felt like nails driven into my eardrums. I clapped my hands over my ears, and for a second I heard nothing but the terrible echo of that cry.

On the ground Lyle held Mr. Willow down with one hand on the shoulder, but he was looking at Violet in shock. She had both hands clasped over her mouth, but it was too late. There were tears on her cheeks and her eyes were bright, bright green.

Mr. Willow's lips moved. I dropped my hands, touching the side of my face. My ears ached as much as when Brian Kerr had fired the shotgun near my head, but I didn't feel any blood.

"Go on," Willow said.

His voice was a wet gurgle, so weak and damp after Violet's deafening scream. He clutched at his torn midsection; there was blood and shredded skin between his fingers.

"Go to her," he said. He coughed and blood foamed on his lips. "Ask for her help. And your sister will be alone." Another cough.

Lyle flinched away from the pink spittle. "I'm going to kill you," he said. His voice shook. He pressed the claw of his thumb into the skin of Mr. Willow's throat.

"It doesn't—doesn't matter. Nothing matters except . . ." Willow shuddered and grasped at his guts with helpless hands. "You don't know how hungry she is."

"Lyle." Violet's voice was quiet now, a desperate whisper rather than a violent scream, but I felt it nonetheless. It was a ringing in my skull, a hornet's nest buzz of discomfort. Violet pressed her fingers to her lips, afraid to speak again. She shuddered with silent sobs. She looked at me desperately, and something cold and dark and hard curled in my gut. I knew what she wanted. After all, this was why she had brought me along.

"Lyle," I said.

I took a step forward, then another. I waited for him to look at me.

I said, "You don't have to do that."

"He promised he would help us," Lyle said.

"He lied."

"Esme—"

"Esme needs you to take care of her," I said.

One more step and I was at Mr. Willow's side. I looked down at Lyle. His bloody claws were trembling, his eyes damp. He had never killed anyone before. I hated my perverse curiosity about how it would feel if he did it right here, right in front of me, how the shadows would whip and grow.

"You should leave," I said.

"But he's—"

"He's not going to hurt anybody else. He's done. Go to your sister."

Lyle lurched to his feet. He started to say something, his mouth working like a fish's, but there was a gurgle in his throat and he gagged on his reply. He wheeled around and stumbled into the woods. I heard him retching and coughing in the gloom.

"Go with him," I said to Violet. "Take the cars and get out of here."

"What are you going to do?" Her words were nettles in my ears. The sun had set, and in the deepening twilight her eyes glowed watery green.

"You don't really care about that, do you?"

"Don't," Violet said, a sudden desperate plea. "Don't go into the mine. Come with us."

"You should get out of here."

"You could *die*."

"It was never your fault," I told her. I wanted her to understand. "Your brother was sick. That priest was in pain before you ever made a sound. You've never killed anybody. Mr. Willow lied to you.

He lied to you about everything."

"We won't leave—"

"You need to get out of here."

Violet stared at me for a long moment before she turned and retreated into the forest. Just once she looked back, her green eyes eerie and bright, then she was gone.

The ground beside Mr. Willow was damp with blood. I knelt beside him. Touched his shoulder, the undamaged one, and he flinched. He was gasping and coughing.

The blood from his mouth and nose was smeared down his face, his neck, staining the collar of his shirt. My jaw throbbed where he had kicked me. A dull ache spread down my throat and into my chest. It felt a little bit like hunger, a little bit like nausea.

"I don't have to do this," I said. "I can walk right by a murderer. I do it every day. You would not believe how many killers are out there. But I can ignore them. It's easy."

I put my hands on his face. One palm on each cheek, flat against his skin. He was cool to the touch.

"A witch told me it won't always be like that," I said. "Maybe she's right. Maybe someday I won't have a choice. But I do now."

It wasn't like the others. Drawing out the memory of his murders was like pulling something dead and rotten out of sticky swamp mud. There was something deformed about him. Whatever he was beneath his skin had curled into a slippery, wriggling, cowering thing long ago, and all that remained was the echo of other people's pain. I heard, briefly, a child crying. Not like their victims had cried in Brian Kerr's memories, manic and pleading, but the way a child weeps when he's hurt and scared and wants his mother to make it better.

Mr. Willow sucked in one last desperate breath. "You can't—"

It was easy, in that moment. He was already dying, and I was getting better at it. His eyes widened with raw terror, the fear a person can only feel once, and he was dead.

# ⋅⫴⋅ THIRTY-SIX ⋅⫴⋅

A DISORIENTING SHUDDER, an electric snap, and I was overcome by Mr. Willow's memories.

I was small and scared—

No. This was his memory, not mine.

Edward was small. He was supposed to be asleep. The night was alive with restless wind. It made him anxious and scared, but he couldn't go to his parents. Mommy might gather him into her arms and press a kiss to his forehead, but Father would send him back to bed.

The word *Father* echoed dully in Edward's memories. I knew the man by no other name.

He was awake, hugging his knees to his chest and wishing he had a toy animal to keep him company, and he was watching through the window. That's when he saw the strangers. They didn't come up to the door, not like neighbors visiting. They moved as shadows at the edge of the forest, lanky and thin. There were four or five of them.

Edward's throat was tight. Father didn't like strangers. They brought bad influences and dangerous ideas into the community.

As Edward watched, one of the shadows detached from the forest and loped across the grass.

It was coming to the house.

Edward slipped from the bed, padded across his room, and crept down the stairs. He was so afraid—how odd fear feels in memories, distant and cool, a collection of symptoms more than visceral instinct—but he was reassured when he heard his mother's voice. She was already awake, and she had opened the door to greet the stranger.

"It has to be tonight," she was saying. "I can't bear it anymore. Come in. It has to be tonight. You don't have to hurt anybody. Just give me time. It has to be tonight." The words were jumbled and smudged in the way of conversations recalled from long ago, the order uncertain even when the intent was clear. She was pleading for help, and the stranger was agreeing.

Edward peered around the corner into the kitchen. Mommy was at the back door, whispering to a tall man with a gaunt face and glittering black eyes. I felt the jolt twice: Edward's shocked fear and my own detached surprise. That wasn't a human face.

Edward gasped, and his mother spun around. She rushed to him and knelt before him. She had a bruise on her cheek and a black eye; she had been disrespectful to Father after supper. She told Edward to go back to bed and stay there, no matter what he heard, no matter how much noise there was. She made him promise. He nodded solemnly and she kissed his cheek.

"Go back to bed while Mommy talks to some of her old friends," she said. "I love you, munchkin."

Behind her the monster leaned in the doorway, a leer twisting its lips.

Edward climbed the steps, but he didn't go back to his room. He went instead to wake Father. The house was dark, then it was light, and at that point his memory became muddled and disjointed: Men shouted and windows shattered and long shadows cackled, and fires glowed like demon eyes in the night, and everything smelled of blood. Neighbors surged with shotguns. A door slammed; a woman screamed. And screamed, and screamed, and screamed. She pleaded with Edward, with Father, weeping behind the cellar door, she was sorry so sorry she didn't mean it she was sorry it was a mistake they made her they were evil things she had left them all behind she had Father and Edward and their home now she was so sorry so sorry please open the door please not the darkness so sorry please. Edward was small and sank to be smaller, curling himself into a ball, cheek pressed against the wood, and her voice grew fainter, and Father was a tall broad silhouette at the end of the hall, and he was saying, "She brought them into our home," and then she wasn't weeping anymore. She always went quiet, eventually, every time Father punished her, but this time was different. This time she was quiet for so long Father went down to the cellar, and when he came back he was carrying her limp body. Edward thought she was only sleeping until he touched her hand. Her skin was cold and there was blood on her fingers, splinters beneath her fingernails. A roaring filled his head until the house and the hallway and the cellar door were gone in a blinding flash of morning sunlight.

There was a thick fall of powdery fresh snow over the mountains. The trees bent and groaned beneath the weight. I felt the cold biting at my nose, the damp seep of slush through my socks. The glistening snow was so clean, so bright, Edward had to squint and cover his eyes, and my eyes stung too.

Father broke the trail ahead. He was pulling the wooden box on a sled. In some places he stopped and Edward helped him lift it over a ditch or a log. Edward's arms were tired and his fingers ached with cold, but he didn't dare complain.

He was taller now. The same height as his father. Years had passed between memories.

The mountains were quiet in the early morning. It had snowed all night, but the clouds were already breaking. They had left Boulder behind as the plows scraped the roads and the news of a snow day broke to the schoolchildren. Edward would have been excited too, last year, but he was fourteen now and Father didn't send him to school anymore. It would only teach him lies, Father said.

Before Father took him out of school, Edward would sit in class at the back of the room and look at his classmates bent over their assignments, at the teacher before the blackboard, and he would wonder what evil, rotting faces they hid beneath their masks of human skin. He kept lists of the ones he suspected to be monsters. He imagined catching them in unguarded moments, peeling back their disguises and revealing the poisonous blood and malformed bones beneath.

Father said it was more important than ever to keep to themselves. Edward didn't understand, and he knew the others in the congregation didn't either. They wanted to warn people about the monsters in the world. How to recognize them, how to fight them. But Father was in charge. They did as he instructed.

Or they had, before. They weren't so trusting of Father now. Edward had seen the way they glared and muttered as they scrubbed blood from the floor. They said Father never should have taken *her* out of her prison in the mountains. They said he should never have trusted the work of God and men to a monster.

They blamed Father for what had happened, even though Edward was the one who had opened the door and let Mother escape. She had been whispering at the door, pleading and whispering, and Edward had remembered another woman, another closed door, and he thought: It's so unfair that Father keeps her locked away like an animal in a darkened room. It's wrong. It's cruel. She deserves better.

She wasn't his real mother. Edward knew that. His real mother had died. She had betrayed their family and his father by inviting monsters into their home. Father rarely spoke of her, and when he did he only said women were weak and could not be trusted.

Most days Edward barely remembered her at all. He didn't

need her. He had Mother.

But now they had to shut Mother away in the darkness where Father had found her years ago, and it was Edward's fault. He had opened the door and two of their congregation had died before they caught her again.

"We were wrong to ever release her into the world," Father had said early that morning, as he steered the car along the snow-covered roads. "She is safer in the mountains. We will tell the others she has perished. They must never know. Promise me, Edward."

Edward had promised.

On their way into the mountains they had driven past sleeping little Gold Hill that looked like a broken toy town from the Old West. They would have a funeral soon. They would bury an empty box and tell the congregation Mother was gone. Only Edward and Father would know the truth.

The sled hit a hidden branch and there was a thump inside the box. Edward placed his hand on the wooden lid. She couldn't feel his touch through the wood, but perhaps she could sense him out here, with her, keeping her safe. Perhaps she knew how sorry he was.

When they reached the mine, Father took a ring of keys out of his pocket. The sun was already melting the snow on the tailings pile, seeping into naked patches of gold-brown gravel. In the morning sunlight, in his long dark coat and heavy snow boots, Father was tall and solemn and magnificent.

"This is not your fault," said Father. He unlocked the gate; it opened with a rusty groan. "You must understand that, Edward.

It is my fault. We are gifted with the safekeeping of this great and terrible thing, but I grew careless. She is more ancient than we can imagine, and more cunning, but she has only ever been a tool for us to use in our mission. We were foolish to forget that."

Father had never called her a *thing* before. The word made acid churn in Edward's stomach. She was great, and she was terrible, but she wasn't a *thing*. She was a gift, a wonder. There were monsters everywhere in the world. They needed her to cure them. Edward couldn't go back to hunting them like wild animals. There was a better way, and that better way was Mother.

Edward waited until his father's back was turned and picked a sharp stone the size of a baseball. It sat heavy in his pocket, a solid weight bumping his thigh.

"Help me carry it," Father said.

Edward ducked his head to hide his scowl. He heard the quiet *thump, thump* of hooves inside the box and the scratch of claws on wood. He would never forget. He would never make the same mistakes Father had made.

"Yes, Father," Edward said, and he followed.

# ⫸ THIRTY-SEVEN ⫷

NIGHT WAS COMING, and with it a cool whispering breeze.

I felt the rock in my hand and the impact of every blow. I remembered it as though I had killed the man myself only minutes ago. I remembered blood splattering over the wooden box that held the woman who was not a woman, the thing called Mother.

His real mother had died after that terrible night when he was a child. I didn't know her name. She had only wanted to escape. Get away from her abusive and controlling husband, get away from the trap they called *community* but probably meant *cult*. I only knew what Willow had known as a child, so I had no idea how she had known the monsters, what they were or where they came from, only that she had called them old friends. I didn't even know if she was one of them. She only wanted a chance to slip away in the night. A few fires, a few broken windows. A desperate woman's desperate plan. It might have worked if Edward hadn't warned his father.

I wished I knew her name. She deserved to have somebody remember her name.

I left Willow's body on the forest floor. Everything smelled like blood. I found the keys and the flashlight, and I walked back to the mine.

There were three keys on the ring, and only one was shiny and new. The padlock opened with a click. The gate was heavier than I expected. I braced my feet against the soft gravel, gripped the metal bars, and leaned. I pulled it open just enough for me to slip through.

"Okay," I said.

Cold, cold air flowed from within the mountain. The hair on the back of my neck rose. I had Violet's warnings, Brian Kerr's memories, Mr. Willow's promises. Unreliable data, all of it. None of it told me what I needed to know.

I pointed the flashlight into the mine and started walking.

There were no metal tracks along the ground, no wooden beams and frames holding back the mountain. All of my ideas about old western mines had come from *Looney Tunes* and Hollywood, and to my great surprise they hadn't quite gotten it right. The tunnel was rough, blasted and chipped away in sharp angles, supported in a few spots by rusted bolts in the rock.

Just inside the gate, where daylight still penetrated, there were cans and bottles, food wrappers, used condoms, cigarette butts. A charred fire ring stained the stone floor. That seemed like a terrible idea to me, but I guess if you thought getting drunk and having sex in an abandoned mine was a good idea, you probably thought lighting a campfire was too.

The tunnel sloped downward. After a hundred feet or so there was no light from outside and no trash either. The ceiling was so low in places I had to duck. Brian Kerr must have come out with a sore back and a headache every time. Water seeped through cracks and gathered in puddles. There was no way around so I splashed right through, then my shoes were slick, making every step treacherous.

The flashlight caught a glint of something shiny ahead in the darkness. I stared at it. I wasn't watching my step. I set my foot on a crooked cut of rock and lost my balance.

I fell, slammed my elbow into the wall so hard I yelped and dropped the flashlight. It rolled away and flickered and I thought, for one terrified moment, the filament would break and I would be left in the darkness. But it still glowed with sickly yellow light. I exhaled with relief.

I climbed to my feet, leaning on the wall for balance. I had twisted my ankle, but I could walk.

Uphill was out. Downhill was in. I hadn't passed any forks or junctions or obstacles. Even if the light died, I could find my way back. Uphill was out.

The flashlight had rolled to a stop against a pile of broken glass, the remains of a large jar. The shards lay like leaves on the tunnel floor, and the curve of the neck rested against the wall. That was the bright reflection that had caught my eye.

I retrieved the flashlight and hurried past.

The second gate was orange with rust, and its iron grid was dented and warped. This time there was no doubt about it: it had been struck from the inside. I knew the hinges would creak when I pushed it open; Brian Kerr had winced every time. One of his victims, an older woman, had laughed at him.

There was a large round rock just outside the gate that had obviously been set there for the purpose of holding it open. I rolled the rock into place and let the gate fall against it.

The scent of the mountain's exhalations grew stronger as I descended. At first I thought it was only stale air, but it was more than that. It was mold and damp and the dark corners of my grandmother's cellar where strange flat mushrooms used to grow. Meadow and I had dared each other to poke them with a broom handle, half expecting them to recoil. I kept walking and the smell grew worse, like a sick room closed up for too long, or the unwashed clothes and sour scent you catch when you pass a homeless man on the street and can barely see a human beneath the layers of jackets and sweatshirts as thick as plates of armor.

It was oldness, illness, and sweet fruit rotting in an alley Dumpster. I imagined a garbage dump down there in the darkness, carted in from the surface in wheelbarrows of breaking plastic bags, a thought so absurd laughter bubbled and nearly escaped before I caught it. I gagged and breathed through my mouth, but that only meant I could taste it on my tongue.

So I stopped breathing. It didn't cut out the smell entirely, but it helped.

I had no sense of how far I was walking. I didn't know how long I had been underground. The surface could have been a thousand yards or a thousand miles behind me.

Beyond the second gate I found the first skeleton.

It wasn't a complete skeleton anymore. It was a pile of bones strewn along the tunnel, tangled in scraps of cloth that had once been clothes. Skull, ribs, pelvis, clavicle, the dirty white knobs of a scattered spine. I didn't recognize the clothes. Whoever it had been, they hadn't earned a permanent place in Brian Kerr's memories.

The rotten stench grew stronger with every step. I was looking forward, not down, and I kicked the second skull before I saw it. It skittered down the tunnel like a soccer ball, knocking from side to side, until it stopped against the third skeleton, which wasn't so much a skeleton as a mummified corpse. Its desiccated, blackened flesh pulled away from its teeth in a comical grin. Its arms were reaching uphill, toward me, but somebody had carelessly knocked one of its hands free. It still wore a watch on one wrist. Plastic, pink. There was a darker smear on the dark stone around the body. It didn't look like a girl anymore. It didn't look like anything except a corpse.

I stopped counting after that.

I could hear them in the incomplete memories I had taken from Brian Kerr, but I couldn't match the screams and pleas to the withered corpses and loose bones and dried blood. There was no sound except my footsteps and my own thudding heart, but my mind was a cacophony of fear and anger. A man screamed over and over again that he would do anything, anything, please, anything. A child cried for her father. A young woman shouted a stream of creative expletives until her voice gave out. Hands scrabbled on stone, blood flowed and pooled, and one by one they died.

The third gate looked much like the second: iron, rusted, solid but bent outward. It had been rammed repeatedly, with great force, from the inside. The stench was so strong it made my eyes water and my stomach turn.

There was no body slumped against the gate. I could see Father's corpse so clearly in Mr. Willow's memory I was momentarily confused to find it gone, even though it had been more than forty years. The man had collapsed in an ungainly heap and Edward, fourteen years old with blood on his hands, had continued on his own, dragging the box with the creature inside. I had no memory of what he had done with his father's body.

Beyond the gate there was another jar. This one was unbroken and upright, and after it, marching into the darkness, clusters of them set up against the walls of the tunnel. They were stacked three or four high in places, in squat little pyramids, glass jars of all shapes and sizes. Nothing in Brian Kerr's or Mr. Willow's memories told me how the jars had gotten there, and that unsettled me as much as the relentless darkness.

I found the third key on the ring and slid it into the lock.

A soft, wet noise filled the mine, distant and quiet.

She was laughing.

# ᛨ THIRTY-EIGHT ᛨ

SHE KNEW I WAS coming, and she was laughing.

As soon as I recognized the sound for what it was, there was nothing else in my universe. No surface. No gates. No peaceful forest of vanilla-scented trees beneath a clear night sky. The world shrunk down to that throat of stone, the yellow light before me and oppressive darkness at my back, old corpses and old blood, and the mocking laughter. I could lie down at the gate and let that cruel, distant laughter wrap around me, fill me, suffocate me, and I wouldn't even fight it.

This must be what they feel like when I kill them.

The thought was like a slap to the face, and the flash of anger cleared my mind.

I wasn't a screaming captive being dragged into the darkness. I wasn't pleading and begging. If that's what she expected, she was going to be disappointed. I was here to meet her, one monster to another.

The laughter faded, but I could feel it on the cusp of bursting forward again. My hands were sweaty; the broken skin stung where I had scraped my palms. Every muscle in my body was tense, every nerve sparking. I turned the key and stepped through the gate, made sure I could get out again before letting it swing closed. I kept the key ring out and the last key between my fingers, like they teach you to do in parking lots late at night.

The flashlight barely penetrated beyond the gate. I approached the stack of jars against the wall, choosing each step with care. The stone was rougher here, the walls more jagged, the floor treacherous with loose sand and gravel. It looked as though something had scooped great gouges out of the rock. I pressed the toe of my shoe into one depression, studied the parallel lines.

Almost like claw marks, I thought, with hollow disbelief.

I lifted my hand to measure the span of one trench on the wall. Small hands, whoever wielded those claws, no bigger than mine. The grooves were stained dark in places. I touched the stone lightly, curled my fingers away. If it was blood, it was long dry.

I inched forward, slowly passed the first stack of jars. Six large mason jars, the kind Melanie's mother used for making pickles and preserves every fall, each sealed with a rusted metal lid. I pointed the flashlight down the tunnel, and something in the darkness rasped and shifted.

I froze. Took a step to the side, away from the jars.

There was a flutter of motion at the corner of my eye.

It was the sand. My heart jumped, beating wildly without my permission. The sand in the jars was moving, rasping and scraping behind the glass.

But when I looked at it directly, it settled with a whisper.

I turned my head, forced myself to look down the tunnel. The sand moved in a nervous dance at the edge of my vision. When I stared at it, it was still again.

A minute or two passed before I could make myself move forward.

The hiss of shifting sand followed me. The jars were all shapes and sizes, some new enough to have labels still clinging to them, others so old the glass was tinted green. I counted at first, numbers ticking nervously through my mind, but gave up when I got to fifty.

I squeezed myself gingerly through a gap between two precarious stacks, and the tunnel opened up. The flashlight didn't reach very far, but I could see the walls had been scraped out in odd alcoves and hollows, the floor so uneven I had trouble choosing my steps. The stone took on a lumpy, diseased look, as though the mountain's insides had erupted into boils and wounds, giving it a queasy fun house feeling. Every motion of the light caught another glint of glass, another shy shiver of sand, another jagged gap of rock.

I closed my eyes to steady myself, but the rustling of sand rose to an unbearable roar, so I snapped them open again. And I moved forward.

This is where they had found her.

The knowledge rose in a memory stolen from Edward Willow. His father had explained it to him as they had carried the wooden box between the first gate and the second. The elder Mr. Willow had come here with fellow hunters—cruel and violent men, he told his son, not to be trusted—because they had heard of a terrible creature hidden away in the mountain. She had been imprisoned here for nearly a hundred years, but she was unfathomably ancient, unlike any monster they had encountered before. The elder Mr. Willow and the others had come to kill her. She would make a magnificent prize for their collection, so unique and so vile, a foul withered head to hang in a place of honor.

When I glanced back I couldn't see the gate anymore. I turned and the flashlight caught a bright glittering spot in the darkness, but lost it again.

A trophy, that was what they wanted. The elder Mr. Willow had wanted it too. He had wanted it until they found her cavern, and she spoke to him, and she told him there was a better way.

The cavern bristled with the susurrus of restless sand, and something else, a gentle clink like a wind chime. Metal on glass.

She had said to him: There is so much blood on your hands already, and still there are families in danger as yours once was, and still there are children whose mothers will betray them. There is a better way. That was why he took her out of the mine; he brought her back when he realized he could never control her. That brief taste of freedom had only made her angrier.

I shook my head to clear it. Willow's memories were distracting and disjointed, a jigsaw of childish guilt and teenage rage, two dead parents and the monster who had taken their place.

The light caught a golden glint again.

A single yellow eye shone in the darkness.

I stopped. My shoe scuffed on stone. I drew in a long, shaky breath, the first I had taken in several minutes. My mouth was dry.

"Hi," I said.

Her laughter was like thunder, rolling and strong. I felt it in the air, in my teeth, in the ripples of my sluggish blood.

"Most of them don't make it this far down," she said.

The sand in the jars fell still when she spoke. I was expecting an animal growl, ancient, wild, as wretched as the stench that filled the mine. But her voice was human. Ugly, phlegmatic, chain-smoker rough, but human. I had no trouble understanding her. She turned, and there were two yellow eyes before me, round and wide with rectangular black pupils.

Those yellow eyes, and the hump of a single shoulder, that was all I could see of her. I couldn't see how large she was. Couldn't see her feet, her hands, her mouth. She was cloaked in the shadows and I was very, very small.

"Where's my boy?" she said.

"He couldn't make it," I said. Unconscious in a hospital bed, never to wake again. Limp and dead on the forest floor. I didn't know if she was asking about Brian Kerr or Mr. Willow. I didn't want to tell her what I had done.

"Come closer. Let me look at you."

"I'm fine right here."

She coughed and spat. "I want to see you. You are a pretty thing."

She moved with lurching, unsteady steps, vanishing behind a stack of jars and reappearing on the other side, and there I could see more of her body. Her back was so bent her torso was nearly parallel to the floor. She wore filthy rags and a blanket stiff with grime. Gray hair hung in a dirty mat around her face. There was a sound like a sniff, the smacking of lips, but her face was hidden by a fold of cloth. She stepped behind a tower of jars again.

"Yes," she said, her voice floating in the darkness. "I have not seen such a pretty thing in a very long time."

I watched the spot where I had last seen her, but I couldn't hear her footsteps. There was more space down the tunnel than I had realized. I couldn't see how deep the cavern went.

"But you have before?" I said. "You've seen something like me?"

"Oh, yes," she said, and she laughed again, loud and hearty, ringing through the cavern. "Oh, yes, my dear. Did you think you were the only one? Did you think you were so very alone?"

Yes, I thought, but I kept my mouth closed. The sand trembled. I took a step back, bumped my elbow into a precarious stack of jam jars sealed with wax.

"Oh, oh, my dear, it must be so very frightening." Her voice was as rough as a fall of rocks, but there was a softness to it, a gentleness that crept under my skin and soothed my jittery nerves. She wasn't a wild animal. She wasn't a ravenous monster raging out of control with her own anger and spite. She was intelligent, and calm, and she knew about me.

"And you are so young. You have been alive barely a heartbeat."

A little bit longer than that, by our standards, but I couldn't say it out loud. The way she said *so young* made me feel like I was a child again, so small I had to reach up to grab my mother's hand in the grocery store, when comfort had been looking up from the bewildering maze of legs and carts and shelves to see her smile and her eyes, to hear her say my name and tug me along. I swallowed down the sting at the back of my throat.

"By their standards," she corrected gently. "But too short even by that measure. You are far too young to have suffered so cruel a fate."

My vision blurred and I raised my hand, still gripping the keys, to scrub away tears before they fell. In her voice was all the pity I had been pretending wasn't eating me from the inside, the childish wail of unfairness gathering in my chest like a summer storm.

"And why shouldn't you rage? Why should you choke down this anger you so deserve?"

She was moving again, and that time I did hear the soft *tap-tap* of her footsteps, uneven, every step a slow pause and lurch, pause and lurch. She moved with a limp so pronounced it twisted her entire body. She stepped around a stack of jars, turning to fit through the narrow gap. I heard a long scrape—a rasp that set my teeth on edge—metal grinding on rock with slow, slow patience.

"You are too brief and too small to suffer so," she said.

When she turned again, she was holding a large jar under one arm. With the other hand she tipped a handful of sand into it. Stray grains fell from the wall behind her, cascading softly from thin parallel scrapes in the wall. Her fingers—claws—clinked on the jar's mouth. They were crooked and mismatched, oddly twisted, not smooth like Lyle's.

"How it must hurt, my dear, my poor dear."

Another step closer to the light and I had a better view of her hand. Her claws didn't look like claws because they weren't, not in the usual sense. The long blade twisting from her thumb was fashioned from a piece of rusted metal, and curving from her forefinger around the top of the jar was a yellow bone sharpened to a point.

"Oh my dear, my dear," she said, the words like a chant. "Tell me how it hurts."

I tore my gaze from her makeshift claws. "It doesn't," I said, a ragged whisper.

And how I wanted it to be true, but in my mind a different answer screamed: Yes, yes, it hurts. I hate it. I hate this alien body that bleeds and breathes only when I make it. I hate that everything I had before is now out of my reach, however little I had collected in seventeen short years of an unremarkable life.

"You are not alone, dear child, my dear. You do not have to feel this pain alone."

The scream in my head became the screams of a dozen strangers led into darkness and trapped behind iron gates, then the strangers' voices faded and there was only the scream of one girl surprised on a quiet street, face distorted in a windshield, streetlamp like a full moon overhead.

"You know there is a way to make it better." She spoke with

infinite patience, the kind of patience that came from being mother to a thousand recalcitrant children, not one of whom wanted to go to bed on time.

"I don't," I said.

"My child," she said, "you do. Mother knows you do."

There was her laughter again, gentle and fond. The sand quivered around me, dizzying and unsteady, the entire cavern coming to life. I squeezed my eyes shut. She did know. She knew what I needed to hear, knew what I had come to learn. She knew what I wanted, and she was laughing because it was such a simple thing, such a simple little thing for something so ancient and as fearsome as her. I only had to ask, and she would laugh again, and I would laugh with her, and everything would be better.

When I opened my eyes, I couldn't see her. My heart thumped— had it been still until that moment? I was losing track of my own pulse, losing the feel of blood in my veins. Every heartbeat, conscious or not, trembled in my throat and through my skin to sink into the stone. I couldn't see her. Not her eyes, not the crooked hump of her shoulder, not her mismatched claws. The cavern was dark but not very wide. She couldn't have slipped away.

I held my breath and listened. There was no *tap-tap* of feet— shoes? Bare feet wouldn't make that sound. It was too solid, a click.

"I don't know what I can do about it," I said again. "That's why I came to you."

I aimed the flashlight into the shadows, looked forward and back. Took a couple of steps farther into the mine and stopped. With every movement I was too aware of the tight space growing tighter, as though the jars were shuffling behind me to close off my escape.

"I really don't," I said. I cleared my throat, hoped my voice sounded steadier than I felt. "Know anything. I don't know anything."

"Oh, my child," she said.

I spun around. The words slithered over my shoulder, teased the cup of my ear, but she wasn't there. There were only the jars full of sand, shuddering at the corners of my eyes.

"How lonely it must be," she said.

Her voice bounced and carried unpredictably. I turned again— my back to the gate now. I had to remember that, remember where the gate was. Down was in. Up was out.

"And if it is lonely now, how lonely it will be as years and years and years go by."

"We're supposed to be talking about me," I said, "not you."

Her laughter rippled through the sand. The more I cast the light around, looking for her, the more confused I became, every scraped alcove, every stack of jars taking the shape of a stooped old woman.

"Yes," she said. "It was a human thing not too long ago, was it not? I can smell its blood. I can taste its breath. Mother knows. It cannot lie to Mother."

A scrape, a scattering fall of sand on glass. Filling the jar. I edged forward and searched along the walls, in the dark spaces behind the stacks and piles. She had to be hiding somewhere.

I stepped sideways between the jars, back toward the gate. I had come too far in. I shouldn't have put that much space between myself and the way out. That was stupid. Careless. I could hear the dying screams of Brian Kerr's victims in my memories. I had brought them in here with me, but I was so used to the memories of strangers dying I had forgotten to listen.

"Yes," I said. "I was human not that long ago."

"I know, little lamb. Mother knows."

Her breath was hot and rancid on the back of my neck.

I turned slowly, slowly, my heart jumping uncontrollably. I hadn't heard her approach. I hadn't see any flicker of motion from the corner of my eyes, hadn't heard the *tap-tap* of her feet on the floor. But she was there, barely two feet away, stinking and crooked and grinning. She had a fat round jar under one arm, and from the other hand she was dribbling a trickle of sand through its mouth. Her fingers were long and filthy, stained dark deep in the creases, each one ending in a knot of scar tissue and a fashioned claw. Twists of metal, sharpened bones, curving dirty and bloody from her fingertips. Fresh red blood welled from one knuckle.

"Did you bring me a gift?" she asked.

I stepped back, kicked a jar behind me. It rocked but didn't fall. "What kind of gift?"

"Gifts of stupid girls who ask questions they already know the answers to," she said.

"Yeah, that was kind of a stupid question." My voice was shaking; I pretended not to notice. "But I have another one that's not as stupid."

"Look at you," she said, laughing. How could I have thought she sounded like my mother? There was no kindness in her voice, no gentleness. "The dead thing with all the questions. Three keys and three locks and it thinks it can ask me questions."

She stepped closer.

"Go on, then," she said. "I like a present that talks with words."

I spoke quickly, before I could change my mind, "Why do you let some of them go? The ones who don't die or go insane. You let them walk away. Why?"

"Why?" She was laughing again. "Why? Why? It wants to know why?"

"Yes. I want to know why."

The sand in the jars hissed around me. I flinched one way, then the other, but there was no space for me to shrink away. When I stepped back, she stepped forward. I didn't want her near me. I didn't want her close enough to touch. Her feet, hidden behind her cloak of rags, clicked on the stone. There was something wrong with her legs.

"That is not what it wants. Nobody comes to Mother to ask questions."

The jars quieted.

I stepped back, and again. I couldn't remember which way was out. I didn't know if I was moving uphill or down. My foot crunched on a broken jar. She caught me with those yellow eyes, and I stopped.

"Ask me what it wants, dead thing. Even a dead thing can ask what it wants."

I swallowed.

"Oh, my dear, dearie dear," she said. "Let Mother take its pain away. You know what it will become if it keeps it for itself, greedy little creature."

I shook my head. I couldn't make myself speak.

"It knows, it does. I can taste its fear. I can taste how much it *wants*. All the wicked, wicked things in the world and now it can see them. Now it can hunt them. Stalk them through the night and they won't even know it's there. They won't ever see the nasty black thing behind the pretty child's mask until they're already dying. I can taste how much it wants that."

"No," I said, and I was shaking my head, and I was remembering what I had seen in Ingrid's house, that vision of myself powerful and strong, moving over the landscape like a shade that left no trace except the bodies of fallen killers. "No, stop, that's not what—"

"I can taste how scared it is. Little child, what a wretched thing you will become."

She was right in front of me. Her mouth was a red gash.

"I know it is frightened. Mother can help. Ask me if I can take it away. Ask me if I can carve it out like a festering wound. They told it, wretched dead thing, go to Mother, she has an appetite like maggots, go to her in the darkness and she will take away the putrid rot, the stink it carries. Mother will gnaw and gnaw and gnaw until it's gone. She'll take your gift and keep it here in her pretty glass cages."

All around us the sand shivered.

"Go on. Go on, ask. Ask me if I can reach inside and tear out all its ugly worms and keep them here with me. Ask me if the dead thing can be alive again."

I couldn't speak. I wasn't breathing. My heart wasn't beating. I was shaking so much the flashlight beam danced over the tunnel, glinting off the smooth curved jars, but her yellow eyes with their angular black pupils never wavered.

*"Ask me!"* she roared.

The walls shook and the trapped sand quivered. My heart jump-started with a painful kick. One small jar, still carrying a label for baby food, slipped from a stack. It fell to the floor and shattered. The sand snaked away in twisting, spidery lines.

When the sand was still and the ringing in my ears faded, I whispered, "Can you?"

She laughed again, but quietly, an amused chuckle so much worse than her loud, wild laughter. Limping and swaying, she shuffled a few steps, gathering up her blanket with one hand. Beneath the folds of fabric, her legs were covered with coarse black hair and they bent the wrong way and the feet at the end weren't feet at all, but hooves.

"Sweet dead thing. Give me your rotten little heart. It's a *good* gift. You won't miss it a bit."

She reached out to me and I mirrored the motion, my hand moving without my permission, drawn up as though lifted by a puppet string. My fingers were still curled into a fist around the keys. The long bone claw of her forefinger traced over the inside of my forearm, its tendons and veins, and her twisted metal thumbnail pressed into the bone of my wrist. She broke the skin and blood welled.

I jerked my hand away, but she didn't let me go. My arm hit a jar; it toppled to the side, knocked into another. They both fell and shattered. The sand hissed and crawled away from the broken glass, rolling like worms toward her split black hooves.

Not worms.

Fingers.

The sand gathered into the shape of a hand, twisting and reaching, fingers curling up from the stone. Lumps rose through the hand and there was the shape of a nose, the curve of a jaw. Mouths opening in silent screams. Blank eyes, crumbling jaws, creeping along the floor, pressing against the glass.

I tugged my hand again. Her thumb and forefinger pressed deeper into my wrist. The pain had been distant before, a mild sting, subdued and softened by the beseeching tone of her voice.

But when I tried to break free it surged to the surface in a flash of crippling agony. My entire arm was on fire, every muscle and tendon spasming in pain. I cried out and doubled over, but still she didn't let go. Blood flowed over my fingers and dripped to the floor. Where it struck the ground, the creeping sand recoiled and scattered.

I hit her wrist with the flashlight, tried to break her grip, but she only laughed.

"Give it to me to keep," she said, still laughing, still laughing. "It will be so happy here."

The pain spread up my arm, a white-hot cascade, and I could feel it in my skin, in my blood. Pure mindless instinct had me sucking in quick, painful breaths, and my heart was beating wildly, out of my control. Every jolt of my pulse drew the gritty-hot press of her claws deeper into my body, deeper, deeper, until her hand was part of my wrist, my arm was her arm, my heartbeat and her laughter, her hunger and the cold, cold fear coiled deep in my gut, all the same, twinning together in an unbreakable tangle, and it hurt it hurt it hurt, but it would hurt worse to stop her, I couldn't stop her I should just let her take it take me take me apart lock the dark monstrous heart of me away it was better that way she would keep it safe it was a *good* gift—

The flashlight fell to the floor. Flickered, blinked, but it didn't go out. I hadn't felt it slip from my fingers, but I heard the clatter, and I saw the yellow light momentarily fail, and in that brief space between noise and darkness her voice faded from my mind, and the cries and pleas of all her victims, captured for me in Brian's memories, returned. She had made me forget them, but she couldn't silence them completely.

"My dear, my dear," she said. She wasn't laughing anymore. "Stay with Mother."

I grabbed the nearest jar and swung it at her face with all my strength.

She shouted in surprise, and I grabbed another, and another, flung them at her head as quickly as I could. The first hit with a dull *thunk*. The second cracked, and sand slithered from the break. The third shattered, an explosion of shards slicing into my skin, and she bellowed with outrage. Her grip on my wrist loosened, and I flung another jar at her, this one aimed at her arm.

She let go and I fell backward. I crawled after the flashlight and scrambled to my feet, turned as she was grasping at my shoulder, my upper arm, slicing through my shirt and my skin. I dove away from her, knocking jars down behind me, one after another. They crashed across the narrow tunnel, a racket of breaking glass and rasping sand. Her breathless laughter and the galloping clatter of hooves followed.

I didn't remember the keys clenched in my fist until I saw the iron gate ahead. I pushed through the gate and swung it shut, but I wasn't fast enough.

Her hand closed around my upper arm and she pulled me back, yanking my shoulder and head into the gate. The blow stunned me for a moment and I sagged, my head spinning, my legs weak. Her fingers were cold, her touch like ice, like wind off the lake on a winter day, like the emptiness of space. I leaned into the iron bars and swung at her arm with the flashlight, hit her wrist with a loud crack of plastic on bone.

She shrieked with laughter and slammed into the gate. Metal groaned, bolts ground against rock, and gravel showered around us. She was holding my arm and I couldn't pull free, so I grasped at her claws with my fingers. The blades cut into my hand and her laughter was a cold mist, a falling night, a shadow.

A suffocating, overpowering shadow. She had killed so many people.

I let go of her claws and grabbed her wrist. Her face was inches from mine, her yellow eyes with those long black slits for pupils, her filthy skin, her dark hair matted with dirt and mud and blood and straw. Her smile was wide and wet and red. She grinned with all of her teeth and shook me, hard, lifting my feet a few inches from the ground and knocking me against the gate. But I didn't let go. I held on, my bloody fingers on her clammy skin, and I pulled.

I couldn't finish it, couldn't do to her as I had done to the others. She was too strong. It was like trying to hold the ocean in the path of a tsunami. But I didn't need her to snap apart at my touch. I only needed to surprise her.

Her laughter broke off with a gasp. I dropped to the ground, twisted, and lunged away. The flesh of my upper arm tore free of her claws.

She rammed into the gate again, bellowing with fury, the agonized creak of metal and grind of rock lost under the strength of her cry. It filled the tunnel and made the mountain tremble, but I was already running. I jumped over the corpses, kicked through the skeletons, ran and ran and ran and didn't look back.

# ᐁ THIRTY-NINE ᐁ

AT THE SECOND gateway I shoved the rock out of place, closed the gate, and locked it. My hands were shaking so badly it took me three tries before I got the right key. She was still shrieking. Sometimes it sounded like laughter, sometimes like screams, sometimes so loud it felt as though she were right behind me. I forced myself to look back.

There was nothing in the tunnel behind me. No yellow eyes, no cloven hooves, no stoop-backed bundle of rags.

But I didn't slow down. I kept running.

I didn't know I was near the surface until the final gate was in front of me. I inhaled the clean scent of the forest, and it was the best thing I had ever smelled. I stumbled through the gate and shouldered it closed, took the padlock from my pocket and snapped it into place. It was such a little thing, a tiny metal lock, but I didn't have anything else. I pulled on the gate. It didn't budge.

I rested my forehead against the cold iron and listened.

I couldn't hear her anymore. I didn't remember when her screams had stopped, or if they had only faded with distance.

Three gates and three locks. I didn't know if it was enough.

I shone the flashlight into the tunnel, almost certain I would see her yellow eyes. But there was nothing. There was only darkness.

I kept the flashlight on as I made my way down the trail. Past the old cabin, past Mr. Willow's body. I could barely look at him. He was a blink of khaki trousers and blood. My shoes kicked noisily through the underbrush and fallen needles. I stopped every few steps to listen to the babbling creek and the wind, to hold my breath and still my heart and wait.

I waited to hear a laugh, a wet-rough cackle, bending iron, breaking glass. The whisper of sand on a stone floor. Sand that had once been a person, or part of one, whatever parts Mother decided to keep for herself.

The night was quiet. I walked faster. The wounds on my wrist and arm were closing; my fingers stung, but the blood was drying. They were far from the worst injuries I had received recently. I probably wouldn't even have scars.

A mile or so from the mine, the old dirt road intersected another. There was a wooden fence and a metal farm gate. I climbed over and looked at the crooked PRIVATE PROPERTY sign before turning away.

I had no idea which way to go, so I chose uphill, toward the starlight and the clear open sky. In the car it had felt like we had driven forever into the heart of the mountains, but when I reached the top of the ridge, the city lights were close, bright and enticing just over the hills.

I put Lyle's flashlight away and took Zeke's phone from my backpack. Two rutted, unpaved roads met on that ridge. There were no houses nearby, no passing cars.

But I did get a cell signal. I found the number for *J* and hit Send.

It rang a few times, then there was a sleepy, "What?"

I winced. "I, uh, sorry. Jake? This is Breezy, um, from yesterday. Zeke gave me his phone and told me—"

"What the hell?"

"I'm sorry, I—"

Something rustled on the other end, following by a soft thump and "Wake up, asshole," and a muffled "Ow."

"It's the middle of the night," Zeke said. He didn't sound like he had been asleep.

"It's—really?" I looked at the phone screen. 3:46. It had been twilight when I went into the mine. "I didn't—sorry. I didn't realize."

"What do you want? Are you okay?"

"Yeah," I said, my voice shaky. "I'm fine. I'm just kind of stranded? I was wondering if you could give me a ride. Um, again. I mean, yeah, again. But I'm not all the way in Wyoming this time,

and I swear I'm not going to try to blackmail you or anything, and—
and there's something in it for you, at least, if you want, but I don't
know how you usually—"

"What— Hey, stop. What are you talking about?"

"Dinner for a week," I said.

Zeke was quiet for a moment. "Where are you?"

"Oh. I have no idea. I was in the trunk when we drove up here."

"The trunk?"

"Not my idea. Wait a sec." I had to cross the road to get a closer
look at the signs. One was a name, the other a county road number. "They're both dirt roads. There's nothing around here. But we
didn't drive very far from Boulder, I don't think."

Zeke said something away from the phone, then came back and
said, "Yeah, whatever, we can find it. Are you sure you're okay?"

"Yeah. Definitely. Fine." Saying it three times absolutely made
it more convincing.

"Is there anybody else there?"

"No. Just me."

"Okay. We'll be there."

I tried to say, "Thank you," but he had already hung up.

I put the phone in my pocket and sat down on my skateboard,
hugged my legs to my chest. Even with the glow of the city lights,
the sky was filled with stars. The Milky Way was a bright smear
overhead. I tilted my head to the side to look at it edge on, imagined
myself floating in space outside the galaxy, seeing it as a massive,
elegant spiral, and our sun as an insignificant speck. I spotted a
satellite, gnat tiny and swift, and watched it until it disappeared

behind the trees. Too slow to be the ISS. It was farther away, lifeless, empty.

The wind rose. I shivered and rubbed my arms.

Three gates. Three locks. It had kept her in for decades. She couldn't get out.

I reminded myself to breathe.

# ⊪ FORTY ⊪

I STOOD WHEN I saw headlights and heard the growl of the truck's engine. Jake was driving. Zeke slid over to let me in the passenger side. They didn't ask me anything except, "Are you hurt?" and "How far?" and I didn't offer anything more than "Not very."

Jake stopped the truck in front of the gate. I jumped out to open it, but when I had my hand on the latch, metal cold beneath my fingers, I couldn't do it.

The headlights cast long, distorted shadows over the narrow dirt road. Me, impossibly tall, and the horizontal bars of the gate like a silhouetted prison. The tunnel of trees stretched into the forest in shades of washed-out yellows and greens. Somehow that artificial light was worse than darkness would have been.

"Breezy?"

Zeke got out of the truck behind me, and a second later Jake did too.

"What is it?" Jake said.

The last thing I wanted to do was follow that road again.

I was shaking my head before I realized what I was doing. "I can't. I can't go back there."

Even where I stood, in the light, behind the false security of a green farm gate, it was too close to the mine. Too close to her.

"We should leave," I said. But I couldn't turn around. That would mean putting my back to the forest and the road. My hand was still on the gate; I flicked the latch open and closed, open and closed. "We shouldn't be here. We need to go."

"Okay," Jake said gently. He put his hand over mine, didn't even flinch at the blood caking my fingers, and stopped the soft metal click of the latch. "Can you tell me what's up there?"

I felt a burst of annoyance that he was talking to me like that, like I was a little girl afraid of the gaping black space beneath her bed. But it steadied me too. It was better to be annoyed than addled with fear.

"I'm not going back up there," I said. I tried to sound stubborn, not terrified. He wasn't fooled. "You want your dinner, go get it yourself."

"Okay. Zeke can stay here with you. Tell me how to get there."

"It's past the end of the road. There's a trail, it goes over a creek, and this old cabin—" I pulled my hand away and turned to face

Jake. "You can't go past the old cabin. Even if— He's there, by the old cabin. The body." I didn't want to say his name out loud. He wasn't a person anymore. There wasn't anything left of him except the memories I had stolen. "But you can't go past that point. You *can't*. For any reason. Don't go to the end of the trail."

"What's at the end of the trail?" Jake asked. He wasn't afraid. Worried, yes, but mostly curious.

"Something you're not going to see, because you're not going that far," I said.

Jake hesitated, then shrugged. "Fine. I won't."

"Promise me."

At that he started to look more concerned. "All right. I promise."

It wasn't enough. "Promise him," I said, pointing at Zeke. "Promise him you won't go past the old cabin."

Jake said, "Okay. I swear to both of you that I won't go past the cabin. I'll be back in a few minutes."

I opened the gate for him, and he drove away. The red taillights disappeared into the forest.

"You are completely freaking out," Zeke said.

"I am not."

"Yes, you are. What's down there?"

"Will he be able to find it?" I asked. *It*, because that was easier than *him*. "I didn't give him very good directions. Does he even have a flashlight?"

Zeke's answer was wry. "We're not good at much of anything, but finding dead bodies in the dark is one thing we can do."

"Oh. Right. Makes sense." I inhaled slowly, tried to get control of my breathing, tried to slow my heart rate. It wasn't working. "Will he do what he said? Will he— I mean, he won't get curious or something? Keep going?"

"No, he'll come right back," Zeke said. "Maybe if he were alone he'd do something stupid, but not with us waiting for him."

"You're sure?"

"I wouldn't have let him go if I wasn't."

"Okay. That's good. Okay."

I felt exposed and unsteady standing there in the middle of the road. My knees felt shaky, my feet were sore, my head aching. The torn skin of my fingers stung with sweat and dirt. I was tired. I was so damn tired. I sat on the top rail of the fence and let my shoulders slump.

Zeke said, "What happened, anyway? How did you get up here?"

"Violet," I said. "The girl I was looking for. I found her. She was . . . she was having doubts about her life choices. She wanted me to do something for her."

"What do you mean?"

I didn't want to go through the whole afternoon. "It's a long story."

Zeke came over to sit beside me on the fence. "Why would you help her?"

"It's not like she was going to kill me."

"Someday you're going to get tired of saying that."

"I'm already tired of it. I've only been a reanimated corpse for a few weeks and I've already used up all my zombie jokes." I rubbed my hands over my face, regretted it when I felt the scrape of grit and dirt on my skin. "I don't want to talk about it."

Not in the dark. Not in the mountains. Maybe in the morning, with the sun burning hot in the blue Colorado sky, miles away from the mine, maybe then I would explain, if he still wanted to know. Not here.

He wasn't going to leave it alone. "But you went with her. Why?"

"Figure it out, Einstein."

It seemed so stupid now, that I had ever thought I could ask anything of the woman in the mine. That I could walk in there and leave behind only the parts of me I didn't want anymore, these powers and this darkness, and keep everything else. She would take exactly what she wanted, nothing more and nothing less, from everybody who stepped into her prison.

"It didn't work out the way you wanted?"

"Can't you tell?"

"You still smell kind of dead," Zeke said.

"Aw, I bet you say that to all the girls."

"Shut up. Are you sure you're okay?"

"Well, I'm still an undead monster who rose from the grave, but at least I'm not a drooling, brain-dead monster who rose from the grave. I'm great. Awesome. Couldn't be better."

Zeke kicked at the low fence rail and looked up at the stars. "Whatever. Next time you're stuck in the middle of nowhere, call somebody else."

I didn't remind him that I had nobody else to call. He knew it;

he was here. "I got you dinner. That's got to be worth at least a tank of gas."

He glanced at me. "You killed a guy and called me to get rid of the evidence."

"I know. Worst first date ever."

He laughed a little. "You are seriously the most annoying undead person I've ever met."

"He was a really bad man," I said, after a minute or two of silence. I hadn't told him much, but Zeke knew Rain's story, and he had seen Brian Kerr's house. He knew what they had been doing. I asked, "Do evil people taste evil?"

"Uh, no," Zeke said, like he wasn't sure it was a serious question. "They all mostly taste the same."

"Huh. Okay." It didn't seem right. There should be something rotten inside somebody who did things like that, something that made them taste like sulfur and decay and maggots. Something that made them different. "That would have been interesting to know when I did that report on the Donner Party in fifth grade. Why did nobody dig me up?"

"What?"

"When I was buried. Before I woke up."

My thoughts were racing, my legs jiggling on the fence. I hated sitting there at the edge of the woods waiting for the first sign of headlights in the dark. It was taking too long. We shouldn't have let Jake go by himself.

"I was there for a *year*. If you can smell a body well enough to find it in the woods, why didn't anybody figure out I was stuck in the ground in somebody's backyard?"

"You don't smell *that* bad. It's not like you're rotting or anything."

"You said you can—"

"I can tell you're not completely alive," Zeke said.

"You mean it's a magic thing, not a smell thing? Like how I can tell when somebody is a killer?"

"I guess. Sort of. It's both. There aren't any ghouls in Chicago," he added, like that was an important detail. "Too many magicians."

"But somebody did find me. When I first woke up."

"The birds weren't exactly subtle."

"Yeah, my magical bird flu epidemic was big news. I didn't do that on purpose. Would that be enough? For somebody to find me?"

"If he knew what he was looking for, maybe." Zeke shook his head. "Probably? I don't know. Ask a magician."

Thinking about the man by my grave only reminded me of his hands on my face and his excitement. *You're beautiful, you're perfect*, as though he had known exactly what he was going to find. And his memories. Especially his memories. I didn't want him in my head.

"Mr. Willow . . ." I stumbled on his name. "His whole deal was telling people they were evil whether they did anything evil or not, and promising to fix them."

"It doesn't work that way," Zeke said.

"He convinced a lot of people it did." I thought of Violet with her glowing eyes and her hands clamped over her mouth. "And when he couldn't convince them, he didn't give them a choice."

Zeke shrugged. "That's what humans always do."

"You don't like humans very much, do you?"

"I would like them more if they weren't always trying to kill us."

I couldn't argue with logic like that. "Thank you for helping me in spite of your prejudices."

"You're not human anymore," Zeke said.

"I'm thanking you anyway."

"Uh, yeah. Okay. It's no big deal."

I closed my eyes for a moment, tilted my head back, and when I looked again the stars were still there.

"You know *Challenger*? The space shuttle that exploded back in the eighties?"

Zeke gave me a quick, confused look. "Yeah. I think so. We learned about it in school."

That threw me for a second. "You go to school?"

He made a face and kicked the fence again. "Jake makes me."

"You're a man-eating corpse-stealing creature of the night and your big brother makes you go to school." For some reason that felt like the most bizarre thing I had heard in a long time. "Does he check your homework too? Go to teacher conferences? Sign field trip permission slips?"

"Yes," Zeke said. And after a beat: "The conferences never go very well. He picks fights with the teachers."

I laughed. Something dense and tangled in my chest began to ease.

"What about it? The space thing?" Zeke said.

"*Challenger*. The space shuttle. I was just thinking about—there's a transcript of everything that happened when it exploded. And right before it happened, everything—everything was fine. They thought it was fine. The shuttle was taking off and everything was perfect, right up until it wasn't. The last voice picked up by the flight cabin recorder was the pilot."

I scrubbed my palms on my knees; my jeans felt grimy and gross. I was so tired of being dirty and hurt and bloody all the time.

"Michael Smith. He was the pilot. He said, 'Uh-oh.' Then it exploded. They all died. Seven people. They think some of them might have survived the explosion and they were still alive for—for the fall. Back to Earth." I swallowed; my throat was dry. "But the last thing mission control heard from them was just that. 'Uh-oh.'"

Zeke didn't say anything. He was waiting for me to go on.

"My best friend Melanie tells me—used to tell me—it was morbid that I knew things like that. She said it was creepy and stupid to think about tragedies all the time. But I always thought . . . I only thought it was sad. They didn't even make it into space. They just died."

I took a deep breath. My heart wasn't racing anymore. My hands weren't shaking.

"I was lying when I said I couldn't remember who killed me."

"I know," Zeke said softly.

"I thought I was lying better than that," I said.

"No, I mean . . ." Zeke trailed off. He bounced his leg nervously, shrugged his thin shoulders. He wasn't looking at me. "I think if you keep trying to tell yourself and everybody else that you don't remember something because it was . . . I think that mostly means you remember it really well, and wish you didn't."

I looked at him, at his profile in the darkness. "Yeah. It's like that."

I thought he would ask. I waited for the inevitable question, tense and uncomfortable, but he didn't.

"The person you killed," I said. "Who was he?"

"Does it matter?"

"I don't know. No. Sorry."

"He was a really bad man," Zeke said, a mocking echo, but he meant it.

"What did he do?"

He was trying to decide what to tell me. In the end, he only said, "He hurt Jake."

"What does it feel like?" I asked. "When you kill someone. What does that feel like?"

Zeke was quiet for so long I didn't think he was going to answer.

"Nothing," he said finally. "It doesn't feel like anything."

He was lying, lying, lying. I let him. It was an unfair question anyway.

"I didn't think I could be scared anymore," I said. "I've been imagining that worms or something got into my brain while I was buried and ate away the amygdala. That's the part of the brain that feels fear. I forgot what it felt like, to be scared. I don't know. Maybe it doesn't even feel the same for me anymore. Now it's like—"

"Like what?" Zeke said, when I didn't go on.

Like being lost in a haunted house. Like throwing up on a carnival ride. Like kicking toward the shimmering light above when you're turned around under water, like digging your feet through the hot outer surface of sand to the cool damp layer beneath, like skimming your fingers over a boy's bare chest and feeling his heart stutter. Like riding a skateboard on the smoothest road you can imagine, faster than you've ever dared, wind in your hair and on your face, sun baking the asphalt below you, grass and trees and barbed wire passing so quickly they smear into a blur of color.

"It feels like being alive," I said.

# ᐧᒡᐧ FORTY-ONE ᐧᒡᐧ

WHEN JAKE RETURNED he didn't say anything except, "Get in."

Several minutes passed before he spoke again. He drove with one hand tight on the wheel, the other on the gear shift. I was sitting in the middle; I could feel how tense he was. The dirt road took us down off the ridge and into a canyon. The windows were down and night air flowed in from both sides, cool and crisp, smelling of pines.

"Did you do that to him?" Jake asked.

"I don't have claws." I didn't need to tear out a man's insides to end his life. My rage didn't look anything like that. "Did you go to the mine?"

"No," he said. "But I could feel it."

"Her. You could feel her. She's not an *it*."

"What is she?"

Hooves, eyes, handmade claws. She was ancient and terrible and angry. I could feel her laughter underneath my skin. I wondered how long she would laugh before she realized nobody was coming to feed her anymore.

"I don't know. I don't—I don't have any idea. He thought she was the only one."

"Can she get out?" Jake asked.

"I don't think so."

Jake glanced at me.

"No. She can't."

The dirt road led to a paved road that spilled us out of the canyon and onto Boulder's quiet early morning streets. Dawn was approaching as a faint light in the east, shades of yellow and pink climbing into dark blue. There were a few cars on the road, joggers and cyclists out for their morning exercise. I listened with every turn, but I didn't hear anything heavy rolling in the back of the truck.

It was still dark when we pulled up to their house. Jake backed the truck into the driveway, and Zeke got out to open the garage. They had done this before. I looked away and tried not to think about what they were unloading. When they went inside I followed because I didn't know what else to do. They carried the body into the bathroom. He was wrapped in plastic, his face hidden. He didn't look like a person at all.

"You do that in the same place where you shower?" I said.

Jake looked at me over his shoulder. "You have a better idea?"

I didn't know how people normally went about butchering bodies in the privacy of their own homes, and the moment I started thinking about it, I couldn't stop.

They were going to *eat* him. He had been a person yesterday, and now he was a piece of meat. A dead thing. A *meal*. I had killed him, with Lyle, and now he was food. There were going to be knives and freezer bags and teeth and a lot of blood. They weren't taking their time. They were impatient. They were hungry.

Knowing what they were was one thing. Seeing it was different.

Jake took pity on me. "Come back in an hour or two," he said.

I grabbed my skateboard and slammed the door behind me.

# ⫸ FORTY-TWO ⫷

JAKE GAVE ME some money before I left Boulder.

"Take a bus," he said. "Less chance of getting kidnapped by a crazy human."

"And one hundred percent more chance of getting propositioned by a fifty-year-old recent parolee. No thanks." I waved the cash away. They didn't have a lot. They needed it more than I did.

Jake rolled his eyes and tucked the folded bills into the front of my backpack.

"Are you going home?" he asked.

"No."

Not like that. Not to stay. Not to see my family. Not to watch my sisters through their bedroom windows like a creep in the yard. Not to see Mom pull the car out of the driveway in the morning, Dad clutching his travel mug of coffee in the passenger seat. Mom always joked that Dad was just as likely to fall asleep during his morning lectures as his students.

I wasn't going back to hide where they might see me and tell myself it was up to them whether they looked or not. To let them decide for themselves if their daughter still existed.

"What could I even say?" I said. "'Hi, Mom and Dad, I got murdered but I'm better now and I kill people but only the bad ones and I kind of like it'? I can't—I can't do that to them."

Jake leaned against the counter and looked at me for a long, uncomfortable moment. The bathroom door was closed and he had changed his shirt. There was no blood, no mess, no sign of what they had been doing—no sign except the basement door, standing open just wide enough for me to see a single dark eye through the gap. Steve was waiting to get to work on the bathroom with its toothbrush and bleach.

Jake started to say something, changed his mind and stopped.

"What?" I said.

"It won't matter what you say to them," he said. "They won't care."

I closed my backpack and played with the zipper. I didn't look at him.

"They won't, Breezy. You could tell them anything and they'll just be happy to have—"

"Really? I can tell them what I am now? You think they won't care about that? You think they'll be *happy?*"

"They—"

"Shut up. You don't know what you're talking about." I hooked the backpack straps over my shoulders and picked up my skateboard. "You've never been human."

I meant it as an insult, but Jake didn't take it that way. "No. You're right. I haven't. Okay. Don't do anything stupid." He smiled crookedly when he said it, like it was something he said a lot but never expected anybody to listen. Then he said "See you later" instead of good-bye.

Zeke was waiting outside. He walked with me to the end of the driveway.

"Where are you going?" he asked.

"I haven't decided yet," I said. It was a lie, but I didn't care if he believed me. "I'm not going on a murderous rampage like Ingrid said I would. I promise."

Zeke nodded. He was looking down the street, not at me. "Yeah, well. That's probably smart."

I dropped the skateboard to the ground, put one foot on, but I didn't kick away yet. "I remembered it wrong, what I told you last night. About *Challenger.*"

"Okay?"

"I mean, not about *Challenger* itself. That was right. But I remembered the wrong person. Maybe there are worms in the memory part of my brain too. It was my sister Meadow who made fun of me for knowing that about their last words. And she didn't tell me it was morbid, she just told me I was a giant nerd and she was embarrassed to be related to me. But there was this other time, I don't know, a while ago. I was sleeping over at my best friend's house."

For a few years we did that every week: me at Melanie's house, or her at mine, a routine our parents accepted and encouraged. Melanie's parents planned their date nights around it; my parents referred to our air mattress and spare comforter as Melanie's bed.

"I had just read about *Apollo 1* for the first time," I said. "Most space books for kids kind of gloss over *Apollo 1*. I guess it's not kid friendly to say, 'And then they all died horribly in a fire right there on the launch pad.' But I read about it, the real story, and I looked it up, and there's a recording of it. An audio recording. I don't know if it's real." I rolled the skateboard back and forth a few times. "The astronauts, they're—one of them is complaining about how the radios aren't working, saying they'll never get to the moon if they can't even make things work on the ground, and then another one starts shouting about fire in the cabin. And that's it. They're dead. I made Melanie listen to it. She wanted to watch a movie or call our friends, and I made her listen to people dying in a fire. That's when she told me I was morbid. It was one of our vocabulary words from school. She was using it all the time."

"She was right," Zeke said. I couldn't tell if he was teasing or serious. They looked pretty much the same on him.

"I know. I'd never heard anybody die before. I'd never thought about how awful it would be to die like that."

I tucked my thumbs into the straps of my backpack. There was no fire on the list in my NASA notebook. I had considered it, tried to work out the logistics. There was too much risk of hurting somebody else. It wouldn't work anyway.

"It wasn't even a real launch, that day of the fire," I said. "It was a practice countdown. They went to work that morning, thinking they were running a test. Is that how it always is? When people die?"

"Most people aren't around afterward to think about it."

"Lucky me. I'm the one who gets to stay."

"You'd rather be gone?" he asked. His tone was flat, but the question was earnest.

What I wanted was to go back to the night I died and change it. Don't go to the party. Don't fight with Melanie. Don't leave by myself. I hadn't done anything wrong, not one single thing, but still I wanted to do it all differently. I wanted to not die that night. I wanted to not wake up a year later and stagger home to an empty house and an unfamiliar world. Not become something else, something strange and monstrous, but still human enough to fall for a dangerous promise and impossible hope.

Give me your rotten little heart, she had said. You won't miss it a bit.

"What I want is for none of this to have happened," I said. "But that's not an option, is it?"

I couldn't bear to talk to him anymore. I couldn't stand there on that quiet Boulder street, outside a house with a blood-splattered bathroom and a homicidal house elf in the basement, pretending everything would be fine.

"I'm leaving now," I said.

"Don't get yourself killed for real," Zeke said.

I kicked off, and I waved as I rode away.

# ᛃᛁᛚ FORTY-THREE ᛃᛁᛚ

IT TOOK ME four days and five different rides to get back to Chicago. I could have made the trip faster if I had tried, but I didn't, and I didn't think much about my reasons for taking my time. I hitchhiked from Boulder up to Cheyenne with a couple of engineering students on their way to Montana for a camping trip, turned east at Cheyenne with a trucker named Joe who spent the entire time telling me about his daughter who traveled around the country just like me, relying on the kindness of strangers, sometimes on the highways and sometimes on the trains.

"Sure I worry," said Joe, in response to a question I wasn't going to ask. "But she's a smart girl. She can take care of herself."

Joe and I parted ways in Kansas City, and from there I rode to St. Louis with two college lacrosse players with identical blond ponytails who spent half the trip arguing about how Taylor Swift had become a feminist icon, then up to Bloomington with a cheerful, chatty woman named Sandra who was road-tripping after her divorce, and the final stretch into Chicago with a Northwestern journalism student named Laurie who was thinking about giving up the news entirely to go learn yoga at an ashram in India.

"It's just so hard to care when nobody else cares," she said. "Nobody wants to hear about anything that matters anymore."

But her car radio was tuned to NPR and she turned it up for the international updates, shaking her head and offering out-of-context commentary I pretended to understand. She was dismayed to learn that I didn't have an opinion on the situation in Gaza. I didn't try to explain that I had spent an entire year underground and missed a lot of important world events.

None of them were killers, the people I rode with, and if they were monsters, they hid it well. The only shadows they dragged behind them were the ordinary kind, the kind that everybody collects going through life, waking up every day to make a series of good and bad decisions, going to bed with the consequences, doing it all over again in the morning.

I didn't approach any old women. Sometimes when I closed my eyes I felt her claws on my wrist and heard the whisper of living sand, but when I opened them again there was only the car, the country, the driver who was kind enough to help a stranger.

Laurie would have taken me into Evanston if I asked, but I

wasn't ready for that yet. After she dropped me off, I used some of Jake's money to head downtown. I used a little more cash to buy a phone, because tucked in with the bills was a note with their phone numbers and the admonishment to let them know I was okay. It made me roll my eyes, but it also made me smile. It felt odd to have a phone in my pocket again and somebody to call, like the earth's gravity had increased and every step I took carried a bit more weight.

I spent the rest of the day at the Field Museum, which was probably not what Jake had given me the money for, but rooms full of dead dinosaurs and noisy school kids were soothing after days on the road. I wandered around, reading displays and staring at skeletons, and nobody noticed, nobody cared, nobody wondered if I belonged.

I stayed with Sue the T. rex and all of her dinosaur friends until the museum closed, then I took the train to Evanston.

# ⑈ FORTY-FOUR ⑈

I WISH I HAD a better story to tell about the night I died.

That should be part of the deal. Die young, come back to tell about it, at the very least it should be an exciting death.

But nothing about that day was unusual. There was only one more week of school before summer. I went over to Melanie's house in the afternoon before Nate's party. Her parents were more easygoing than mine. Not that Mom and Dad were ever very strict, but Alan and Lillian—they insisted I call them by their first names—let Melanie take the car every time she asked, never enforced a curfew, only laughed when Melanie's little brother, Ryan, tried to tattle on us for breaking the rules. We were good girls, mostly. We never gave them much reason to worry.

Melanie had been dating a senior since January. His name was Lawrence but everybody called him Lucky. He even called himself Lucky, because he was the kind of guy who sometimes talked about himself in the third person. He was going to William & Mary in the fall to study English literature, and he had been trying to convince Melanie to apply to the same school, casually at first, almost a joke, but more and more insistently as graduation drew closer.

"I mean, I like him," Melanie said. She was always careful not to say *love* when she didn't mean it. "But every time he brings it up I just want to stab myself. Seriously, who wants to go to college in Virginia?"

I was lying on her bed, flipping halfheartedly through my World History notes, glancing over names and dates but not absorbing much. I never had to study much for math or science exams, but anything involving people required work. Melanie was sitting at her computer, playing music from indie bands Lucky wanted her to like. Melanie started each song, listened for a few seconds, clicked to the next.

"Where do you want to go instead?" I asked.

"Somewhere besides Virginia," Melanie said with a laugh. "New York, I think. I'd love to live in New York. Maybe Boston, since you'll be at MIT." She played another song, made a face at the vocalist's reedy voice, moved on. "I don't know. Why do I have to decide now? Lucky's acting like I should know everything I want already or I'm going to end up taking accounting classes at community college. Does he really think anybody our age has everything figured out?" She spun around in her chair. "Except for you. But you're not exactly normal."

I could remember when Melanie had wanted something as much as I wanted to be an astronaut. For her it was medicine. She wanted to be a doctor, a pediatrician. Not the vaccines-and-lollipops kind of pediatrician, but the kind who took care of kids with cancer, with genetic disorders or degenerative diseases, the kind of pediatrician whose patients were too sick to play or go to school or have a normal life. When most of us were signing up for community service to fulfill the National Honor Society requirements and add another accomplishment to our college applications, Melanie was already volunteering at the children's hospital. She read to the kids and talked to their parents, commiserated with the nurses and shadowed the doctors. I hadn't realized until that afternoon it wasn't her dream anymore.

Melanie did end up going to New York. I looked her up eventually, when it didn't hurt so much. She was studying film at NYU. I found a picture of her with her freshman roommate at a Halloween party. They were dressed up like starlets from 1940s Hollywood, with clinging dresses and curled hair. Red plastic cups in hand, bright matching smiles, skin shiny in the camera flash, they looked happy. "Me and my bestie!!!!!" Melanie had always used too much punctuation. It looked like a night on another planet, in another universe, one I could barely imagine anymore.

But that was later. That afternoon, the last day of my human life, I didn't ask when Melanie had stopped dreaming about helping sick kids, and she didn't notice my silence.

"You think Devon will be there tonight?" Melanie said, and I understood that there were things she had missed too. Devon was a guy I had hooked up with a few times in the winter, but not since March, when his ex-girlfriend in Portland had called up to say she wanted to try the long-distance thing for real. We had never been into each other that much anyway. The full extent of our relationship, if that was the word for it, was to head over to his house after school, do our calculus homework, have sex, and play video games until his parents got home. It was fun, for a while, but two months later I didn't think about him much anymore.

Later, after I disappeared and the police interviewed everybody I knew, Devon had only nice things to say about me. I appreciated that. Everybody else in school was getting a lot of mileage out of sharing every sordid story they could remember or make up about me, but all Devon said was that I was a friend who was good at math but terrible at *Call of Duty*.

"I don't know," I answered truthfully. "Maybe."

"Everybody will be there," Melanie said, and she moved on to talking about our friend Tatiana's car, an old Firebird she and her stepmother were rebuilding in their garage. They were taking classes, buying books, peppering every employee at every auto parts shop in town with questions. It was all Tatiana talked about anymore. We were already planning a road trip for after graduation.

There should have been something significant about that day. Something ominous. A sign, in retrospect, that it was the last day of my life. But there wasn't. It was an ordinary day.

For dinner we had Indian takeout with Melanie's family. Ryan was going through a phase where he claimed to be training himself to eat the hottest foods he could find. He spent the meal teary and red-faced, gulping water between bouts of laughter. We cleaned up the dishes. We got ready for the night. Melanie promised not to drink and drive; I promised not to let her. We went to Nate's party.

I had a few drinks. I danced. I hugged my graduating senior friends. I kissed my best friend and her lips were warm, sticky with mint-flavored gloss. She said, "What the hell?" and she slapped me. It was no secret I was bisexual, and Melanie had never cared, but she cared about that. I wasn't even sure why I kissed her. I had never wanted to before, and probably wouldn't have again, if I had lived. It seemed like a good idea at the time.

I locked myself in Nate Havers's upstairs bathroom and looked at myself in the mirror. Melanie's hand had left a red smudge on my cheek. Somebody pounded on the door and shouted that he was going to piss in the hallway if I didn't let him in. I wanted to go home. My dad always said I could call if I needed a ride when I was out with my friends, for any reason, even if I had been drinking, even if I was somewhere I wasn't supposed to be. I wouldn't get into trouble, he said, that was a promise.

I didn't call my father. The police found my phone in the bathroom at Nate's house. I don't remember leaving it there.

I decided to walk. I stopped on Nate's front steps to take off my uncomfortable sandals, and a girl I recognized but couldn't name said, "Awesome shoes!" She lifted her Corona in a toast. I stared at her, didn't even remember to smile, and she was gone, dragged laughing into the house by a friend.

Nobody noticed me leaving. That's what they all said later.

The grass on Nate's front lawn was cool beneath my bare feet, a soft tickle on my ankles. I wanted to walk in the grass all the way home, cutting through yards, over hedges and fences, staying in the shadows.

I was standing there at the edge of the grass, trying to decide if I could jump the flower bed into the next yard over, when I heard my name.

"Breezy. Hey, Breezy. Hey, are you okay?"

I turned around and I thought: God, it's that kid, what is he even doing here?

And: What's his name, what's his name, he's always saying hi to me in the halls, what is his name?

And I thought about the stupid letters he used to send to me, his messy handwriting on the envelopes and torn-out notebook paper. I had a whole stack of them from middle school, from freshman year. Melanie and my other friends used to laugh, told me I should be flattered, maybe he was a nice boy beneath all the shyness, maybe I shouldn't be so mean to him. I stopped telling them, eventually, when it wasn't funny anymore. I wondered how he had even known there was a party at Nate's house. He wasn't friends with Nate. He was on the track team; he hung out with a different crowd.

"Hi, Ricky," I said.

"Are you leaving?" Ricky said. "Do you need a ride?"

"No. I'm fine."

"Are you sure? I can give you a ride."

"I'm sure."

"Come on, Breezy, I just want to talk."

I said no. I said I was fine. I kept walking.

And he followed me. Nobody saw him. Nobody was watching. The cops never talked to Ricky Benning.

I don't remember dying.

I remember telling him to leave me alone. I remember that he grabbed my arm. I remember that he shoved me and I stumbled into a car and hit my head on the window. I remember shouting for help, or trying to, dazed and dizzy and nauseous, and the pressure of his hand on my mouth, his fingers on my neck, his babbling, panicked plea for me to be quiet, be quiet, please shut up, shut up, *shut up*, somebody might hear. I don't remember the snap of my hyoid bone. I don't remember my trachea collapsing under the pressure of his hands. He shouldn't have been strong enough, but he was angry and scared. I don't remember the blood vessels in my eyes rupturing.

It only takes a few seconds for a person to lose consciousness from strangulation. I don't remember anything after that.

# ⑴⑴ FORTY-FIVE ⑴⑴

THE BENNINGS HAD lived in the same house since Ricky was in kindergarten. For a few years they had invited everybody in the class over for Ricky's birthday. I remembered those parties in a vague blur of sticky frosting, melting ice cream, colorful paper streamers, and once, maybe, a clown that made Jill Patterson cry, but that might have been somewhere else.

The house was dark. It didn't look like it had in the nightmare I'd had at Ingrid's. It was smaller, brown rather than gray, and there was no light in the upstairs window.

He was home. I could feel him.

I stashed my skateboard at the edge of the lawn and ducked

into the shadows. I changed into the mud-stained party clothes I had been wearing when I died. The shirt was Melanie's; I had forgotten until I pulled it over my head. She had told me not to spill beer on it and not to have sex in it, and we had both laughed. She hadn't said anything about getting murdered in it, but I felt guilty anyway. It was one of her favorites.

I left my backpack in the grass and walked around the house, looking for a way in. They had locked all their doors and windows on the first floor. I could break a windowpane, but I didn't want to wake anybody up. I found my way in when I spotted the dog flap in the back door. It was closed up with a plastic board on the inside, but the board wasn't locked into place. I slid it out and squeezed myself through the dog door.

I was in the kitchen before I remembered that *dog door* means *dog*. A low growl rumbled in the darkness. A big, angry German shepherd.

But it was only a dog, and I'm not human anymore. I stepped toward it and growled right back. That big German shepherd backed away with an alarmed whine and cowered in the corner by its food bowl.

"Good dog," I whispered.

I followed the shadows upstairs, slipped into Ricky's room, and shut the door behind me. In the light from the street, I could see him asleep on his twin bed. There were clothes and shoes scattered all over the floor. On the desk was a square graduation cap with the tassel dangling over the edge. The room smelled like teenage boy: sweat, dirty socks, the chemical offense of cheap body spray.

The clinging shadows of his guilt filled the room with a darkness I felt more than saw. It reminded me of a nature program I had watched once, a diver's view of a kelp forest off the California coast, impossibly tall dark stalks swaying and drifting against the distant, wavering sunlight.

I sat on the edge of the bed and put my hand over his mouth.

I said, "Hey, Ricky."

He woke slowly, eyes blinking, lips moving beneath my fingers. His breath was warm and damp on my palm. First there was disbelief, confusion, the narrow-eyed squint of somebody who thinks he's in a dream.

Then he inhaled, and he was awake. He tried to sit up and scramble away from me.

"Shh." I pressed my hand harder over his mouth, pushing his head into the pillow. "Don't do that. I just want to talk."

Ricky's eyes were wide and pale and he began to shake his head, back and forth, back and forth, hair whispering against his pillow.

"Isn't that what you told me? You just wanted to talk. You didn't care if I wanted to listen."

He made a noise in his throat. It sounded like the scared whimper of the dog downstairs. His hands clenched uselessly at the edge of his sheet.

"I'm wondering how surprised you are to see me," I said. He flinched and his eyes twitched rapidly. "You must have freaked out when you heard about that dead guy they found where you buried me. You must have pissed yourself, thinking they would find me next."

He shook his head.

"I'll let you talk, because I want to hear the answer to that," I said. I put my other hand against his neck. His skin was warm, sweaty; I made a disgusted face but pressed my fingers into his throat. "If you try to scream, you'll be dead before you take a breath. Just tell me. Are you surprised to see me?"

I removed my hand from his mouth.

"You're dead," he whispered.

"Wow, you're a genius. You want to see something?" I tilted my chin up, let him get a good look at the bruises around my neck. "See that? I still have the bruises. The bruises *you* gave me."

I caught myself as my voice rose, pressed my lips together and breathed.

"I didn't," he said. "I didn't, I didn't, I didn't mean—"

"Shut up."

He obeyed.

"I don't care. Shut up."

He was making fists in his blanket and he was trembling all over, like a rabbit hiding in an open field. I had never seen anything more pathetic. I pushed my thumb into the side of his neck. I could feel his pulse racing.

"Did you know this could happen? Somebody told me things like me mostly come out of war zones and epidemics. Are you an epidemic, Ricky?"

"No," he said, a weak little moan.

"Did you do it on purpose? Did you want me to be *special?*"

"No, no, no," he stuttered, his breath catching in half-formed sobs.

Maybe he was lying, maybe he wasn't, but I didn't care any-more. I didn't care what Ricky knew. I didn't care why he had killed me. He had put me in a grave, but I had climbed out, and he didn't matter. I was so fucking tired of men deciding whether or not I got to go on existing for another day.

"I have this problem," I said. "I really want to kill you."

"No!"

I slapped my hand over his mouth again. "Shut up. You don't get to have an opinion. I really want to kill you. I don't think I want revenge, exactly, although I do want some payback for all that shitty poetry you sent to me. I bet you thought I didn't read it. I did, you know. I read it to my friends and we laughed about it, but I had to ask somebody to point you out at school because I had no idea who you were."

He was crying now. I dug my fingernails into his skin; they were still flecked with the blue polish I had put on that afternoon at Melanie's house, and just long enough to draw blood. Ricky was saying *"please, please"* behind my hand, the word little more than an ani-mal whine. He squirmed and kicked his legs, drew up his knees, and grasped at the blanket over his crotch; he had wet himself. But he didn't push me away. He was too scared to try. My fingernails left four half-moon specks of blood on his neck. In the morning he would see them and know it hadn't been a dream.

"I want to kill you." I looked down at him pressed into his pil-low. I felt his hot breath on my hand. His shadows surrounded us like a forest. "But I'm not going to. Not tonight."

Ingrid thought I didn't know how this would end, but I did.

Nothing on my list could have worked. There was only one way out for me, and I wasn't going to take it.

He blinked rapidly and tears streaked down his face, and suddenly I felt bored and annoyed and angry that I was wasting my time with this gross little creep in his childish bedroom while he cried and pissed his pants. I took my hand from his mouth. He wasn't going to make a sound. He was an irrelevant little rodent.

I stood to leave. At the door, I looked back.

"I'm going to be watching you," I said. "You won't see me, but I'll be there. I might change my mind someday."

# ⫸ FORTY-SIX ⫷

IF KAREN GARROW is right, and all the other physicists who imagine such things, there's a universe out there where I call my dad and get a ride home. There's a universe where Melanie kisses me back. There's a universe where I scream for help and somebody hears me.

There's a universe where that night happens just like in this one—party, kiss, Ricky, death—except they find my body and they catch him. The police interrogate him in a small dingy room with his parents and a lawyer at his side, and he cries as he says, "I didn't mean to hurt her, I didn't mean it, I swear, I'm sorry, I didn't mean it." News articles talk about what a surprise it is, that such a nice young man could do such a thing. Surely it was an accident. They mourn his lost potential, his lost track scholarships, how tragic it is that one night ruined his entire life. They write articles and have meetings warning teenage girls about the dangers of drinking and partying. Nobody writes articles telling teenage boys not to stalk and kill girls who don't like their stupid adolescent poetry. Maybe they mourn me, as an afterthought, but I'm already gone. It's too late for me to matter.

There's a universe out there, or several, where I survive the night. I fight him off. I get away. There's a universe where I'm too ashamed to tell anybody, and there's a universe where I call the cops, give a statement to a sympathetic officer in the glow of the cruiser lights. I go home to be hugged by my mother and tucked in by my father, and maybe a few months later I write about it in my college essay. I tell the faceless admissions officers what it felt like to be that scared, to face danger that real, and I make up some bullshit about how it only made me more determined to do what too many people said women couldn't do, and it works, and they love my essay and they admire my determination and my grades and my test scores, and I go to MIT, or maybe Caltech with its palm trees and smog-shrouded desert mountains, and I'm good at college. I have fun and I work hard and my classes are challenging and rewarding, and after a year or two I move into an off-campus apartment with a nice girl or a nice boy, and we take turns cooking dinner and argue about the dishes. Maybe my nice girl or nice boy comes with me to graduate school, to my first postdoc, or maybe by then I've found somebody else to hold my hand and share my bed and take me to mind-numbing action movies when I'm stressed and drag me on a camping trip for distraction when I'm waiting to hear from NASA.

Or maybe there's nobody at all, maybe Melanie was right all along about how I'm good at casual hooking up but bad at dating, and there's nobody beside me when I get the phone call and I can barely hear the words over the roaring in my head, and I pack up to move to Houston alone, but Mom and Dad are there to help me carry boxes of books out to the moving truck, and I'm still single years later when the mission to Mars gets the green light, and the news media and bloggers talk about that more than they talk about my role on the crew and my scientific accomplishments. They speculate that I was chosen because I'm unmarried and childless, and is it even fair to make a decision based on a lifestyle choice they all suspect is unnatural anyway, and they argue about whether it's ethical to send a woman into space for so long with the radiation and risk of infertility, but I don't care, I don't care, I'm too busy to care in the months before the launch, too busy to do more than endure their stupid questions and give carefully vetted replies, firm, quotable, sharp but not offensive, never offensive, and I always smile, and then there are preliminary tests, and there is lift-off, and in the final moments of the countdown I vow not to look back, not even a glance, not until the earth is no more than a distant blue speck I don't know that I'll ever see again.

There's a universe somewhere where I sit on the edge of Ricky's bed, surrounded by the grasping shadows only I can feel, and I touch his fever-hot skin, and he dies, and I die with him. In the morning his parents find us, him in his pajamas and me in my party clothes, two empty bodies and answers nobody wants.

There's a universe, or several, where I die. My body rots away to bones and nobody ever digs me up and that's it. That's the end.

# FORTY-SEVEN

I LEFT RICKY'S HOUSE and wound through the empty streets to Centennial Park. I didn't go anywhere near my neighborhood and the house that had always been home. I didn't want the temptation.

The lake was inky black and there were clouds gathering over the water, blotting out the stars. It took me several minutes to work up the courage to step onto the sand, and when I did I held my breath, expecting it to shift and rasp beneath my feet, roiling into imprisoned faces and hands at the edge of my vision.

It didn't. It was only sand.

I changed out of my party clothes right there on the beach and jammed them into the bottom of my backpack. I didn't want to touch them again, but I didn't want to throw them away either.

I sat at the edge of the water and listened to the waves dragging on the shore. It was just me and the lake for a while, until the most dedicated early morning joggers and dog walkers emerged and the sky began to lighten. The first runner who came close startled me so much I jumped to my feet and whirled around. In the darkness I was certain she was hunched and lurching on crooked legs and split hooves, but it was only a woman with a ponytail and bright silver reflectors on her shirt. She didn't see me gaping at her.

I sat down again and breathed until my heart was steady. There was a thin line of clear sky between the water and the clouds. I watched it shift from gray to pink.

I dug my new phone out of my backpack and typed a message:

*almost had to add "torn apart by angry dog" to the list.*

Several minutes passed. It was barely five a.m. in Chicago, which meant it didn't even qualify as morning in Colorado. I leaned back to rest my elbows on the ground and looked up, but the clouds had overtaken most of the sky.

My phone rang with an obnoxious tone, so loud it made me jump.

"What kind of dog?" Zeke asked.

"German shepherd."

"I hate those."

"I made this one cry."

"It probably deserved it." He sounded tired but alert. I didn't think I had woken him up.

"Are you naturally nocturnal?" I asked.

"No. Are you naturally annoying?"

"Yes. Been this way since birth. Hopeless case. Sorry." I dug my heels into the sand. Somewhere over the lake the wind was rising, the waves coming in faster and choppier. "Were you really asleep?"

"Not really. Where are you? Jake's been worried about you."

"Seriously?"

"Yeah, he's like that. I don't care what happens to you," Zeke said, and I laughed. I considered, for a moment, embarrassing the hell out of Zeke by telling him that that I liked his prickly discomfort more than Jake's unearned concern, but I didn't want him to hang up. I hadn't wanted them to worry about me. I hadn't even known until I sent the text that I was going to contact them again.

"I'm sitting beside Lake Michigan," I said. "We used to come here on the weekends. Family picnics and stuff. We had five-person Frisbee tournaments. Do ghouls do stuff like that or is it just a human thing?"

"I do know what a picnic is," Zeke said.

"My mom has a special basket and everything." I watched the water for a few moments. "I just wanted to see it one more time. It's different in the dark, with nobody here."

"Watch out for the mermaids."

"There aren't even any mermaids. Just me, and I'm just sitting here thinking. . . ." I cleared my throat. "I was going to be an astronaut, you know? I had it all worked out. It's the only thing I ever wanted to do. I was going to be on the first manned mission to Mars."

I sat up and wrapped my arms around my knees. Zeke didn't say anything.

"And I could have done it. I could have. So why couldn't this have happened to somebody else? Somebody who was never going to do anything. Some loser who was going to spend her life getting high in her parents' basement and telling everybody she was starting a band. Why couldn't that girl die? I'm supposed to be going to graduation parties and packing for college and writing stupid shit in people's yearbooks. Why couldn't he have picked somebody else? Why did he have to pick anybody at all? Why didn't—didn't anybody hear me scream? I did. I tried—I tried to fight him. Somebody must have heard. Did they even care?"

My voice caught and I stopped, pressed the heel of my hand to one stinging eye, then the other. I took a ragged breath. There was something hard and cold opening in my chest, a flower made of razors, pressing outward from the inside.

"I just keep thinking, well, now I'm perfect for the job," I said, quieter, all of my anger run out of me. "Who needs a space suit when you don't need to breathe and your cells can heal any radiation damage? I probably wouldn't even lose bone density. Not with magic on my side. Now I'm perfect."

Zeke still didn't say anything, but he didn't hang up on me either. Tears ran down my face in hot lines. The patchwork girl I had stitched together was gone. She had never existed at all. She had been less real than the wisp of a shadow. There was only me.

We sat there in silence for a long time. I heard the scuff of shoes and rattle of a leash behind me; a woman was running with her golden retriever. She didn't pay any attention to me.

"I didn't kill him," I said eventually. My voice was rough. It was hard to speak. "The guy who did this to me. I wanted to. But I didn't."

"Okay." Zeke's voice was quiet.

Okay. It was okay.

I wiped my nose on the edge of my T-shirt and cleared my throat. "What do people like me even do if they're not running around on quests of magical vengeance? How do I . . . I don't know what I'm supposed to do next."

"I don't know," he said. "You live, I guess. Same as everybody else."

"I can't *live*. I'm dead."

"You're only kind of dead."

I laughed at that, a short damp sound. "That's not helpful."

"You want helpful, call me when it's not the middle of the night."

"I'll do that," I said. "This is your warning. You're going to regret ever being nice to me."

"I already do," Zeke said, but he probably didn't mean it.

So I said, "Thanks," and I said, "See you around," and I let him go back to sleep.

After I hung up, I took Mr. Willow's keys out of the backpack.

Three keys, three locks, three gates.

I twirled the ring around my finger, caught the keys against my palm. I could throw them into the lake. Let them sink to the bottom with all the other trash. Nobody would ever find them. I could be rid of them.

But I didn't. I tucked them away in my pack again, down at the bottom with the party clothes.

Everybody kept telling me they had no idea why I had returned when everybody else stayed dead. Maybe there was nothing to know. Maybe there was no explanation for it. Or maybe there was. Either way, if I wanted to find a reason, a purpose for walking around outside my grave when I should have stayed buried, I was going to have to find it myself.

I headed back to the road. The city was slow to wake. I couldn't remember what day of the week it was. Saturday, maybe. It didn't matter. I went back to Ricky's house and stood on the sidewalk across the street until I saw the curtain in his window twitch, his pale face peek out and disappear again.

I wasn't going to haunt him. I was going to leave and never see him again. There was a whole world out there to explore, magic and monsters and a million inexplicable things, and he was no more than a smudge of filth. But I wanted to give him that one glimpse. I wanted him to think I was always there, always watching, wherever he went, whatever he did. I wanted him to be scared for the rest of his life.

There's something Karen Garrow once said about the fate of the universe. It was on one of her television shows, an episode I watched a dozen times on the basement TV. All of us, she said, all of us and all of everything that had ever existed and ever would exist, it was all made up of matter that formed in the very first moments of the universe, and it would all last until the very end. The atoms would decay, the particles would break apart, everything would disintegrate and shatter until it was unrecognizable—*too degraded*—but that would take so many billions and billions of years we didn't even have words for time scales that large. Everything had come from the same hot explosion and everything would end in the same empty darkness. It had nothing to do with what we believed or what we wanted or how desperately we needed to reassure ourselves that the brief, bright moment in which we lived meant anything at all. None of it would matter in the end.

And Karen smiled her playful smile, and she said, "But it isn't the end yet. It matters now, everything we have, for as long as we can hold on to it."

The sun was coming up.

I turned away from the house and the boy hiding behind the window.

Once I thought I heard, beneath the rumble of skateboard wheels on pavement, the slither of sand and low rolling laughter.

I kicked again, and I skated faster, and I didn't hear it anymore.

# ⑾ ACKNOWLEDGMENTS ⑾

Thanks first and foremost to my agent, Adriann Ranta, for taking a chance on me and believing in the stories everybody else said were too gruesome to be released into the wild.

Thanks to my amazing editors, Anica Rissi and Alex Arnold, and to everybody else at Katherine Tegen Books for all the work they've put into making this novel better.

Thanks to Kristin McLaughlin and Amanda Poythress for loving these characters from the beginning; to Leah Thomas for reassuring me that it's totally okay and not at all weird to want to spend your entire life writing about terrible things happening to fictional teenagers; to Emily Tesh, Katie Johns, Lindsey Johns,

Brenda Meyer, Cindy Rosenthal, Kerry Given, Siobhan McKiernan, and Carla Spencer for the cheerleading that started long before this novel even existed; to Jennifer Hsyu and Greg Bossert for the commiseration and whiskey and ramen; to Jessica Hilt for all the help and encouragement (and Craft Night); to Tom Underberg for answering my questions about his town; to Ann and Jeff Vander-Meer for their advice; and to the rest of my instructors and fellow classmates from Clarion 2010 for making it impossible to give up.

And finally, a million thanks to my family for their patience and support, but especially to Sarah and Pete for letting me be the monster in the basement for a few years while I was figuring things out. Next time we're in Hawaii the princess room is all yours.

Read on for the sneak peek of

# THE MEMORY TREES,

a darkly magical novel about a mysterious family legacy,
the bonds of sisterhood, and the strange and powerful ways
we are shaped by the places we call home.

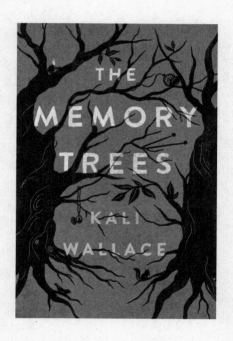

1

BEYOND THE WINDOW the morning was bright and glittering, the sky a breathless blue, and the hotels on Miami Beach jutted like broken teeth across the water, but all Sorrow could see was the orchard. There were trees whispering behind the walls of the office, and she almost believed if she turned—if she was quick—she would glimpse their sturdy thick trunks and rustling dead leaves from the corner of her eye.

"Your father is very worried about you," Dr. Silva said.

Sorrow rubbed her arms and looked away from the window. That cool breeze touching the back of her neck, that was only the air conditioner.

Dr. Silva was, as ever, perfectly composed in a pencil skirt, a cream blouse that complemented her dark skin, and heels so high Sorrow wondered how anybody could walk in them without risking ankle damage. Sorrow had seen Dr. Silva regularly when she first moved to Florida, but it had been two years since her last appointment, and the doctor had moved her practice from a hospital in Coral Gables to a Brickell skyscraper overlooking Biscayne Bay. Boats crawled through the no-wake zone far below, and cars glinted like jewels on the bridges.

Sorrow was leaning in the corner of the leather sofa, her legs sticking painfully to the seat. Dad was in the waiting room, probably paging through a glossy travel magazine, checking his email, checking the time. He had made the appointment, gotten Sorrow out of bed, fixed her breakfast, taken a day off work to come with her even though she was perfectly capable of driving herself. Sorrow's stepmother, Sonia, had watched it all with worried eyes and a concerned pinch to her lips, but she hadn't argued or interfered. She hadn't offered any opinion at all except to say, "I think that's a good idea."

Dr. Silva was waiting for an answer. Sorrow thought about rolling her eyes, didn't. Thought about giving an unimpressed snort. Didn't. The silence stretched. There wasn't a trace of impatience on Dr. Silva's face.

Finally Sorrow said, "I can't stop thinking about my sister."

It was the first time Sorrow had admitted it out loud since the party, and once she started, the words were tumbling out: she had been thinking about Patience when she disappeared that evening from her grandparents' house on the edge of the Everglades, and she had been thinking about her day and night since then. She thought about Patience when she woke in the morning and when she tossed and turned in bed at night, when she went to school and when she came home, when she hugged her stepsister, Andi, good-bye at the airport, when Sonia asked about her day, when she shrugged away from her father's concern. She had been thinking about Patience when she was blowing off meeting her friends, when she was supposed to be doing her homework, taking a trigonometry exam, writing an English essay, and she had been thinking about Patience when her teachers had called Dad and Sonia into the school to discuss the recent decline in her already unimpressive academic performance.

Every day, every moment, she was thinking about Patience in their mother's orchard in Vermont, her long brown hair and soft hazel eyes, how she had loved racing playfully through the apple trees while Sorrow tagged along, always smaller, always slower. In her thoughts the seasons turned around them in a film-reel flicker of color—winter brown to pale spring green, summer's deep mossy shadows to autumn's blaze of red and gold—and no matter how hard Sorrow tried, no matter how desperately she reached, Patience was always just beyond her grasp.

She had been thinking about who Patience would have been, if she had lived.

There were blank spaces in Sorrow's memory surrounding the day Patience died. Where before she had always let her thoughts skitter away from those days like roaches fleeing a sudden light, now she turned in to them, examined them, unflinching, and all she found was a thicket of shadows obscuring her view, a tangled wall of branches between her and the past. Nothing she did helped her push through. All she had were questions and the long ago echo of nightmares tinged with fire.

"Why can't I remember what happened?" she asked.

Dr. Silva, her voice as calm and deep as the cloudless sky, said, "Memory is imperfect, Sorrow, even in the best circumstances. Your sister's death was a terrible trauma, and the effects of such a trauma, especially at such a young age, they last a long time. You might never remember everything."

"It's been eight years," Sorrow said, and there it was again, the whisper of wind through remembered trees all around her, the imagined shadows reaching up the walls and bending onto the ceiling. "I don't have nightmares anymore."

"Why is it so important to you?" Dr. Silva asked. "What do you think will change if you remember?"

It wasn't enough to sketch in those terrible days with what others had told her. Dad hadn't even been there when Patience died; he had only visited a few times a year throughout her childhood. She could never talk about it with her mother; their phone conversations were carefully light, deliberately casual, and they never, ever mentioned Patience. A girl who couldn't remember, a man who had been hundreds of miles away, a woman who would not even say her daughter's name. A few lines of empty fact: unexplained fire, unexpected tragedy. It wasn't enough.

Dr. Silva was speaking, but her words were a murmur at the

edge of Sorrow's awareness. Sorrow was staring out the window again at beaches and bridges and keys, and what she was seeing was the orchard not as it would be now, in the first blush of spring with apple blossoms opening pink and white, but as it had been before Patience died. It had been winter-gray and barren, the naked branches of the trees silver in the moonlight, the nights so bitterly cold she felt it still as an ache in her chest.

The Lovegoods of Abrams Valley, the family of her mother and grandmother and the long unbroken braid of women before them, they had always lived and died by stories they told, their remembrances held dear long after most families would have let old names and old deeds disappear into history.

"I want to go back," Sorrow said. "I need to go back to the orchard."

Patience deserved that. She deserved to be remembered.

# 2

# REJOICE LOVEGOOD
## ?–1790

DAWN CREPT OVER the mountains, and the land breathed. She felt it beneath her, a living thing, as she climbed the hill away from the cabin. The newest saplings, one year old, were knee-high now on the cusp of summer. The hills were mottled brown and green, shapes indistinguishable in the murky half-light before sunrise, but the sky was an extravagant smear of pink and orange and gold, such glorious colors they felt like fire in her eyes, embers beneath her skin.

At the summit of the hill waited the gnarled old oak. It was a magnificent tree, so broad and so towering she had thought it might have a story, a history, some weighty reverence due to its great age and imposing height, but the villagers had laughed when she asked. It was only a tree, they said. A tree in a sea of trees, a world of trees, but even so, she had not the heart to cut it down. It would stay here. She would clear the hill around it, bring her apple trees up the south-facing slope in clean curving rows, over the top and down the northern side. By the end of this summer she would have this hill ready for her rootstock. The land was stubborn, the roots hard as iron and the stones plentiful, but her stubbornness, she had learned, was greater.

Last year's planting had the look of spindly sticks, offering a shy spattering of leaves as they broke from their winter dormancy. Those from the year before, no longer saplings but still skinny as colt legs, were branching into proper little trees. The oldest, the first she had planted, they were three years old, and their branches were innumerable, their early summer leaves lush and supple, and their blossoms as shy and pink as a smile.

Four years now she had toiled alone in these dark woods. That first winter, after she had cleared the land and planted her first precious roots, but before she had known if even a single apple tree would take, she had huddled in her cabin as the wind snaked through chinks in the mud. She had been barely more than a girl when she crossed the sea, spring-fresh and unformed, not yet twenty years of age, and though she felt ancient in her heart as the cold closed around her, old as the mountains in her bones, she had wept like a child when the storms wailed. Wept for the girl she had been and the misty green hills she had left behind, wept for the family across the sea that would never again speak her name except in shame and, someday, perhaps, regret. She had wept until she was scraped raw inside, empty but for the leaden weight of every memory of the life she had left, the grasping thorns of every choice that had brought her to this bleak and howling place. When darkness fell she poured rivers of tears into the wood and soil and stone beneath her, a well of loneliness that felt as though it would never run dry.

But slowly, slowly, winter had broken its hold on the mountains. Gray skies cracked apart to reveal searing blue, and the call of songbirds and drone of insects chased away the mourning wind. Spring came with a crush of green, a blush of pink, and she did not have time to weep anymore. She had work to do. The tears she had spilled nourished the land, softened it for her ax and spade, flowed through the earth, feeding her trees both wild and tame. Her sweat sank to join it, her blood as well, so much through that first year, so often, the land might have been an extension of her own body, flesh and stone, water and blood.

The wind turned, a gentle breeze tugging at wisps of unbound hair. The work never stopped, but she allowed herself this small luxury of watching the sun rise. Today the dawn was joined by a hint of smoke in the air. It had become a familiar scent these past few days, and she wasn't yet sure how to feel about neighbors planting themselves so close. She had met them yesterday. A man and his family, grim stern-faced folk lately of a plantation in Massachusetts. The boys were strapping and strong, the wife unsmiling and silent; one of the sons, a child of about ten, had spat on the ground and glowered, mumbling *witch* to the earth before his mother herded him away. The man had asked to speak to her husband, her father,

her brother, each question lifting his voice and brow with increasing disbelief that he had come so far into the mountains to find a woman alone on a piece of land she had cultivated with her own hands, and no man to rule her.

She had told him she was a widow—handily dispatching the imaginary husband she had invented to secure the land—and she had watched the calculating spark appear in his eyes. Her land was rich, the soil good, and most of all it was already cleared. Her apple trees were young but thriving. His own land promised years of toil to come.

She patted the trunk of the magnificent oak and felt its warmth beneath her fingers, its welcoming strength. She had acres to tend, and the sun was rising. The smoke of the neighbors' fire was as delicate as spider silk against the brilliant dawn. The man would be waking with avarice in his heart and deception in his eyes. As the summer bloomed he would try to clear her along with the shrubs and stones and snags, as though a woman were no more than another obstacle on the landscape.

But she had shed tears and blood to make this land a part of herself. She was not so easily frightened away.

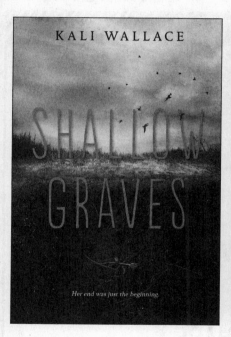

## JOIN THE

# Epic Reads

## COMMUNITY

**THE ULTIMATE YA DESTINATION**

 **DISCOVER** ▶
your next favorite read

◀ **MEET** ▶
new authors to love

◀ **WIN** ▶
free books

◀ **SHARE** ▶
infographics, playlists, quizzes, and more

◀ **WATCH** ▶
the latest videos

www.epicreads.com